FACTORY 4-80

Gordon A. Long

Delta, B. C.
2019

Factory 4-80

Gordon A. Long

Published by
Airborn Press
4958 10A Ave, Delta, B. C.
V4M 1X8
Canada

ISBN: 978-1-988898-14-8

Printed by Kindle Direct Publishing

Cover Design by Gordon A. Long

A STRANGE FIRST CONTACT

Lieutenant Jones caressed the radio controls, and the alien factory's scratchy voice cleared...*if we had visual contact, this would be a good point to transmit a smile, I think. Do I have that right?*

Natalia raised her eyebrows. This wasn't what the Space Arm boffins predicted in the briefings. *Yes, a smile would be appropriate.*

Do you want to open visual channels?

We have security concerns. We have no knowledge of your computing capability and no guarantee of your intentions.

Ah. Astute, but likewise, I have no idea of yours. A certain level of trust is necessary when any two entities do business.

She glanced at Jones, who shook his head and shrugged.

"It's all on me then." *All right, Factory Four Eight Zero. We're opening a standard video frequency.* She nodded to Jones. Snow blurred the viewers, and then a familiar scene came into focus.

"What the he..." Murmurs echoed through the bridge. "That's a cartoon!"

Would this be an appropriate avatar? An animated character strolled into view. A very familiar character.

The bridge crew exploded into laughter. "Mickey Mouse?"

"I do not understand your reaction." A pleasant male tenor voice came over the com. "Was that a mistake? I felt it appropriate to assume a non-threatening mien."

Natalia forced herself to be serious. "That was laughter, Factory Four Eight Zero. That image comes from children's entertainment so it is not threatening, but hardly serious either. Perhaps not a perfect fit for a businessman."

Mickey shrugged and grinned. "Well, if this avatar is not offensive, I will maintain it until I have learned enough about human culture to make a more appropriate choice." He made a sweeping bow. "And now, madam, since I assume I am viewing Commander Natalia O'Rourke, it is a pleasure to meet you."

i

CONTENTS

THANKS

To my Beta readers, Alain, Don, Matthew and Zachary, who held my feet to the fire on many technical and other issues.

1.   OTHERWHERE

Life's a gamble, and if you want to play the game you have to ante up.

– Mariel Collingwood

Commander Natalia O'Rourke stepped onto the bridge and gave the brass plaque by the door the traditional swipe with her sleeve. "Planetary Community Space Craft 9108 *NightHawk*, Reconnaissance Cutter." She tried to suppress her smile, but even now, four months of travel and three light-years from Earth, she couldn't stifle the once-again realization that this was her ship.

Sure, she's only a 100-metre Scout, but she's mine.

A clear, three-dimensional view appeared in her augment.

Image: tall, broad-shouldered woman standing on bridge with her hand on the shoulder of beautifully patterned auguar. His coat shines with the markings of a cloud leopard, but his shoulder reaches her waist. She is a handsome human, but his beauty outshines hers in every way.

Yes, Chakka, your ship and mine. NightHawk?

The ever-present aura of vast knowledge and competence in her augment snapped into focus.

Aye, ma'am.

I take the bridge.

"Captain on the bridge."

This sounded over the ship's com in NightHawk's gentle voice.

Natalia's mood dimmed as she turned to face her First Officer. "Lieutenant Jones, I relieve you."

"I stand relieved." A tiny smirk curled his lip; then he raised his eyes to meet hers.

1

She refrained from stepping closer, because she knew her size intimidated him, tall though he was.

Was he watching me?

The view in her augment took on a lower angle, looking upward from the bridge hatchway.

Image: Adrian Jones glancing across the bridge towards her as she polishes the plaque. His lip wrinkles.

Emotion: simmering protective anger.

Thank you, Chakka. Calmly, now. He doesn't mean anything by it.

Emotion: supreme feline disdain.

Natalia smothered a chuckle. "Anything to report?"

"Nothing to report, ma'am. All checks complete, all systems normal. Fuel at 87.3%, within 0.5 % of predicted consumption."

"Thank you, Lieutenant." She decided to make another try at cordiality. "Jonny's whipped up some dynamite eggs for breakfast."

"Thank you, ma'am. I think I'll stick to my usual porridge."

She dredged up a smile. "Yes, the eggs were a bit explosive."

"Juanita can't fight that Mexican heritage, ma'am."

She nodded, hiding her surprise. *He almost sounded human for a moment, there.*

Jones flashed her a wooden smile and marched off the bridge, his dark head bobbing like a metronome.

How the man can march in 0.3 Gs is beyond me. No, that's being snarky. He's a good officer and a wizard communications specialist. Too bad he never learned to communicate with humans.

Slapping herself mentally behind the ear before Chakka could, Natalia did her habitual scan of the crowded bridge — really just a large cockpit — noting everything in the same order as usual. The viewscreens showed only the depthless black of Otherwhere, framed by the comforting glow of the control panels and readouts of the electronics that lined the walls. Except for those readings, *NightHawk* and her crew could have been floating in a sea of nothingness. Which explained Otherwhere as well as anything could. Five weeks of that scene had not inured her to the shudder that ran down her back every time she looked out.

Chakka did his own patrol, pausing by the helmsman for a scratch under the chin before flowing up to his deeply padded perch behind the Captain's acceleration couch.

"Anything to report, Pete?"

The helmsman's blond head tilted, his eyes fixed forward. "Point zero, zero three drift to galactic east noted at oh four thirty-two, ma'am. Navigation adjusted accordingly."

She stopped beside him. "You made that up, didn't you?"

He grinned up at her. "Oh, no, ma'am. It happened just like I said. You can check."

"I will." *NightHawk? Course report.*

"Point zero, zero three drift..."

"All right, all right. The two of you are in cahoots. I don't know how you persuaded the ship, though. ArIns don't get bored." A sudden thought struck her. *Or do you?*

I wouldn't exactly call it boredom, ma'am. We are programmed to use times of little action to monitor the more subtle aspects of the ship's operations and environment.

Fair enough. Any sign of the radio signal we're out here chasing?

Not expecting anything on that band until oh eight forty-three, ma'am. The carrier from the mine is coming through five-nine-nine. The Mine Manager sent in his weekly report at oh seven hundred. They are back to full production after their shutdown for repairs last month. Would you like a précise?

The mine's business is none of our business, NightHawk, and anything we add would take too long getting there to be of any use.

She considered that problem in a new light. *But if you're bored, keep monitoring their messages for any indication of*

3

trouble. They're in Barnard's System, with our supposed alien radio signal coming from the same area of space. Anything could happen, which is why they sent a Commando team.

Plus the fact that we're the fastest thing in the solar system.

We're no longer in our solar system: Keep your ears on.

Thank you, ma'am. That will help with the boredom.

You're welcome, NightHawk.

A pleasure doing business with you, ma'am.

I'm sure. And NightHawk, do you know what happens to a ship's ArIn who develops a sense of humour?

It wasn't in my training protocols so I don't know, ma'am.

Nor do you want to, because I haven't had time to think up something appropriately nasty. She switched to external speech. "Pete, we're scheduled for some radio calibrations this morning. If you're bored, we can start now."

"Right away, ma'am. *NightHawk*, please take the helm."

The ship's pleasant contralto came over the bridge speakers.

"I have the helm, Master Pilot Jager."

He swung his legs out of the pilot's accel couch so he could reach the radio controls. "Right, ma'am. Shall we start with long-range, ultra-high and work down and in for a change?"

She stifled a sigh. "Anything for a change, Pete."

* * *

One duty that helped relieve her boredom was the simulation training. She spent several hours every watch on her augment with *NightHawk*, Chakka and often Lieutenant Jones, working through every possible attack and defense situation the fertile (and she suspected, bored) minds at Headquarters had thought up.

"I don't know why we even bother with this configuration, ma'am."

4

"Why not, First?"

"Because it always comes out the same way. When you and Chakka pair against the ship's ArIn and me, we end up in a stalemate."

"Yes. You in a defensive shell like a turtle, us dancing around outside in frustration."

"Every time. So what's the value in that?"

She glanced over to where the lieutenant somehow sat at attention in his accel couch. "Two things I can think of. One, it tells us which combination to use, depending on the situation. Two, and perhaps more important, it tells each pair that there is a certain type of response that we can't beat. We probably ought to work on this specific teaming more, rather than less, because it strengthens a weakness. Want to try again?"

"Of course. But please, let's change the teams."

"Fine. You take Chakka; I'll go with *NightHawk*."

"Sublime to the ridiculous. At least I have a chance to win."

"Ready?"

"Ready."

"*NightHawk*, run attack simulation 45B with the teams as mentioned."

Ready, ma'am. Go...

Natalia's vision was blanked out by the stars of the Milky Way Galaxy, sweeping out in a brilliant display, the three-dimensionality of her augment giving them the same depth and immediacy she would feel if she were swimming out there among them. But their beauty contained a threat.

Three corvettes confronted her, their hulls bristling with projectile, plasma and laser weaponry. Her heads-up display showed one destroyer backing her up. She watched the trajectories of the enemy ships while *NightHawk* fed her weapons analysis, and a plan began to form...

* * *

5

Action on mission band, ma'am.

"Damn. I was just about to finish them off."

"No you weren't, ma'am."

She sent a querying glance at Jones.

He gave a grim smile, but his hands were busy on the control screens. "You didn't take Chakka into account."

"I always take Chakka into account."

"And he knows that you do."

"Chakka! Have you been playing me?"

Image: auguar lounging on his bed in the mess hall, licking his stretched-out hind leg in a show of casual disdain.

I'll deal with you later. Back to business.

Natalia dropped out of her augment with a grin of satisfaction. As long as her new partners were surprising her with original ideas, the team was growing and learning.

She glanced at the viewscreen, where the graph of a familiar audio signal zigzagged its usual pattern. "Same message?"

The ship also spoke aloud.

"Right on schedule, ma'am: oh eight forty-three on the nose."

"Pete, what do you make of that?"

"The regularity? I can't see anyone, alien or not, setting up a schedule like that for any reason. Earth has been receiving alien messages ever since we invented the tech to hear them. The usual explanation for a schedule is due to planetary rotation, and they always turn out to be natural phenomena."

"So they're broadcasting a narrow signal from the planet's surface, and we catch it as it sweeps by? The boffins at Space Arm disproved that. This signal shuts off. It comes on, pointed straight as a die at Earth, then shuts off after, what, ten hours?"

"Ten hours, thirteen minutes...give or take, as if that matters."

"Anything could matter. We just don't know what or why."

First Officer Jones had been leaving the bridge, but he turned in the doorway. "Solar power."

"Solar power?"

"If the rotation of the planet was twenty hours plus, and the signal was sent by solar power, it could only be sent during half the day."

She raised her eyebrows. "And that would in turn suggest that it is a real alien message."

"Also that it is set on automatic and could be centuries old."

"It follows. Where did you hear that theory?"

"I thought of it myself." His brows were drawing down.

"Not bad, First. I haven't heard a new idea in weeks. I'll put it in tonight's report. Space Arm will get it in...what... three months or so?"

"Three months, seven days, three hours, twenty-six minutes, if you send it right now, ma'am."

At your leisure, NightHawk. I don't think there's any rush.

"As you wish, ma'am."

Natalia dropped into her accel couch, trying to look industrious.

A nagging sensation in the back of her brain alerted her. She focused on the crew vitals, where the change originated. *Second Engineer B'kose, why am I getting elevated readings from your augment?*

Nothing, ma'am.

No it isn't, Fiona. Sergeant Jacobs, you too. What's going on?

It's Fiona. She just won't...

It isn't Fiona, Sergeant. It's Otherwhere getting to you, and that's a fault on your part, no matter what small, niggling character flaw one of the other crew exhibits. We are Commandos. We are part of a team. We do not let our personal feelings get in the way of our function. Do you follow, Toni?

Yes, ma'am. I'm sorry.

7

Don't apologize to me. Second Engineer?

Totally my fault, ma'am. I was…

I'm doubtful it was totally your fault, Fiona, and I'm not interested in the details. You and Toni settle it between you, or we'll set up the training ring and you can do some training on each other.

She let an evil chuckle escape. *At least that'll keep the rest of the crew entertained.*

A spate of denial washed through the augment, and Natalia closed them out. *What do you think, Chakka? Do we need a bit of training?*

Emotions: boredom and the need to hunt.

Yes, well you're not going to get that for a while. Don't worry, Barnard's Star has at least one oxygen-atmo planet. Maybe we'll get to stretch our legs in four months or so.

Emotion: instant enthusiasm!

Don't get set on it. This isn't that kind of a mission. Come to think of it, I'm not sure what kind of a mission this is going to be. So far, a boring one.

She straightened her posture in the couch. *Can't let it get to me. Show a good example and all that.* She called up another image in her augment and got to work. *Hmm…crew eval reports. What fun.*

2. CONTACT

At the morning watch change, Lieutenant Jones strode onto the Bridge, his uniform as sharp as the day he arrived on the ship. "Ready for duty, ma'am."

Probably sharper. He has all the time in space these days. "I stand relieved, Lieutenant. Nothing of interest to report."

"I relieve you."

"First Officer on duty."

NightHawk?

"Aye, ma'am."

I'm going off duty. Keep an eye on our two signals.

"I'll check them now, ma'am."

Joe Karaka was on helm this morning, and he reached out a languid hand to change the radio frequency. Then he shot alert. "Signal, ma'am. On the mine frequency."

"Put it on the ship's com. The crew wants to hear this."

Karaka slid aside and the First Officer dropped into his couch, fingers brushing his control screens. The signal cleared and strengthened.

"NightHawk, NightHawk. This is El Dorado 12 Mine calling PCSC 9108 NightHawk. El Dorado 12 calling NightHawk. Just got the message from Head Office about your imminent arrival. All is well, here, and we'll be rolling out the red carpet for such a distinguished visitor. And for you and your crew as well, Captain Anderson. Welcome to our neck of the woods. What is your ETA? We need time to hang the tinsel."

"Return message, Lieutenant."

"At your leisure, ma'am"

She re-connected to *NightHawk* on her augment, still speaking aloud in order to keep the crew in touch with what was happening. *"Return message. 'El Dorado 12, El Dorado 12, PCSC NightHawk calling El Dorado 12. Captain Anderson regretfully declines your invitation due to being on Earth, 6 light-*

9

years away from you. I guess that message hasn't reached you yet. Commander Natalia O'Reilly on the bridge, here. Our ETA is one hundred twenty-seven days. Do you read that? Four months, seven days. Plenty of time to bang the dust off your red carpet. NightHawk out.' Send immediately."

"When will they get that, *NightHawk*?"

"Three hours plus change, ma'am."

"I can't begin to calculate how long it will take to get a message back. Just let me know."

"Wilco, ma'am. Think of it as shooting a gun forward off a fast train. The speed of our message is already travelling with us at 7 lights. When we send a message forward at lightspeed, it is then travelling at 8 lights."

Time for a lesson for the crew. "But the speed of light is only the speed of light. Radio waves can't go any faster."

"Not in Otherwhere, ma'am. Out here they can go at any velocity we can boost them to, just like the ship does. The only problem is for the receiver to notice a message moving that fast, hook it into re-ti and translate it. The Doppler effect is horrendous unless you have a receiver that peeks into Otherwhere. Which the mine has, of course. Nothing too good for the El Dorado Corporation."

"Thank you for the lecture, Doctor *NightHawk*. Crew, there will be a quiz on Friday."

"I will post the data to all crew's private boards. Do you want me to include the info about sending messages backwards, and why they take so much longer?"

"No, they can apply the "bullet off the train" analogy if they really care. Post it as is. If we keep it short enough, some of them might even read it."

"Wilco, Commander."

There was a moment of satisfied silence on the bridge. Then Natalia smiled at her First Officer. "Well, Mister Jones, it seems at least there will be somebody home at the mine when we come knocking."

"It seems so, ma'am."

10

"I'm for breakfast. The Bridge is yours. Carry on."

"Aye, Ma'am."

"First Officer in command."

She slipped down the slideway ladder at a brisker pace than she had used for a week, Chakka padding beside her. By the time she reached the galley word had spread, and smiles greeted her. An outside communication took on giant proportions in the insular claustrophobia of endless nothingness. Space Arm regs frowned on showing the black, vacant Otherwhere image on screens in public areas. With good reason.

She glanced at the galley main viewer. *NightHawk, that picture of the Painted Desert in Utah is one of my favourites, but it's been on too much lately.*

The sweeping vista of warm banded rock and sparse cacti faded, to be replaced by a stark planetscape from Calisto, the second largest moon of Jupiter. And incidentally one of the least inviting.

Thanks, NightHawk. That makes me feel much better.

Query, ma'am?

Yes, NightHawk

Was that ironic, ma'am?

Very good, Nighthawk. That was ironic to the point of sarcasm. Start learning the difference between the two if you find yourself getting bored. And yes, that was ironic to.

I thought so, ma'am. Thank you.

We live to serve, NightHawk.

11

3. NON-STANDARD MAINTENANCE

Natalia took her breakfast and sat opposite Nelson Lundeen, the Chief Engineer. He was a tall, well-built man of about forty, old for the Commandos, but useful because of his knowledge of the workings of the prototype Otherwhen engine of the *NightHawk*.

He looked up at her. "Nothing's wrong. Save you asking."

She flicked her fingertips against his arm. "Spoiled my opening line. I'm looking ahead. The Otherwhen sphere maintenance schedule."

At the centre of gravity of the ship, just aft of the habitation ring, sat the great Otherwhen sphere, which had little to do with external propulsion and everything to do with the ship's inertio-temporal relationship to the universe.

Natalia had been given a tour of the machinery before it was locked away in its own little pocket of space-time. All she had recognized was a dark orb almost hidden by the kilometres of superconductor windings that turned its external shell into a huge generator of Otherwhen power. Essentially the Otherwhen engine absorbed energy while making the Lightspeed transfer, then ran on whatever was happening in Wherever it was as long as it was there, leaking power back to the ship in the process. This neatly solved the weight-of-fuel problem for long voyages. In essence, a ship could travel in Otherwhere as long as it had reaction mass for the engines that in normal space were fired by plutonium fission. In practice, the constant Otherness grated on the crew's nerves, limiting allowable exposure to a few months.

Juanita came over with fresh cups of coffee and plunked her stocky body beside the engineer. "*No entiendo*, Nelson. Why do you have to do the maintenance way out here? They could do it at Space Dock when we're not in range in case they blow it up. *¿No es verdad, Señor?*"

Lundeen stretched his arms and cracked his knuckles. He loved talking about his favourite toy. "Once it's up and running, the engine is Somewhere and Somewhen else, and it stays there, hopefully until the ship refits in five years or so. All we have to do is be in contact with it and get the ship up to Light Transfer Speed, which is about zero point two Lightspeed. At that point, the Sphere kicks us above the Light Transfer Ceiling into Otherwhere, and the rules of normal space don't apply. We can accelerate up to any speed we want with no time or mass distortion. When we drop below the LTC we kick out, but the Sphere doesn't. That's why it's locked away when we're in re-ti. It isn't really here. So I do the maintenance while we're on a voyage and in sync with it. Do you follow?"

"*No lo se, señor.* You know, back in Mexico my family farmed on the side of a volcano. Always rumbling, always threatening to explode. When I joined the Space Arm I thought I would be safe from things like that. Now my farm is on top of this thing. Hah!" She shrugged. "*No importa.* As long as it makes my vegetables warm enough to keep them growing, it can stay wherever it likes."

"Your wonderful and life-giving hydroponics garden is as close to the Sphere as possible to keep everything toasty warm. Don't complain when I go in to fix it."

"Don't blow us up, and I won't complain. *¿Acuerdo?*"

"Want to lay a hundred planetoids on it?"

"*De ninguna manera.* I know better than to bet against *el anciano.* It will be a trick."

He shrugged and grinned. "If I blow us up you won't be here to collect. You won't even know it happened."

"Ah, but I will come back and haunt you." She wiggled ghostly fingers at him.

"Not if I'm dead, too." He wiggled back.

"If we're all so happy at the prospect of being dead, I think we've been in Otherwhere too long." Natalia kept her sigh to herself. Keep the crew's spirits up. Duty of the captain.

13

"Oh, and I've been meaning to talk to you, Nelson. Jonny, here, says there were some pretty weird noises during mid-flight turnover yesterday. Any ideas?"

Lundeen grinned. "Besides the sound of her puking in the sink? I told everybody. Stay out of the centrifuge section during turnover. Gravity goes all wonky."

"*Si*, and you don't want to know what it did to my angel-food cake!" Her stubby fingers clenched, then flew apart. "It took an hour to clean the oven."

Natalia nodded. "But it's a good thing she was there, or we wouldn't know about those noises. What do you think they are?"

He winced. "I know what they are. The bearings on the centrifuge. I told them they were too small. If we do a turnover while the ball is turning, it puts a lot of pressure on them."

"We can't kill the gravity to the living quarters every time we do a flip. It takes too long to spool down."

"No, but we could do the flip slower."

"I'll talk to the pilots. We don't want anything to interfere with Jonny's angel-food cake."

"We sure don't. This crew exists on its stomach."

* * *

By day 192 of the voyage they had decelerated to the LTC and it was time to drop out of Otherwhere. The whole crew looked forward to it, because proper gravity would be back. Real cooking could resume, and that unpleasant look-over-your-shoulder feeling would go away.

They seated themselves securely at their posts, ready to do their duties.

Natalia clicked onto ship-wide com. "Just a reminder, folks. Dropout is weird, but nobody's ever had a negative reaction. We did this once on our commissioning trip, so it should be no problem. However, we've been in point 3 Gs for ten weeks, and

14

when the emergence burn hits it won't be pretty. Hold fast in position, and remember, no matter how you feel, don't react when we come out. Whatever you do, don't move. Accidents have been known to happen."

Silence descended on the ship.

"Emergence burn in ten seconds. Light Transition Ceiling in two minutes."

"Emergence burn in five...three, two, one. Burn."

Pressure increased as the engines fired up to three full Gs.

An eerie wailing began to build, a grating whine that teetered on the edge of conscious hearing.

"Dropout. Engine shutdown."

The noise chopped off and weight disappeared, along with a certain edginess that Natalia had got past noticing, that uncomfortable awareness of *wrong* that had permeated the ship for the last ten weeks. Then the elation of re-ti flooded through her like the full starlight of the Milky Way Galaxy now bursting from all the bridge viewscreens. It was like coming out of a dank tunnel into a fine, sunlit meadow, and the urge to jump and run was irresistible...

She stamped it out fiercely. "All hands stay at stations! Do not move. Repeat, do not move!"

The order was relayed throughout the ship: on every screen, in every speaker, through every augment. There was a moment of complete stillness...

"Warning! Prepare to resume deceleration."

"Ready down here in Engineering. Or is that up here?"

"It's going to be down the moment you hit that button, Lundeen. *NightHawk*, take the count, please."

"Decel burn in ten...five...three, two, one. Burn."

"Engines firing at ten percent."

"Increase power to seventy."

"Increasing over twenty seconds."

As the vibration and roar of the engines increased, the heavy hand of gravity pushed on her chest. It reached normal, but still rose. Finally, at 1.3 Gs, it levelled out.

"Replace inertial grav."

"Inertial gravity reset in five...three, two, one, activating."

The weight eased off in the bridge area, leaving them at the more natural-feeling 0.8 Gs.

"Report in order, please."

"Captain on duty."

"Helm on duty."

"Bridge on duty."

"Engineering on duty."

The reports cycled in from the whole crew, ending with "Galley on the boil."

Chuckles filled the coms and augments.

"The cook will put herself on orders for disregard of proper procedures. Her penalty will be strawberry Pavlova for the crew at the next possible opportunity. And a double serving for the Captain."

Applause and one faint wolf whistle faded back into silence.

And then the tedium began again. Three months of deceleration. *Oh, well, better than the ten weeks of Otherwhere.* She gazed fondly at the viewscreen, which displayed the Milky Way in full colour, the Horsehead Nebula, one of her favourites, front and centre. *Especially the scenery. And point three Gs loses its novelty after a while. I wonder what other goodies are going to show up that we didn't hit on our two-week commissioning run? Probably a lot, with all this new tech aboard.*

Natalia pulled up another document on her internal visuals and began to read.

* * *

But the weeks passed with little incident, and soon they were crossing the orbits of the target system's outer planets. It looked like Barnard's had experienced a rougher evolution than Sol. Twenty-two planets, depending on one's definition of planet, orbited the star, along with two separate asteroid belts. The sweep of space between the fourth and fifth planets was their first target because of their orders to visit El Dorado 12, which mined one of the planetoids that peppered the zone and happened to be on the near side of the system as they approached. The rest of the belt was far denser than Sol's, and spread over a larger area of space, fading only at the lines swept by the gravity fields of the confining planets.

Spectacular images of the target grew in the viewers every day, as did the crew's anticipation of the end of the voyage. The usual monosyllabic interactions blossomed into mealtime chats.

"Well, Master Pilot Jager. What does an experienced spacer like yourself do on his first shore leave in seven months?"

He shrugged. "It's an ore extraction plant, ma'am. The women are all married, everything will have a layer of dust on it and the air will smell like our engine room. No offense to Engineers." He grinned at Lundeen across the table. "I think I'm just going to walk around in a different place and look at strangers' faces. The crew is on shifts, so the bar will be open whenever we get there. I guess a couple of drinks are in order if I can find the planetoids to pay for them. After that, who knows?"

"You're a real adventurer, Pete. Don't worry; you've got a lot of pay coming to you." She glanced at him. "If you haven't lost it already playing poker with the Chief Engineer."

He smiled. "Oh, I don't do so badly."

"Well, have a good time, then."

"Is the duty roster set?"

"Let's not go overboard. We don't know when we'll be getting in, yet."

"A man can dream."

"Not while you're on watch. We still have seven days to go."

"Right you are, ma'am." He returned to his toast and reconstituted eggs.

She accessed her augment. *Lieutenant Jones, do you have a reading on the mission wavelength?*

We're getting better angles, now, and I was able to do some triangulation. It's not very accurate yet...

I'm sure it will be better than what we had.

I hope so, ma'am. Our target is farther outsystem than El Dorado 12, but farther around the planet. The good news is that Eldorado has a faster orbit, so it's catching up to the source. Will do so for the next...I'd say three months or so, after which it will race on ahead.

Great. Our plan to go to the mine first remains unchanged, and we have plenty of time to prepare for the unknown part of our adventure.

I'd say that is accurate, ma'am.

Thanks, Adrian. We depend on you for this sort of expertise.

Um...you're welcome ma'am.

4. S.O.S.

At Day 251, four days out from the mine, Natalia sat in the quaintly termed chart room — her office just aft of the bridge — getting ahead on her docuload in anticipation of arrival.

Alert, ma'am.

What is it, NightHawk?

Message from El Dorado 12. Urgent. It's a mayday.

Put it on the ship's com.

This close, the messages were coming in pretty much re-ti. Fear and anger radiated through her head. "Mayday, mayday! *NightHawk, NightHawk.* This is El Dorado 12 calling *NightHawk.* Please come in. Mayday! Please come in. Please! Anyone?"

"This is *NightHawk*, El Dorado. What's the problem?"

"We are under attack, *NightHawk.* Repeat, we are under attack!"

"What kind of attack? Who?"

"Bombardment. We don't know who. We're getting hit badly."

"What kind of armament? Are your defenses coping?"

"Huge chunks of rock. Someone is throwing asteroids at us! Our cannons and lasers can't handle anything this big. They're striking all over."

"Could it be a natural shower?"

"We don't think so. It's too focused, and they just keep coming! Damn! Another one."

A deep boom overloaded the system, turning everything into white noise that bounced around inside her head.

NightHawk, up the audio overload damping, please. I felt that one to my toes. Continue transmission. "All right, El Dorado 12. We're going to turn over and do a quick blast. It'll be complicated, but we'll maximize our G-loads and get there as soon as possible."

If we can stand 3 Gs deceleration for one hour, we can be there in two days, ma'am, and 4 Gs makes it 33 hours.

"El Dorado 12, we have recalculated our ETA. We will be there in 48 hours. Do you copy? 48 hours is the best we can do."

"Thank you, *NightHawk*. I hope there's somebody left to greet you when you arrive. We're going down into the emergency shelters in the mine. If you get here and there's nobody around, start digging. El Dorado 12 out."

"Good luck, El Dorado 12. See you ASAP. *NightHawk* out."

NightHawk, replay that over the ship's com, then set us up for the 4 G burn.

I don't understand, ma'am. You told them 48 hours...

And we don't know who was listening. Arriving a little early won't do any harm, and we just might catch someone napping.

Understood, ma'am.

All-band broadcast. Put it on the ship's com, too.

All channels open, ma'am.

"This is PCSC-9108 *NightHawk* contacting any and all ships involved in the bombardment of El Dorado 12. Cease and desist immediately. I repeat, cease and desist. Under the Interplanet Treaties, Section five, Subsection twelve, any bombardment of a facility with civilian occupants is an act of war. The Planetary Community Space Arm orders you to cease and desist this act of war or suffer the full penalty of the law."

"Repeat for the next hour, *NightHawk*. Any response so far?"

"All frequencies empty, ma'am. Repeating for one hour."

"Best we can do." Natalia boosted the com volume. "General alert. You heard the situation. Vacate the living quarters and strap in for turnover and a quick burn. *NightHawk* will count down the numbers. Captain out."

Now the endless drills and refinements paid off. The ship and her crew made a perfect turnover and a short burst of power to increase speed as much as possible.

Two hours later they turned back again and resumed deceleration, but at a lower rate. Now they were rushing towards El Dorado 12 with more speed than they should have been. They would pay for it at the end, when they had to dump the excess velocity in a hurry or slide right on past.

Now the drills changed.

Not fast enough, Sergeant Jacobs.

The portside lasers aren't recharging like they should, ma'am.

Engineering, what's going on?

Right on it, ma'am.

Charlie, can you reload your Space to Space faster?

No, ma'am. The commando's deep voice filled the augment's battle com. *She's a sweet weapon, but they tacked her on at the last minute, and there's no room anywhere near the launcher to store the extra missiles.*

In that case, take your time aiming and don't waste your first shot. Toni, if the lasers aren't there fast enough, don't hold back on the plasma bolts. We have fuel to spare, and we're heading for a plutonium mine. Let's try the left-right-left sequence one more time while Fiona works on the lasers. Ready?

Any time, Cap'n.

Fire!

Damn! It's hard making this work flying backwards, ma'am.

She opened her voice to full ship's com. "Listen up. We don't know if this is a human attack. We don't know at what stage in our deceleration we will engage the enemy. We have to practise everything because we have to be ready for anything, forwards, backwards or in the middle of a flip. Do you follow?"

A chorus of "Yes, ma'ams" rang through the ship, and everyone set up and tried it again.

* * *

21

The morning of the last day she left Master Pilot Jager alone on the bridge and called the rest of the crew together in the mess hall, the only place on the ship large enough for all ten of them.

"This is the way it will go, folks. Starting at 09:32 we will have a 4.1 G deceleration burn for one hour. Everyone in space armour, G-suits and oxygen masks, strapped in tight, perpendicular to the axis of the ship. You've all been through it in training, but this time we must be keyed up to fight at the end of it. Questions? First..."

Jones wasn't showing his habitual snap. His face was even paler than usual, but there was a glint in his eye. You didn't get to his level in the Commandos without having a touch of the joy of combat. "Your best guess as to what we'll meet when we get there?"

"Worst case scenario, which is most probable, is that whoever hit the mine has loaded up all the stockpiled plutonium triiodide and is a day gone, and most or all of the miners are dead. That makes it easy for us. We check for survivors, collect data, and go on about our mission. If the miners were lucky, the attackers heard our threat and backed off to see who shows up to support it.

"Worst case for us is the attack was by someone with heavy firepower; we drop in and they're waiting for us. That's the one we're planning for. We'll all be strapped in with G-suits and space armour, so we'll be ready for some serious hijinks. Make sure your helmet is secured at hand and set for quick access. Our maneuverability will be the only thing that will get us out of a firefight, so be quick on the triggers. I'm not waiting around while you take aim."

She scanned the strained faces in front of her. "The *Hawk* is a state-of-the-art bird with the very best arms and equipment, a ground-breaking ArIn and a crew honed to the max. Nobody in human space will be ready for how fast we move and how quickly we target. It will all be hit and run. Remember, we're not here to save a mine. We're on another mission that may be more important. If we're outgunned, we simply leave."

"But the miners..."

"Sergeant Jacobs," she towered over the young commando and nailed her with a glare. "The miners are a tough bunch, and they knew the risks. There's no use losing the Space Arm's only ship in the area by playing heroes. We duck in, we assess, then I make the decision to stay or go. There will be no discussion, because there might well be no time for discussion. Do you follow?"

The gunner's shorn head bobbed. 'Yes, ma'am."

The captain spread her stare to the others. "You all got that?"

A series of nods and murmured, "Yes, ma'ams."

"Right. To your positions. The *NightHawk* is about to enter her first battle. Good luck to us."

They all repeated the mantra and filed out of the mess hall.

5. FIRST BATTLE

It was the toughest hour of Natalia's life. The stress of the G-force was nothing compared to the agony of complete immobility when every nerve was crying out for action. The only thing in her body that functioned was her mind, and she spent the whole time cycling through the possible scenarios, finding holes in her plans, moaning in frustration when she had no strength to speak and relay her thoughts to the crew.

The saving grace was her augment, which kept her in re-ti contact with the sensitive skin of the *NightHawk* and everything the designated sensors could relay.

NightHawk, report.

Velocity at 0.005 Light. Deceleration at optimum. All crew vitals stable. Chakka is not happy.

What do you mean? Chakka?

Image: auguar rending spaceships to small ribbons of metal and batting them around space.

I know, love. I want the same. Hold on like a good cat.

Image: endearing auguar rolling over for tummy rub.

She couldn't laugh very well with a ton of bricks on her chest, but she croaked out a chuckle. "We...will...hit...them...so...hard..."

Message from station. Bombardment stopped 9:23.

Respond: Received. Send real ETA

Change on mission waveband.

What? What kind of change?

Mission waveband has gone active in one of its sleep periods. No message incoming.

I don't have time for this. Send: Standard Query.

Sending as ordered: Query.

Keep an ear open, but concentrate on the battle ahead. No point trying to talk to these beings if we're going to be dead before we can get there.

True, ma'am.

NightHawk, report.

Velocity 0.004 Light. Deceleration at optimum. All crew vitals stable. Mission waveband open and empty.

Graphic interface. Play Action Parameter 5. Thank you. Play Action Parameter 4. Good. Insert Action Parameter 4.5; place NightHawk 500 kilometres closer to station.

Highly unlikely, ma'am...parameter 4.5 recorded.

I know it's unlikely, NightHawk, but I want it to be even more unlikely that we come out of this engagement dead.

Opinion accepted and approved, ma'am.

Your approval does wonders for my apprehension. Report.

Velocity 0.003 Light. Deceleration at optimum. All crew vitals stable. Mission waveband open and empty. Mine waveband empty.

I'm going to shut up and let you run this until we hit action. I have some thinking to do.

NightHawk on full alert, ma'am.

All Space Arm personnel were trained in Present Awareness techniques, and Natalia slipped into meditation where her mind floated free, observing the ship and its occupants drifting below, isolated and separated from her internal reality. She revelled in the relaxation, tuning her mind, her augment, her auguar and her body together in one harmonious blend, ready for the fight.

Some time later she slid back to the real world, a crystal view of her ship and its prospects for the coming conflict fresh in her mind. She felt the power of *NightHawk's* senses and knowledge, the confidence in her own training and abilities, and a feral desire to hunt and kill that could only come from Chakka the Warrior, sharpening his claws on the splintered edge of his acceleration couch.

NightHawk, report.

Velocity 0.001 Light. Deceleration at optimum. All crew vitals stable. Mission waveband open and empty. Mine waveband empty. Nominal galley temperature 100 degrees Celsius.

Can the humour, NightHawk. You said something twice, now. What do you mean, "Mine waveband empty?"

No signal, ma'am. The attack must have taken out their antennae.

Let's hope it was the antennae and not the radio room...

A raucous alarm sounded on the ship's com.

...what have we got?

Bogey at position four, one-seventeen, ninety-five, ma'am.

Course and velocity?

Course directly away, ma'am...calculating...velocity increasing from mine-relative zero. Estimate 0.7 Gs acceleration. In case you meant to ask, ma'am, mass approximately 10,000 tonnes. Length 250 metres. No other information.

Spectral readings on exhaust?

Mostly plasma, ma'am. Typical of standard Hall-type thrusters, but due to the high percentage of Xenon ions in them, an obsolete system in less-than-optimum condition. A poor choice of fuel. As I recall from the survey data, there is little Xenon in natural form in Barnard's system.

Nice to know we're probably dealing with humans, even if they are ten times our size. Our ETA?

Plan to sweep through and hit zero velocity 1000 kilometres past the mine asteroid on schedule for 17 minutes, ma'am.

Carry on.

She dragged up the energy to speak. "Listen up, folks. It looks like someone is running away. I emphasize the 'looks like.' It could be a trick. It could be a false reading. It could be Santa Claus making an unscheduled stop. The *NightHawk* WILL BE READY FOR BATTLE in 10 minutes."

A weak cheer went up, then silence.

She scanned every piece of information the ship could give her. Nothing new.

"Here's the plan if nothing else happens. Six minutes to zero velocity, a slow turnover and approach head on. One minute later a sharp starboard turn-drop-and-burn 45 degrees both ways. Puts the mine and its environs above us to port. Do NOT pre-aim your weapons. *NightHawk* counts down; you prep at the two-count." She paused to take a gasping breath.

"Five seconds accel on that course. Then — helm, listen up — a faster turnover — sorry, Engineering, I know how you feel about those — to original heading and resume decel. That stops us 100 klicks past the station, five klicks below it by galactic north, headed inbound, sliding to galactic west. If you can't picture that, don't worry. I made it impossible to predict. We then adjust course and accelerate as needed.

"Anything after that depends on our reception. Questions?"

Only the sound of breathing filled the com. Roiling emotions of anger, fear, and excitement spilled out of the augment system.

"Fine. Start the turnover on my mark...mark."

It was a move for the textbooks. It would have given *NightHawk* a sidebar in the history of space warfare. They executed with a precision that would have made the captain's heart soar if she hadn't been so worried.

Unfortunately — at least for Space Arm history — this perfect maneuver was the prelude to a battle that never happened. When the ship's nose finally came to bear on the target, the rest of space was empty. The huge asteroid that housed the mine twisted majestically along its orbit, its rotational movement barely perceptible. It was eleven kilometres long, a rough pyramid with the mine on the centre of the sunlit face. Smaller asteroids scattered the space around it, each tumbling its own private route around the star, oblivious to the human disaster that had just occurred.

Magnify.

Little was left of the mine superstructure, which looked as if a mountain had fallen on it. The whole area was scattered with hunks of rock of all sizes, many still floating nearby with deceptively gentle movement until they crashed into each other or the main planetoid. A glint of metal showed a huge ore carrier tucked behind the asteroid. *NightHawk* could detect no obvious damage to the hull.

Everyone with eyes and ears open!

Bogey disappearing into asteroid cluster. Course and acceleration unchanged along the belt down-spin. Mine entry on course, velocity 1200 kph.

Any other report?

Natalia waited a count of ten.

Easy turnover. Resume deceleration for zero velocity one kilometre from the mine entry.

With slow grace, *NightHawk* pivoted and her engines roared again. Normal gravity returned.

First, what do you have on the radio?

Mission band open and empty. Mine band empty...one moment, ma'am...there! I've got it. Emergency com repeater is still operating...a weak signal, but I can work with that..."

She watched the First Officer's expert fingers flying over the screens and reminded herself why he had been assigned to this mission.

As he chased the elusive signal the crackle and hiss gradually faded, and voices began to sift through. His frown of concentration faded, and a smile lit his face. He looked up at her, speaking aloud, now. "There we have it, ma'am. Three frequencies. One broadcast, two suit channels. They were still under battle protocol. Once I sent the handshake codes, we're through loud and clear."

"Multi-channel broadcast, please."

Ready to send. The moment he was back at his duties, Jones retreated into his augment. Which, she had to admit, was the usual protocol while under hostilities.

Hello, El Dorado 12. This is NightHawk. Anyone home?

There was immediate silence. Then a radio crackled.

NightHawk? El Dorado 12 calling NightHawk.

We're knocking at the gate, El Dorado. What's your status?

28

Where is the enemy?

If you mean the ten thousander, she's running. Was there another ship?

We saw no ships at all, NightHawk.

Then let's hope there aren't any more. This is Commander Natalia O'Rourke. Who am I talking to? Again, what is your status?

This is Mine Manager Nicholas Ludge, Commander. We're down in the emergency shelters. We had three deaths and five injured in the initial attack. Everyone else is fine.

May I assume the ore carrier is yours?

Yes. She was loading when we saw the incoming rocks, so we slid her out of danger. Is she damaged?

Not that I can tell.

Natalia paused, the adrenaline and heavy-G relief causing her hands to shake. She couldn't think of what to say.

How do you want to handle this, NightHawk?

I was about to ask you the same question, El Dorado 12. She grinned to herself and flipped her radio signal to the ship's com. "It's safe for you to come out. We aren't in a hurry. We'll stand guard until we're sure the enemy is gone and give you any assistance we can in assessment of damage. You probably have better medical facilities than we do, but our corpswoman is available if needed.

"We have two shuttles, both 4-man with a small payload capacity, if you need mobility. I can't think of anything else. You'll have to ask for what you need."

Thank you, NightHawk. I can only think of one thing. Communications are crucial. Can you send a team from above to look at our antennae?

Send over your equipment specs and we're on it. Ship us an initial report, and we'll launch a com drone to Space Arm and El Dorado Corporation immediately. NightHawk out.

We'll be back to you soon. El Dorado 12 out.

Natalia looked around the bridge. "*NightHawk*, you're on sensors, full power. Everyone else, stand down. Post-briefing in the dining hall in thirty minutes. Fiona, you and Pete are going for a ride after that. Prep Shuttle One and your toolkit."

"Aye, ma'am." Engineer Fiona B'kose was the exact opposite of the Chief Engineer. She was short, black-skinned and slim. Her ability to repair miniaturized components and caress the most precise accuracy out of the battle lasers had earned her the position of "Small-Space Access Engineer," a job with a lot of application on this size of ship.

I take the bridge. Sensor duties top priority.

Take your time, NightHawk, but we laid some stresses on the hull. Full structural analysis second in line, then moving parts.

Aye, ma'am. S and MP analysis commencing.

Natalia glanced around the bridge. No one had moved. *If they're anything like me, the adrenalin is still pumping.* She took conscious control of her breathing. "Ship is at zero V. Bridge is in shutdown. Carry on."

As they filed out she slipped into the chart room and flipped on the screens. Tucking her feet under Chakka's warm body, she settled into her chair. *Replay last ten minutes before zero V at double time. Thank you...stop there. Starboard laser response?*

Within battle parameters, ma'am.

Continue...stop there. Coolant temperature?

Ten degrees above spec. Five under battle parameters, ma'am.

No surprise. Flag that for Engineering. Continue...

* * *

Natalia stood with her hand on Chakka's neck, surveying her crew. They stared back, some worried, some puzzled, shooting side glances at the images of the destroyed facility on the viewers. Finally she threw up her hands.

"Well, I did a quick run-through of the battle record. For our first fight, it was a wonderful drill. We were all where we should be and did what we should do. The ship performed right up to specs, and all systems stayed within parameters. I will expect all of you to review your personal records and write me up a short report. You've done plenty of practice write-ups, but this one's for real and will go in the official log. Now, before it all fades in our memories, does anyone have any impressions? Was anything not as you expected? Anything at all might be important. Nelson?"

The Chief Engineer had been hesitant about sticking up his hand, and now he put on a tentative grin. "I'm not sure what was going on, but before the battle...just after the burn started...was that you...chuckling, ma'am?"

She regarded him from under lowered brows. "And if I was?"

He shrugged. "...share the joke, ma'am?"

"The joke...? Oh, yes. It was Chakka. He would like to play with the enemy ships. Serious play."

The auguar bared his teeth with a gentle hiss that faded away, his eyes firm on the engineer.

Nelson raised his hands. "Whatever he says, ma'am. No argument from me."

"That's a good attitude, Chief. In any case, a great performance all round, and Jonny has promised to dive into her special store of strawberries for another of her famous Pavlovas. Well done, everyone."

6. A SENSE OF HUMOUR

"Permission to enter, ma'am?"

She slid her chair back. "Come in, Adrian. What's happening in radioland?"

"I've been taking a close look at the mission band, ma'am. I think the news is important."

She sat up. "Go ahead." Jones had won his position on the ship over fierce competition because of his hobby: knowledge of historical radio signals. *He certainly isn't here because of his personnel skills.*

Image: Auguar slapping Commander behind the ear with soft paw.

I know. I'm just being catty...no, scratch that last comment as well...oops!

Image: auguar with disapproving stare.

Yes, they warned us about post-battle euphoria. She dragged her attention back to her duty.

"There is greater evidence to suggest this is a machine-generated signal. *NightHawk* and I have been comparing the stream to every supposed alien radio signal for the last two hundred years, and not one of them exhibits such a regularity of wave form and narrowness of band." He perched on the stool she kicked towards him in the low gravity.

"So we're talking to an alien?"

He gave the ghost of a smile. "We're listening for an alien, ma'am. If it's a real intelligence, why hasn't it said anything?" He shifted on the stool. "What we have is, at the greatest stretch, an invitation. An open hand requesting response. That's all. There's a very good chance it's an automatic system hundreds, even thousands of years old."

"But still, evidence of alien life."

"It points that way."

She grinned. "Well, that's great, Adrian. Better than anything any of the other signals have given us."

He nodded, then shifted again, more uncomfortable on the stool than the low gravity should make him. "There's another thing, ma'am. I hate to bring it up…"

She sighed, but only inwardly. "What is it, First?"

He looked around the chart room as if expecting an eavesdropper. "It's our ArIn, ma'am. Could we speak in private?"

She regarded him, then spoke aloud and in her augment. "*NightHawk,* privacy in the chartroom, please. No recording."

"Aye, ma'am. I'm gone."

He pointed at the ceiling. "There. That's what I'm talking about."

"What?"

"That last comment. It was unnecessary and informal. Flippant, even."

"Ah. You have noticed *NightHawk's* growing sense of humour."

"Exactly. Of what use is a sense of humour in an Artificial Intelligence? A sense of humour overlays discussion with an extra tier of social context and leads to misunderstanding, waste of time and a potential for error. I think we should discourage this development."

"I agree with your analysis of *NightHawk's* progress, Lieutenant Jones, but I don't think it will be a problem. ArIns are learning creatures, and she's a young one. The reason they don't program them with a sense of humour is because it can't be done. They have to experience it first hand. They need to know about humour in order to interface fully with the crew. I know an ArIn making a joke could lead to misunderstanding, but an ArIn misunderstanding a joke by a crewmember could be just as dangerous. If Space Arm didn't want them to have a sense of humour, they wouldn't have programmed the ability."

Wondering how much of this problem stemmed from the First Officer's own inability to recognize a joke, she considered her next speech carefully. "If you think about a human's sense of humour as we mature, one element that always needs tuning is knowing when it's appropriate to joke. Some people never learn." She mentally steeled herself. "If you don't mind my saying it, I don't think you have, yet."

His shoulders stiffened and his face went pale. "Pardon me? You are telling me that I don't know when it's appropriate to joke?" His breath rate increased, and his hands trembled. "Name me one time. Just one time that I have made an inappropriate joke. One time..."

She stayed dead still, her hands held up in gentle defence. After a moment he stopped, staring at her. "That's my point, Jones. You never joke. I don't know why, and it's not my business to ask. But I wanted to take a moment when we are all in a very pleasant and positive state, so you will not think I am saying this for any other reason than for your personal development as an officer. I think it would be good if you let down and made the odd joke." She gave him a tentative smile. "Or even a normal joke, if you can't think of an odd one." Then she waited.

He stared at her. Then the light dawned. "Oh." He thought it over for a moment. A smile tried to twitch the corner of his mouth. Finally he allowed it. "You just demonstrated a moment when a joke was appropriate. As a way to reduce tension."

"That's right, First. Now, let's drop this conversation. In the future you and *NightHawk* can tell each other jokes. Don't expect me to listen.

"And now to business. *NightHawk*, back on duty in the Chart room."

"Listening in as usual, Commander."

"Anything else, First?"

The firmness around his mouth showed that *NightHawk*'s turn of phrase had bothered him. Had the message sunk in? He shook his head. "I looked at the analysis as well. I hate to admit

34

it, but I can't find anything but fine tuning needed." He stopped and glanced at her. "No, I don't hate to admit it. I'm proud to say our crew did a fine job, battle or no battle. Coming out of hard-G and performing flawlessly was a fine test of our abilities."

She smiled. "And here's something I don't hate to admit. Your methods of crew training and mine are very different. I'm a great motivator. The crew will do anything in their power that I ask. You aren't. You're a great trainer. Your standards are high, and you make sure the crew comes up to them. We will clash in the future on this element, you can bet on it. But between the two of us, we can create a crew that does everything they are able, and their ability to perform is as high as it can be." She stuck out her hand. "Well done to both of us."

He nodded gravely and shook her hand. Then he looked at his hand, ducked his head, turned out the door and strode down the slideway. Which was difficult, as the ship was stationary, and the inertial gravity from the cockpit plates faded as he went aft.

Was it something I said?

Image: auguar rubbing head against captain's hand, fading to officer rubbing head against Captain's hand.

What? You're saying he's sweet on me?

Image: large, soft paw clouting captain firmly behind the ear.

That's a relief. You're just saying that he doesn't get much praise and he doesn't know how to handle it. And there's me bragging about how good a motivator I am.

She jumped to her feet. "Come on. Let's see how our aerial repair mission is getting on."

7. ON THE MOVE

Natalia mentally disconnected her augment from the ship's systems, leaned back in her chair and stretched mightily. Then she dropped her hands to pat the blocky head that had deposited itself on her knee.

Image: auguar and mistress running through jungle.

She laughed and keyed into the ship's com. "General warning. Clear the running track. All hands who value their hides clear the running track. Guests who think they're up to it are welcome."

She leapt from her chair and dove down the slideway to the living area. At the exit she pivoted gracefully into the increasing rotational gravity and dropped gently down the wall to the rubberized path that girded the inside circumference of the living pod. She started a gentle jog, intending to work up to a full run in time.

Chakka had no patience with such practicalities. He hit full bound in the first three steps, circling high above her head and coming around from behind in no time flat, his tail flicking the small of her back with a "thwap" as he passed. She laughed aloud and pushed forward,

Once they were thoroughly warm they moved into their routine, Natalia leaping the big cat, then rolling as he leapt over her. Running backwards, then forwards, stop-and-go and general silliness with Natalia doing zig-zag handsprings along the track and Chakka ducking underneath each spring. They followed this with leapfrog and tag, improvising until even their melded minds could not keep up and they tumbled in a mass of flailing arms, legs, and tail to land in a panting heap in the middle of the track.

As they disentangled themselves, footsteps approached, and two other figures jogged by at a sedate pace.

"You ever hear of a warm-up, ma'am?"

36

Natalia jumped up and sprinted to catch the smaller commando. "You presume to instruct your Team Leader, who has a whole year more battle training and three levels of command school on you?"

Toni laughed. "Do you wish to challenge my 'fitness' to teach you running?" Her pace increased. She usually took the point position on the Commando team, moving through city streets or dense jungles with such stealth the enemy rarely noticed her. Until it was too late.

"Unfair. You sent your cohort to wind me first."

Chakka bounded past again, pushing it now, his hind paws hitting the mat in front of his nose at every leap.

Image: lazy humans in panting pile.

The two women continued to accelerate, passing Charlie, who plowed ahead at his own ponderous lope, his heavy body moving with grace nonetheless. They split on either side of him, Toni tagging a shoulder and ducking away from the sweeping hand that threatened to flatten her. Natalia used her long reach to jab a knuckle at his ribs, then moved out of the danger zone as well.

"Feels good to be moving."

Toni nodded. Her breath rate had risen, but her voice still came normally. "Can't let ourselves get soft."

Natalia shot her an evil grin. "Don't worry, I've got something planned for you."

"Such as?"

"Next planet in-system."

"What about it?"

"Look it up. Plans aren't complete, but you're going down."

"Recon?"

"Yes, but plans..."

"I know. Not complete. I'll check the surveys." She glanced over, grinning. "Coupla fast laps?"

Natalia waved her companion ahead. "Those were my fast laps. Go for it."

Despite their original pace, Toni added more power and zoomed away, her lithe body moving like a dancer's as her captain slowed to a cool-down jog.

Chakka loped along for the company. He also needed the exercise; this length of voyage wasn't really his metier. That was part of the reason they had been selected for the mission: to test the psych limits of the augments and the individuals that contained them.

* * *

It was a more relaxed crew that lounged in the mess hall an hour later waiting for their orders. Natalia strode in with Chakka, who decided to bless Toni with his attention. She laughed and made room on the couch, hauling his head into her lap.

"So. Plans are going ahead. We've been tossing around ideas, but here's the finished product." She slipped a video feed on the screen: the camera panned past battered metal walls, cracked domes, fallen beams, crushed conveyor systems. Piles of rock everywhere. Impact craters that looked like bombs had gone off. Figures in space suits poked through the rubble with disappointed lethargy, their tiny dimensions emphasizing the vastness of the desolation.

"The installation is toast. Every building has damage; despite our repairs, not one is airtight up to specs. Crushers are intact but industrial power sources are off line and likely to stay that way awhile. The mine itself is undamaged. It's only rock, after all. However, there's no chance of the miners resuming production without major help. It will be four months before our com drone gets home and their headquarters even knows they have a problem, probably nine more before a rescue party can be organized and get here.

"They could just sit tight, but the real problem is life support. The mine's 'ponics system took heavy damage, and their biomass was severely degraded by extended exposure to space. They don't have enough plant volume to support their population for a long stretch in the leaky environment they are stuck with.

"So they have decided to go home. Luckily the ore carrier isn't full. It has two empty bins that can be adapted to rough living space. The rotational-grav travel quarters in the bow will give them enough gravity, combined with the acceleration, to stay healthy." The ore carrier was usually unmanned but carried basic accommodation for the transport of personnel. "It's a good thing this ore is easy to refine into plutonium fuel and iodine reactant mass, so they won't suffer from a lack of propellant. Iodine is not as good as Xenon, but it's convenient, especially in a system where Xenon is scarce."

Lundeen raised his head. "But the biomass?"

"Partly solved by the smaller area and the tighter seals. But that's where we come in."

Toni bounced upright in her chair. "The third planet."

"Give the lady a kewpie doll. We take a run over there and pick up whatever's big enough to bundle together and haul home. Hopefully only one run will do it."

"Compatibility? The survey says the plants are carbon based, but nothing else."

"Apparently it doesn't matter much. We'll test before we harvest, but the 'ponics system busts it down to cellular level, so anything that produces oxygen as a by-product will be fine.

"We break orbit tomorrow. A quick jaunt over to the next planet to harvest our crop, then back here. The miners are already at work on the modifications to the ore carrier. By the time we bring in the load, they should be ready to move. Then we're back on our original mission, having lost only two or three weeks on this little detour. Well within mission guidelines, and I think Space Arm Control will be happy. If

39

they're not, they can take it up with El Dorado Corp, who ought to be very grateful at our timely intercession."

Charlie raised his hand. "And the miners? They heading straight home?"

She shook her head. "Too dangerous with a warship in the vicinity. The pirates are probably waiting for us to leave so they can come in and take over the mine. We have to make sure the miners aren't their target. An experienced staff is a valuable commodity."

Toni laughed. "What's the enemy waiting for? It's a ten thousander, isn't it? All we could do is run."

"I doubt if they're worried about us. More likely waiting to see if reinforcements show up.

"So the miners will be following along in their big, clunky ore carrier. Since our radio source went full-time live, we have better data on it. It's orbiting the next planet outsystem, not more than a week away, even at the ore boat's speed. Then we can go home. Questions. Charlie?"

"When do we get the Pavlova?"

Juanita jumped to her feet to stare down on the bulky commando. "It's three days to the planet. Once we get under acceleration and there's gravity elsewhere, you lot won't be under my feet constantly in the mess hall. Then you get Pavlova, *muchacho. Nada antes.*"

"Couldn't have put it better myself. Say goodbye to your girlfriends on the ground, spacers, because we're under acceleration at oh nine hundred tomorrow."

* * *

"Um...ma'am?"

Natalia turned in her chair with a sinking feeling. The hesitant approach, tinged with determination, meant trouble. "Come in, First. Pull up a stool. What can I do for you?"

40

"It's the Tree Planet, ma'am. We're going there to harvest a crop."

"What?"

"You said it yourself, so I looked it up. By the definition of the Treaties, we're accessing a viable crop on an unknown planet."

She shrugged. "I suppose that could be argued." Then she regarded his face again. That determined look, even firmer. Oh, great. "So, what does that mean?"

He gave a wry grin. "Documentation, of course. Feasibility, potential ecological damage, effect on indigenous animal life. Possibility of intelligent life forms."

She considered. "I did a check before I planned the mission. We have the complete reports from the Planetary Survey. No intelligent life forms. Bountiful flora in a wide range of species. Widespread fauna at all levels but none anywhere near intelligent, even compared to Earth's cetaceans. Most of the concerns you mention will be minimal if we only remove a few tons of general biomass. Still, I agree we should exhibit due diligence. I might have missed something."

His face relaxed. "Fine. I'll get on it. I have already accessed the appropriate forms," his augment sent her a file name, "and as far as I can tell, you're right. At first glance. Just for the record, I'll dig a little deeper."

"Great. Use *NightHawk*'s research function and push her a bit. You'll get better results."

"Push her?"

She grinned. "She's not a computer. Think how you'd help a crewmember who wasn't quite sure how accurate or thorough his work was supposed to be. I'm sure you have had that experience before."

He raised his eyebrows. "As a matter of record, I have." He frowned again, but it was a thoughtful look. "I'll consider that."

He jumped up so fast his feet left the deck plates for a moment. "I'll get right on it, ma'am."

"You do that, Lieutenant. I look forward to what you dig up."

He paused and put on a smile. "And if I don't dig up anything, we can all be happy."

She nodded, and he marched out the chart room door, his step as jaunty as you can manage in light gravity.

8. DOWNPLANET

The next three days were uneventful, as the crew settled back into familiar routines. The Pavlova was a hit, and they slid out of empty space and swung into the gravity of the planet looking forward to their next challenge.

Natalia gazed at the panoramic image that splashed across the bridge viewscreens. "Interesting."

Nobody argued. The system of the fourth planet resembled nothing from back home. Like Barnard's other satellites, it had space debris of all sizes orbiting it. Three bodies were large enough to have orb shape and be called moons. Each of them cut its personal swath through the thick asteroid ring that girded the equator. The composition of the ring was partly visible even at this distance, because boulders, asteroids and uneven bodies with enough mass to be called planetoids jostled their way along the rainbow path of dust and ice.

"Looks like Saturn with a case of the mumps."

"Mumps?"

Nelson chuckled. "An old disease that made the glands in your throat swell up. No fun at all, I gather. Wiped out fifty years ago."

"I thought you meant it put a lump in your throat to see anything that beautiful."

Instead of laughing the Chief Engineer nodded and was silent.

After another pause to appreciate the beauty of the universe, Natalia brought herself back to business.

"Readings, Fiona?"

The tiny engineer looked up from her screens. "Lots of biomass, even from this distance. We'll need to do a complete orbit to figure the spread and then take a shuttle in for samples."

"Good enough." She switched to general com. "Let's have a team ready in the port shuttle bay sixty minutes after we finish the orbit. Full EV suits."

They were straining the capacity of the four-man shuttle to five, with the commander, pilot, engineer and Chakka. For that reason, Toni got the jump seat, much to Charlie's disgust.

"It's sizeism, that's what it is. I'm contemplating a human rights suit."

"When you can fit into Toni's suit, we'll consider bringing you along. You and Pete stand by Shuttle 2 in case you're needed."

"Aye, ma'am. Have a good time."

They belted in and soon were dropping towards the atmosphere, the crew eyeing the viewscreens with nostalgia. It was a typical carboxygen planet, with green vegetation and blue seas, amazingly earth-like. Natalia switched to a close-up view of the landing spot.

Toni had chosen a solid green area on the coast of one of the larger islands in what might be a temperate belt, according to the data from the survey. Axial tilt was minimal, so seasons shouldn't be a problem.

Shouldn't be...there are no guarantees in space; there are even fewer on an alien planet.

"Find a place to put her down, Joe. No rush."

As the image grew, the earth-like similarity persisted. A rocky headland pushed out of a dense forest, small waves breaking on jagged, water-darkened stone. The top was rounded, with a scuff of green that looked quite a bit like moss.

"Aye, ma'am. That peninsula's mostly bare rock. Weather's clear. Wind's light, if the size of the waves hitting the shore are any indication."

"You would know better than I do."

"Looks just like Te Karo Bay on the Coromandel Peninsula, ma'am. On a really bad surfing day."

"I bow to your experience. In your time, Pilot."

44

It was a simple landing, and soon they were lining up for the airlock. "The air is supposed to be breathable, but we'll use EV protocol this time. It'll save us decontamination hassles when we get back to the ship. Lieutenant Jones didn't find a close connection between our biologies, but they're near enough that we should worry about contaminants, so we're at Level 3. That means decon in the airlock going both in and out of the shuttle, and we leave nothing behind, as per regs."

It was good to get feet on solid ground again, despite the 0.9 gravity. The only one unhappy was Chakka. He wasn't a big fan of space suits, but he'd been through the drill often, and the weight of the armour was balanced by its extra protection. The extendable raking claws on all four feet were also a consideration, if it came to trouble.

All sensors alert. What do you see, Toni?

As if there was any doubt. Trees. Massive trunks stretching up into the gray-blue sky. The equivalent of limbs were thick fans of interlaced fibres all the way around the bole every metre or so, expanding as they got higher up the trunk, then contracting near the top to create a roundish ball.

This looks good, ma'am.

It does. We don't even need to bring them inside. We'll boost a load of them onto a course and pick them up as they roll past the mine.

Joe was frowning behind the cockpit window. *Catching them and bringing them to a stop is gonna be a problem.*

It might be if we were going to stop them. But we'll just grab them on our way out-system. The miners can process them en route. We'll have to make sure they rotate to keep the sunlight hitting all sides. A hard freeze would damage the cells.

Sounds easy.

It won't be, but it will work. NightHawk, are you getting this?

Nine-nine-five, ma'am. Nelson is dancing a jig.

Can't see why. He's the one I'm counting on for a way to harvest them.

Says he already knows, ma'am. Done it before.

Are you telling me that Nelson has already lifted giant trees out of the forest and lofted them into space? This I've got to hear.

The Chief Engineer's voice came on. *The only thing important is the roots. Size, spread, and depth of ground penetration. Those dense limbs indicate either light winds or deep roots.*

Fiona clicked in. *These are growing on solid rock, near as I can tell. Thin soil.*

Look for one that's fallen over. We want to see roots.

Right you are, boss. The smaller engineer signed off and glanced at Natalia.

Okay. We're looking for a fallen tree. Chakka, Toni and I will go in and patrol a perimeter at about 100 metres, depending on the thickness of the ground cover. I think we're capable enough botanists to recognize a fallen tree.

Traditionally they assume a horizontal position, ma'am.

Thank you for that informative lecture, Professor B'kosa. Our development as scientists continues. You get what you need inside our perimeter: soil, wood and animal samples. Joe, you still awake in there?

Ready when needed, ma'am.

That didn't answer my question, did it? Bird's-eye view; up you go. Find us a big fallen tree, either nearby or close to a good landing spot.

The shuttle lifted and the team scattered to their jobs. Natalia and Toni followed Chakka into the undergrowth; it wasn't easy. The auguar, despite his bulky suit, was able to force a path between the stems of the bushes that grew in profusion among the tree trunks. The taller humans found themselves at the same height as the longest limb-disks, battering their way through by main strength.

Natalia's suit coolers were moving towards redline, so she stopped to listen. Chakka froze at her thought, and Toni, always watching her Team Leader, did the same.

Silence. Small creatures made non-threatening noises, and now that she was still, Natalia could detect something tiny dancing in the air. She sent a query to the auguar.

Image: small, four-legged something scuttling away: long snout and webbed, three-toed feet.

Anything bigger?

Image: long line of tiny six-legged creatures filing across a log.

Fine. We have flies, mice and ants.

Toni chimed in on her voice com. "Broken branches to our left, shoulder height. Something big."

They slid as silently as possible in that direction, hands on pistol butts. The ground was covered by some kind of spongy moss, and no tracks showed.

"Let's move on."

The real break came when Chakka penetrated another thirty metres.

Image: undergrowth thinning, large trunks spaced out, fading away into the gloom.

She slid onto wide-range com. *Good news. It's like Earth rainforests. The sun only penetrates at the edges. Once inside, there's not enough light for underbrush. Good visibility, easy travel. Toni, let's spread out. Follow the edge of the brush west. I'll go east. Chakka, sweep another hundred metres inland.*

The auguar and the commando slipped away, and she took her own assigned path. *Look inwards for more brush and sunlight. If one of those giants fell over it would cause quite a break in the canopy.*

Her quiet progress was broken by crackling in the brush and a wordless shout on the com.

Toni? What's wrong? Chakka, support.

Heavy breathing on the com, then...*reporting a creature, ma'am. A big one. A hundred metres west. It must have been standing still, but broke when I got too close. Rushed away through the trees, headed inland.*

Video any good?

There was a pause while Toni replayed her visual. *Not great. I oughta be able to clean it up, back on the ship. Tall as me at the shoulder. Four skinny legs, heavy body. Sorta like a moose.*

As long as it hides and runs away, we're good. Prey behaviour. Continue recon.

Long as we don't run into what preys on something that big.

Got trees down, ma'am.

How close, Joe?

Pile of them along the shore. A big, wide fan of roots, just like the limbs. No taproot. That's what it's called, isn't it? A root that goes down deep?

Fiona, you reading this?

That sounds good, ma'am. I've got soil and wood samples and several unclassified wrigglies.

Then let's go home. We have a logging operation to plan. Anybody bring a chain saw?

There was a notable dearth of responses, so they all trudged back towards the landing spot.

Joe's voice broke in. *Uh, ma'am, I'd hurry that up a bit.*

What do you have?

Predatory behaviour, ma'am. Seven blips, smaller than Toni's moose, but big enough to show on my screen. They're following it, spread out in a line.

Direction?

Straight away from us, ma'am. But they're fast.

You heard him, folks. Let's move it.

Coming in, now.

They rolled into the airlock together the moment they hit the shuttle: a tight squeeze, but Chakka took up the space at their feet, and they were off the ground and safe in forty seconds. They deconned the suits as well as the shuttle's facilities could and left them in the airlock. Joe did a quick scan over the region, but the animals had disappeared into cover at the sound of the engines.

They blasted out and soon were back on the *NightHawk*. When everyone was cleaned and safe to board, they met for planning.

"Nelson, now you're going to tell us what you're so happy about. A misspent youth hugging trees?"

"Not quite, ma'am. I worked my way through engineering school as a logger on Vancouver Island."

"Lifting the trees into orbit?"

"Of course not. We used an old-fashioned high-lead logging show with a portable metal spar."

"Whatever that is. How about our situation, here?"

"Heli-logging. I've seen it done. There's stuff in the database if we need it. On the West Coast in rough terrain they fell, limb and top the tree they want. The chokerman loops the choker around the log, The helicopter lowers a grapple, the chokerman hooks on the choker, and away it flies."

"That sounds like a lot of skilled people with special equipment."

"Sure, but that's only a helicopter. We've got a shuttle that'll lift ten times as much, and trees with shallow roots."

"You think we can pull them out?"

"Like carrots from the garden, ma'am. You lower me a cable, I loop it as high as I can on the trunk and run like hell. When I'm clear, you haul it away. Our big advantage over earth helicopters is our sensors. In the old days those poor guys had to navigate by line of sight.

"Depending on the size of the trees and how long it takes, we could take them up one by one or drop them off at a landing and gather five or six together to lift them into orbit. How much mass do we need?"

"They told me 100 tons would be bare minimum, 200 tons optimum."

The engineer paused and his eyes focused upward as he accessed his augment. Then he grinned. "Four trees."

"That's all?"

"Just a guess based on Fiona's samples. A two-metre-thick tree will weigh in the range of 50 tons, depending on the taper. The shuttle can lift more than that. Getting it out of the ground will be the most difficult part. Once it's in the air, they might as well keep right on going. Orbit about 200 klicks up. If we have two cables, when the shuttle gets back we'll have the next one roped up for lift with extra time for a coffee break, and you can match orbit with the first tree as it comes around."

"What kind of special equipment do you need?"

"The shuttle winch is fine as is. I'll make up a couple of 20-metre chokers with snap hooks on them. We can use them later to bundle the load for transport."

"This sounds too easy."

"It might be. If the shuttle can't get them out of the ground, we'll have to cut them off. That won't be fun, especially when they fall. We don't have a saw, and we'd have to burn them down. They'd fall any old way."

"So, let's hope we can pull them out like weeds."

"When do we start?"

"Where are the cables?"

"One hour, ma'am." He started to leave, but turned back.

"Another idea, ma'am?"

"I can tell I'm not going to like this."

"I take down four cables, you bring in the *NightHawk*, and we yank 'em all at once."

"I knew I wouldn't like it. Go make two cables."

As the engineer left, she turned to Toni. "What kind of wildlife do we have?"

The commando sent an image to the viewer. A bulky animal on four legs peered from behind a tree trunk. Two large, dark eyes, spaced on opposite sides of a wide, flat nose. Then it moved forward, revealing a stocky body and humped shoulders with knobbed armour across them. The creature stampeded through the undergrowth and out of sight, its unusual leg joints giving it a strange, rolling gait.

"It's not pretty, but it moves fast."

"An armoured moose, but uglier."

"We'll keep an eye out for those predators, that's for sure."

9. LOGGING

By the time they reached their logging site, the sun was well past noon. "Let's get one tree and see how long it takes. We'll try for number two if the light lasts. Charlie and Nelson get out first, head inland and look for a good tree. I'll get Pete to drop Chakka and me off on that butte over there. I'm still concerned about whatever preys on our moosey friend. It's a good place to watch the logging as well."

Soon the two burly loggers were tramping into the undergrowth, each with a coil of cable slung over his shoulder. Up on the butte, Natalia and her auguar stepped out of the shuttle without even grounding it, and Pete headed back down, the grapple cable already unreeling.

It was difficult, dividing her attention between the fascinating operation in front of her and the wide swath of land she had to watch for danger. Without Chakka and his augmented senses, she wouldn't have tried. She wished she wasn't wearing full space armour. The bright, clear air demanded a deep, cleansing breath, but when she tried it, all she got was a reminder that her suit filters could do with refreshing.

Soon the shuttle was hovering over a particularly tall tree. The grapple hook disappeared into the foliage, and there was a pause. She monitored the com, but the terse commands from below meant little to her. *As long as they're happy, I'm happy.* She switched to her own sensors and scanned for moving masses in the area near the base of the target tree. Charlie and Nelson were close in to the trunk. Nelson's image moved outward, then the grapple line swung inward.

Take up the slack. Easy, now.

She knew what that meant.

Take her away, Pete!

Then the two figures on the ground were running, and the shuttle began to rise. It lifted slowly, the cable coming taut.

Then the airboat stopped moving but the roar of the engines increased.

Nothing happened. Her sensors showed Nelson craning upward to see the top of the tree.

Try a new angle.

The shuttle slid sideways and roared again.

Again, no movement but a tremor in the foliage.

Pete slid his craft to the opposite side and pulled again. This time the top of the tree swayed to follow the cable. Pete reversed, and the top swayed again.

It's working. I can see the soil lifting. Hit it again!

The third pull the top took a definite lean. She imagined the snapping of roots and the groaning of wood at ground level.

She'll go this time. Hit 'er hard!

She bit her tongue to keep from interfering. Pete knew his boat.

The pilot swung around again, heading the shuttle across the axis of the tree. This time the top started to fall, and as the shuttle slowly rose, the branches swooped down and the trunk jumped upward. With a sudden bound the shuttle was moving, and the roots of the tree broke from the forest crown, the top dragging through the disks of the other trees. This looked like a danger point. If one of those disks caught...

And then, with a cowboy whoop on the com, the shuttle was free and flying away to the west, rising rapidly like a seabird with a fish in its talons, its roar diminishing. Soon it disappeared into the clouds, and silence descended.

Whaddaya think, boss?

It seems to have worked.

Seems? That went like a dream.

I hate to interfere...

Oh, go ahead. Tell me my job, ma'am.

53

It occurs to me that if you pick a tree that stands above the others, it's a big tree, sure, but it also gets more wind, so the roots...

I get you, ma'am. Charlie, let's find a shorter, fatter one.

You got it. Look at this one over here.

Yeah, that's great. And he can make his exit over the hole the first one left. I didn't like that dragging-through-the-treetops bit. Hangups and heavy limbs cause most of the accidents in the bush.

I wish you'd told me that ahead of time.

Didn't want you worrying, ma'am. Charlie, it's gonna take him a good hour to get up there and back. Maybe two. Can we get that cable higher on the trunk? More leverage.

Sure enough. Give me a boost and I can get up on that limb. Or disc, or whatever we want to call it.

Natalia stifled a giggle and created a picture for Chakka.

Image: two boys tumbling out of an apple tree.

The response came,

Image: two cubs rolling in the grass.

They shared a chuckle and went back to their perimeter scan. *Not that there's likely to be anything around with all that noise we made. We're definitely the loudest predator on the island.*

Image: powerful male auguar on rock, roaring defiance to forest.

That's you, all right.

With the crew's steep learning curve, the second tree went even easier, and two hours later they were back in the shuttle, heading for home.

"Everything cleaned up on the ground?"

Nelson nodded. "We didn't take anything with us to leave behind. Although I might have seen Charlie drop a sandwich wrapper at lunch time."

54

Natalia ignored this and looked at the forward viewscreen. "Do we need to worry about running into any errant trees in this vicinity?"

Pete gestured towards the screen. "They're tumbling along merrily about a kilometre apart, half way round the world from here. Trans-polar orbit so they don't freeze. I think we're okay."

"Just checking."

"As you should, ma'am. Wouldn't want the crew to get all pumped up about themselves and forget something obvious."

"Like turning on the running lights and radio beacon when we're in the planetary shadow?"

"Thought we shouldn't, ma'am. We don't know there isn't enemy around."

"Probably a good idea. At least it's a good excuse."

"Excuse, ma'am?" His voice dripped injured pride.

"Hmm."

A satisfied silence descended in the cabin as the shuttle winged its way up to the *NightHawk*.

10. STOWAWAY

The miners proved their enthusiasm by having the ore carrier, which was named Santa Maria, already moving outsystem when *NightHawk* caught up with her. They had brought a small ore crusher up from the mine and attached it on the outside of the forward hull. When the *NightHawk* laid the drag of trees alongside, they used the force of acceleration to push the heavy trunks through the machine and into the empty bio tanks. The miners were used to managing high-mass objects in vacuum, weightless or otherwise, and the process went smoothly.

While the ships were in close proximity, the mine manager called Natalia.

She straightened in her chair. "What can I do for you, Manager Ludge?"

The round, forty-something face on the viewscreen grinned. "Please call me Nicholas, ma'am. It only seems right after you came to our rescue like this."

"Seems to me you're doing a good job of taking care of yourselves. I'm Natalia."

"Us miners are an independent lot. That's why they ship us out here where they can't see what we're doing that we shouldn't be."

"You're in good company, then. The Commandos have similar problems with the hoi polloi."

"Glad to hear it. I was going to suggest a social call."

She considered. It was logical, and they had all been too busy with organizing the rescue for any visiting. "Sounds fine. Are you inviting us over for tea?"

Ludge glanced into the dimness behind him. "Not ready for visitors yet, Natalia. I thought I'd just drop round to pay my respects."

"My calendar is rather empty at the moment. If you wait a couple of hours, my cook will have time to prepare something out of the ordinary."

"Anything made by a different cook is a pleasure." He grinned again. "Says the man whose wife is the mine dietician. Shall I come in two hours, then?"

"Do you require transport?"

"No, several of our runabouts survived with minor dents."

"Good. See you in two hours."

"Santa Maria out."

* * *

Two space suits clumped out of the airlock, one normal spacer's gear, the other about half size and a model Natalia had never seen before. The fabric looked highly flexible and light seemed to shift along the surface.

She went to private augment. *NightHawk, what do you make of that suit?*

Nothing like it in the database. Hi res camo, I'd say.

Interesting.

When the helmets came off, they revealed the round head of the Mine Manager and that of a blond boy about ten years old.

"Welcome to the *NightHawk*, Manager Ludge." She shook his hand. "Nice to see you in person after all this electronic communication." She turned and looked down. "And who's your sidekick?"

A frown ghosted across the Manager's brow. "Um...just a friend. He bothered me so much about coming along, I decided it wasn't worth the hassle to keep him away."

The boy shrugged his skinny shoulders out of his suit top with a practised twist and held out his hand. "Crewman

57

Andrew Lundin Collingwood the Third at your service, ma'am. A pleasure to get a re-li look at the ship I heard so much about."

"Hmm." With a thought to nipping potential trouble in the bud, she kept a firm grip on the hand and frowned. "Flattery will get you nowhere around here, youngster. What have you heard about us and where did you hear it?"

The boy slipped out of her grip and shucked the rest of his suit while the mine manager was still struggling with his sleeves. "I dunno. State-a-th'-art buggy like this puts her nose outa spacedock and seven different info nets light up like onea them Earthside Christmas trees."

He leaned closer. "Do you know, on the shadowtech web there's an ad for a full set of specs for this bird, includin' her engines?" He raised a cautioning hand. "You don't wanna believe all you see on the shadow webs, but you catch my drift."

As Ludge pulled a pair of mag slippers from the bin by the airlock door he raised his eyebrows. "For someone with no official bandwidth allotted on the company net, perhaps you're giving away a little too much information, here, with all sorts of official people listening."

The kid shrugged his skinny shoulders and grinned, revealing slightly crooked front teeth. "Aw, I'm just good at lookin' over people's shoulders."

"You'll find the ArIn on this ship a little harder to fool."

"Oh, I'm sure I will, ma'am." He glanced up at her with innocent eyes.

NightHawk?

Aye, ma'am.

You've been monitoring this conversation.

Aye.

You get the drift?

Keep my eyes wide open while he's aboard, ma'am.

Fine...and maybe after he's gone as well.

During this interchange she had been leading the way towards the central pod. Entering, she did her usual economical slide down the wall to the gravity floor, and the mine manager followed at an even more dignified pace due to the mag slippers.

Not Andrew Collingwood III. With a whoop, he launched himself out the hatch at an angle, aiming just off the gravity-less central core, executing a perfect coriolis spin and swooping down and around to land at a trot on the central track. "I just love these centrifugal pods!"

"Where'd you learn to do that?"

"Dunno. Somethin' kids learn, I guess."

"They obviously do." Noting young Andrew for further investigation, she led them to the mess hall. "We weren't expecting two for lunch, but Juanita usually makes plenty, and I don't suppose you burn too many calories."

A glance at Ludge's face told her all she needed to know about his opinion of the situation; he had little idea how to handle the child. She split Andrew off and sent him with a sandwich and a soda to tour Engineering with Fiona while their meeting progressed. She grinned at the manager. "Save the fresh baking for those of us who will appreciate it."

He nodded and looked her up and down as she sat opposite him. "If you don't mind my saying, ma'am, you're a bit...well...larger than I expected. My miners are built stocky. Most spacers we see are on the short, slim side."

"No offense taken, Mr. Ludge. Most spacers aren't Commandos. If you look around, you'll see that this is a small, crowded ship with large doorways. For good reason. Now, tell me about life in a mining colony."

The conversation continued on social topics; there was little business to handle that couldn't be dealt with over the com. Her recent experience on the journey gave her a new perspective of life in such a remote area, and she was astounded at how well the miners seemed to manage. Ludge waved her compliments aside.

59

"You don't get this job unless you can handle it. Thrive on it, preferably. I bet El Dorado subjects potential employees to a more rigorous psych testing than the Space Arm does." He grinned. "We've got more recruits lining up. Pay's better."

Andrew came back an hour later gushing with astonishment and kept up a constant chatter all the way back to the airlock. Ludge met Natalia's glance over the boy's head and wiped imaginary sweat from his brow.

She grinned in response.

"Oh, hey, I bin meanin' to ask. What's with Chakka?"

"Is there something about my auguar that puzzles you?"

"He's called an auguar, is he? Hide's patterned like a clouded leopard, but he's too big. But he's not a jaguar, either. Oh, I get the augment part. He some kinda special project, too?"

"What do you mean, 'too?' Do you see any other special projects around?"

Image: small boy with hands firmly pressed across mouth. "Oh no, ma'am. I musta bin thinkin' 'bout the ship, ma'am."

"That's good. You keep thinking that way."

Hiding her surprise, Natalia contacted Chakka. *Did you send that image?*

Emotion: ???

Never mind.

With a non-committal answer to Andrew's demands for another visit, she saw them through the lock, turned away with her own figurative brow wipe and boosted herself back up the companionway to the chart room.

Ma'am?

Yes, NightHawk.

I monitored the boy closely while he was here. He is very knowledgeable about ship technology.

Pardon me if I don't sound surprised.

And I accessed the mine's records.

And what did you dig up on our little friend?

Emotion: polite laughter.

I get the joke, ma'am. I think you will find this interesting, though. According to their logs, an independent came in for fuel about three months ago. Said they had a stowaway, and if the mine couldn't use him, they were going to space him. Reading between the lines, I got the impression it was more than that.

In what way?

Well, ma'am, you and I both know what the term "independent" means.

A wide range of occupations, services, and ethical viewpoints.

Exactly. From a couple of off-hand remarks on the mine's general monitors, I got the impression that these independents found it difficult to keep secrets with young Andrew looking over everybody's shoulders, and he was an impediment to their way of doing business. If you catch my drift, ma'am.

You and I are drifting along the same vectors, NightHawk. Anything suspicious while he was on board?

Not if asking about a thousand questions an hour is normal for a twelve-year-old.

He's that old? Looks a young ten.

He's not the only one that can be subtle.

Good for you. Anything come up?

Nope. He's clean...but...

It's not like you to be uncertain.

I wondered if I should mention it. He knew he was being scanned. After I finished, he looked straight up at my visual input and winked. He has no implants. How could he feel a scan?

I don't know. If he has no augmentation, how did he send me an image? He's a character, no doubt about it. Fortunately, he's not our problem. She pulled a list up on the monitor. *And these are. Let's start with food consumption rates for a two-week extension on our original itinerary...*

* * *

Her First Officer took the next opportunity to let his feelings be known. They were finishing a meeting in the chart room, and just before he left, he turned in the doorway. "I thought you were rather light on Ludge for bringing that boy over here. He was in no position to take that liberty."

"Ludge isn't military. He doesn't worry about protocol like we do. The kid's probably driving him nuts, and he thought this might shut him up." She grinned. "Faint hope."

"I still don't like it. The protocols are ours, and it's up to us to make sure others follow them. If we let people like Ludge take liberties, they will soon assume that is the norm."

"I agree, but look at it from the manager's point of view. That's one bright kid: a potential resource. If he can train an able assistant, he can work him for room and board until he signs up officially, and then probably keep him on to the advantage of the mine, the owners and the manager himself."

"I don't see much likelihood of that kid hanging around an asteroid mining operation."

"Nor do I, but if Ludge trains up and sends on a viable protégé, he gets credit. That's how the bureaucratic mind thinks, Adrian. I'm giving Ludge a bit of slack. We'll be working together for the next week or even more, depending on what we find at our radio source. A bit of grease on the skids now could go a long way towards keeping the friction down on more important discussions. Besides, there's another way to look at this. Have you heard the old expression, 'Keep your friends close and your enemies closer'?"

"I never give credence to popular wisdom. It is too often skewed towards the popular and away from the wisdom."

"Think about it. The kid knows more than he's saying. He has far greater capabilities than he's letting on. Agreed?"

"With reservations, yes. Mostly he's just a brat who gets away with his sass because he doesn't threaten anyone."

"His game could have serious implications. He also lets slip too much information for someone that seems to be so smart."

"Which gives credence to my contention that he isn't that smart."

"Or else suggests that he means to give us that information."

Jones frowned and thought a moment. "That is possible."

"Are you getting the picture of what this individual is like?"

"Yes, though I think your version is a faulty one based on your enjoyment of that sort of personality."

"A valid point, but the way game is played, my opponent gives me a little more information than I think he should have given. If I fall for his ploy, I think I'm superior to him, and that gives him an edge on me. If I'm smarter than him, I then know about his game, and he's lost both the game and the information he gave me. It's a risk that often pays off, especially if you read your opponent accurately." She grinned. "He didn't."

NightHawk slipped a private thought to her. **Unless he's playing an even deeper game.**

And then I'm counting on you to notice.

The Lieutenant was frowning. "Are you suggesting he's a spy, planted at the mine to infiltrate *NightHawk*? Ridiculous."

"I'm not suggesting anything. You and I are speculating, as good officers do, on probable threats to our ship. My big question is where he came from in the first place. That, plus the presence of the independent, our bogey and our signal, makes me suspicious there is more traffic in this section of the galaxy than Space Arm is aware of. I don't see enough danger to warrant action, but neither do I plan to ignore this kid as a minor irritant."

After a moment, Jones nodded. "I have a different take on the personal situation, but I agree with your risk assessment. Fortunately he is someone else's problem at the moment."

"And as long as he stays that way, we're all happy."

* * *

And she stayed happy as the final chips were cleared away, the hatches were sealed, and the *NightHawk* and the Santa Maria blasted into full accel side by side, their noses seeking out the signal that beckoned from the next planet outsystem.

Her satisfaction lasted until the ships were accelerating at the *Santa Maria's* best rate and everything was settled. Then she strolled into the mess hall for a relaxing cup of whatever Jonny recommended.

To be faced by an interesting pair. Curled on his bed in the corner lay her favourite auguar. Curled against his chest lay her least favourite child.

The boy jumped to attention and snapped her a salute. "Andrew Collingwood reporting as ordered, ma'am."

"What are you doing here?"

The shoulders relaxed and the small, round face grinned up at her. "Came along for the ride."

Faced with that smile, she found it hard to maintain her anger so she frowned harder. "Who said you could come for a ride?"

Vision: A smiling agular with a child curled against his belly

She rounded on the cat. "You? You told him he could come? How did he get on board?"

Emotion: smug satisfaction.

NightHawk!

Yes, ma'am

How did this kid get on board?

Your order, ma'am.

I gave no such order!

Under your authority code, ma'am. I double-checked to make sure. Yes, here it is.

A standard ident image of the stowaway formed in her vision. Under it was her general authority code. The image gradually cross-faded into the auguar and the boy.

"Chakka." She lowered her voice to a growl. "Did you do this?"

Emotion: self-righteousness.

"How long have you been able to forge my codes?"

No teenager can shrug 'I dunno' with more expression than a feline.

She spun to freeze the boy with a pointing finger. "Don't think you're going to get away with this just because something's wrong with my interface." She had a thought. "And if I find out you're the something that's wrong…"

He seemed unimpressed. "Gonna need me."

"I'm going to need you?"

"Mm-hmm."

"In whose opinion?"

Image: a smiling auguar with a smiling child leaning over the cat's shoulders, chin on crossed hands.

"All right, you two. You're up to something, and you'd better tell me right now."

The two miscreants glanced at each other, then each gave his version of a shrug.

"Fine. If you're going to ride this ship, you have to log in. How are we going to do that?"

"Already did."

"What? You have a chip?"

Again the shrug.

Image: a child in a scanner. The viewing screen is empty.

She frowned at Chakka. "He doesn't have a chip."

"I'm squeaky clean, ma'am." Again the grin.

"You have no chip, no augmentation, nothing. And you logged into my ship. How did you do that?"

"How do you communicate to your Helmsman?"

"What…? I speak the orders, he hears me…oh."

The boy elbowed the auguar. "See? She understands."

"I give up. All right, cat. You got him aboard, you take care of him. Figure out a place he can strap in, sleep, stow his stuff. Keep him out of my hair and everyone else's as well. For the next week. Got it?"

The boy snapped to attention and saluted. Chakka yawned and stretched.

"Off you go." She turned away. "I'm going to talk to people that know how to follow orders."

She glanced back as they left. The boy swung his hip into the big cat's shoulder and received a head-butt that flattened him against the wall. He bounced off and jogged away down the corridor, the auguar bounding behind him.

* * *

Dinner was a revelation.

"Well, now we know why you stowed away...no, don't talk with your mouth full."

The boy rolled his eyes in a wide sweep. "Mmm-mmm!"

"The miners don't have spaghetti?"

He chewed mightily and gulped a huge swallow. She could swear she saw the lump slide down his skinny throat. "Not with real meat."

Juanita winked at the Commander. "All depending on your definition of 'real meat.' That stuff has been so freeze-dried, chewed up, tamped down and refried it doesn't know which end of the pig it came from."

The boy snorted. "T'ain't what it is. It's what you do with it."

"Is that a compliment?"

"Sure." He used his last piece of bread to swipe his plate clean. Then he leaned back and looked around. "Y'know, all I seen so far is th' insida this ball we're in. I never even seen th' *Hawk* from th' outside. Space Arm was real stingy with images." He glanced at Natalia. "And I gotta admit, nobody at the mine

66

was interested enough to look any closer. What does th' bird look like?"

Natalia smiled. "I'll let the old man fill you in. He knows the most about her. Hear him talk, you'd think he built her himself."

Nelson was unfazed by the appellation, pleased to take on the role of oldest hand on the ship. "Some of the more recent modifications, I did." He leaned back in his chair and stared at the ceiling a moment. "Well, she's a slim, high-powered, lightly-armed Scout a hundred metres long. She's got this rotational gravity chamber in the centre, making her look rather like a seal that swallowed a basketball."

"A seal? I hearda those..."

"Aquatic mammal. Long and sleek like a naval torpedo."

"I know what a torpedo's like."

"Well, there you go. Engines, fuel and Engineering in the aft section. That's Fiona and me. No gravity back there unless we're under thrust like we are, right now. Otherwhen Sphere in front of that. Centre of gravity of the ship, of course. 'Ponics around the outside of the Sphere where it's warmest.

"Living quarters in the rotational gravity chamber. Optimum point eight Gs. Don't be in the central ball when the ship does the midpoint turnover. Gravity goes all wonky. You ought to hear the bearings complain."

The engineer pointed a grease-impregnated finger at the Helmsman. "In fact, you're the one who needs to hear that one more time. Those bearings are under-specced, and if you keep playing that game, they're going to freeze up. It's only rotational torque. If you would take the flip at about a quarter the speed, there'd be no pressure at all."

Pete opened his mouth, but then his glance shot to Natalia and met her stare. "Sure enough, Mr. Lundeen. The captain mentioned it. All you have to do is say the word."

The Engineer paused a moment to assess this capitulation, then smiled and turned back to the boy. "Weapons control and shuttles and the like in the for'ard hull. Variable gravity there, too. Right forward is the Bridge. Point three grav and inertial damping from plates under the floor. Very new tech.

"Bridge right at the front, hey? I guess if the cap'n piles us into somethin' she'll be the first one at the scene of the accident. Sounds fair to me."

Lundeen stifled his grin. "Three-sixty cubed visuals so the captain and helm can see in re-li what's coming at us from any direction. Or what we're coming at, more likely. Not too many ships in the universe are going to be coming up behind us."

The boy nodded. "'Less we're deceleratin'." He ignored the adults' reaction. "Hull's Permaskin, ain't it?"

"It is. Full sensory response throughout. *NightHawk* feels space like a seal feels the water, through the whole electromagnetic spectrum from ultraviolet to infra-red. Pressure, auditory and chemically sensitive, too, for atmospheric work."

"Can she land on a planet?"

"Nope. Not unless it's a small one. Moons and the like, no problem, but she gets down a deep gravity well, even her big engines couldn't lift her off."

"Why didn't they give her big enough engines?"

"Limited by the humans inside her. We can't stand the acceleration." Nelson leaned his elbows on the table. "It's the size of the inertial dampers. The nature of the beast; they have to be heavy to do their job. If we put in a set powerful enough to neutralize the push of those bigger engines, it would make the ship so heavy that the engines couldn't lift her anyway."

The boy nodded. "I see." Then he grinned. "I guess we'd better not land her on Xeta, then."

Natalia frowned. "Where's Xeta?"

The boy's face froze. "Ain't that...where we're goin' right now?"

She stood over him. "We don't know where we're going right now. We're following a signal, and that's all we know. Do you know more than that?"

"Tha's funny. Coulda swore somebody on the ore carrier mentioned Xeta. It's the next planet outsystem." He shrugged. "I coulda bin mistaken."

Chakka, stretched out on his bed in the corner of the mess, yawned. *Image: Large claw poking small boy in butt.*

He's lying. More interesting. Just a kid playing games?

Image: small boy with large head.

That's what I'm thinking. Good idea to have him where we can keep an eye on him.

Image: large, beautiful cat rolling over for tummy rub.

Don't push it. Anything goes wrong, you're still responsible. He messes up, then turnover would be a great time to reassign ship's personnel.

"Andrew, you're here on sufferance. You don't leave the gravitational ball without escort, and that goes double for the bridge. Do you follow?"

"Oh yes, ma'am."

"See that you remember. Dismissed."

She shook her head as he saluted and spun away.

But her warnings seemed to take effect. Andrew endeared himself to the ship's crew, but spent a lot of time with Chakka, either curled up silently or roaming the ship. The auguar enjoyed the attention wholeheartedly, and Natalia began to see the boy as an asset to the team for that reason as well. Nobody really knew the needs the augmented animal would have, and companionship of an equal seemed to be one.

The visitor worked his way into an unofficial position of errand runner, attentive listener and general entertainment by turnover, and watched from *NightHawk*'s viewscreens as the Santa Maria took a leisurely time to flip the long, heavy aggregation of loaded storage pods around for the decel burn.

At that point, the two ships parted company, Natalia opting for a shorter, heavier burn starting later to approach their objective a few hours ahead of her companion.

11.   FIRST CONTACT

As they approached Xeta, Natalia scanned it closely with all her resources, ending with a visual that she left up on her screen. It was far less inviting than the Tree Planet, with an overall reddish hue, streaked with browns and greys. The Survey had flagged it for mineral content, but for quality of life it rated rather low. The usual assortment of companions orbited it, including one decent moon, but it lacked the striking, multicoloured ring of its sister planet.

Chakka stared at the image, his augment active.

Emotion: disdain and disappointment

You got that right, buddy. We won't be going down there unless we have to.

Action on mission wavelength, ma'am.

Natalia jerked upright in her chair. *What kind of action?*

Echo of our query. Echo of our query. Package of data, unknown format. Echo...echo...data. Same size of package. Repeating over and over.

Put the data package on full military firewall. Use the hardwire to send it straight to the isolated cpu, lock the door and physically disconnect once it's secured. Do the same with one of the echoes and ignore the rest. I don't want you to touch this, NightHawk. I'll work on it myself, first. With my augment turned off.

Aye, ma'am. Data package and echoed query so moved.

"Lieutenant, take no further action unless the package changes. Then let me know. The bridge is yours."

"I relieve you, ma'am."

"First Officer on watch."

In the chart room, Natalia opened her closet, pulled out her stand-alone and fired it up on battery power, disconnecting the cable interface. The data package was there on the desktop viewer when the screen came up. She started to work the manual keyboard, first using the standard capabilities of the SA. She compared the query package to an original, right down to the individual byte, but it proved to be identical in every way. Then she turned to the alien data package.

It opened on the third try. *A string of ones and zeros, just like they taught us to expect in the Command class on First Contact.* There was a base two translator in the SA unit, and soon she had a solid stream of images and words in different languages scrolling down the monitor.

Reminding herself to pay closer attention in the classes she took, she opened the standard First Contact program and followed the prompts.

Standard English rolled across the screen.

She dropped her hands in her lap and stared. *English on the first try. This is too easy. Or maybe it's not. Scientists, linguists and mathematicians have spent more than two centuries preparing for this moment. For once they got it right.*

She started to read.

Two hours later she faced her crew in the mess hall and Mine Manager Ludge on the remote screen. "Here's what we have, folks. You wouldn't believe how easy it all was. Out there, tucked behind the moon of the next planet, the name of which is Xeta," she shot a frown at Andrew, "is a factory. It's looking for business." She tossed up her hands. "That's it. You should check out the info package. It reads like a pamphlet for a multi-functional fabricating shop. A lot of the stuff is technical names that won't translate, but this factory can apparently create just about anything you can bring them the specs for. Electronic, optical, medical, biological, you name it.

"Oh. But they don't do weapons. That's pretty much their only caveat. No weapons. That sounds positive."

Ludge cleared his throat. "How does one pay these people?"

She grinned. "That's the good part. They'll barter. Anything you have. New technology, work time, genetic material, you name it. But you know what's on top of their list? Energy. They need fuel right now, and they'll take any kind. Plutonium, radium, uranium...they'll even take crude oil or coal, if you can believe it."

Ludge's dour face broke into the first smile she had seen. "You mean we can get repairs done and use our payload to cover the charge?"

"Seems like it."

Jones frowned. "Wait a minute. We haven't even made first contact, and already we're doing business? Isn't that rushing things?"

She shrugged. "They told us in the briefings to go along with whatever the alien race seemed to find normal. This is a factory. It stands to reason that they will find doing business normal. What do you think, Nicholas? Shall I call them and give them our ETA? Tell them we're offering energy? Nothing specific, I don't think."

"Yes, let's be cagey about this. We have no idea who we're dealing with."

"We don't even know if these are the people who attacked you."

The Manager's smile faded. "I suppose they could be. But why?"

"Who can tell? Jones, you're frowning."

The First Officer shook his head. "You say this was all too easy, but now you're going ahead."

"We have to. That's our assignment. I followed every single protocol that was laid out in our orders and in the First Contact class at the Academy. I have absolutely no idea of the sophistication we face. For all we know, our heaviest precautions are like kids with sand shovels and beach buckets facing a tsunami. We have nothing else to go on except our intuition."

He grimaced, but said no more.

She knew how he felt about intuition. "So, Manager Ludge, have I your authority to open basic negotiations for repairs and perhaps modifications to the Santa Maria on behalf of the El Dorado Company as well as the PCSA? I won't commit to anything without consultation."

"I suppose we must take some risk. We're heading their way in any case. We certainly could use an upgrade of the ore carrier before such a long trip with this huge crew."

"Fine. I'll get on that and keep you posted." She dusted off her hands. "Let's go see what this factory looks like."

12. FACTORY 480

It was frustrating and possibly dangerous to approach a planet with a potential threat hidden behind it. The small moon held a scattering of asteroids in its orbit, sufficient to hide any number of fighter-sized attack vessels. So *NightHawk* swung wide, dipping closer to Xeta and dumping velocity by turning uphill away from the planet. As they slued around in their course change they began to see the hidden side of the moon.

NightHawk spoke on the com for the benefit of the crew.

"Bogey coming into sight, ma'am. On the ecliptic. Large and circular... correction, toroidal."

I see it. Magnify screen one, please.

The fuzzy image showed a huge, donut-shaped object coming into view from behind the moon. It looked lifeless, just hanging there in space. There was no movement on or near it.

Natalia's heart jumped. "No humans made that."

"Nothing in my data base anything like it, ma'am."

The Commander made eye contact with her First Officer. Both shook their heads in awe.

"Zero Velocity in ten minutes, ma'am, 2000 metres short of the object."

"We'll flip now and use our thrusters at five to stop 1000 metres short."

"Initiating slow turnover for the sake of Mr. Lundeen's bearings. In five...three, two, one, Fire thrusters."

The starfield spun as the ship turned end-over end, settling with her nose facing the toroid.

Well, that wasn't fun.

What? Andrew, is that you?

Image: Boy with green face, hands over mouth, eyes wide.

I'm not going to ask how you got on the com. Didn't anyone tell you to stay out of rotational gravity during turnover?"

Um...yeah, I guess so.

So you'll remember the lesson, now.

Emotion: helpless acceptance tinged with wry humour.

"Zero velocity in ten seconds."

NightHawk eased off on her thrusters and slid to a gentle halt facing the behemoth that spun serenely, shining in the faint sunlight.

"Zero velocity. Objective in view. First stage of mission complete."

"Record that in the log, if you would, along with a full set of readings on every sensor we have."

"So recorded, ma'am.

Without a request, *NightHawk* zoomed in to cover all the forward viewscreens, giving them a re-li view.

The outside of the factory was a torus about a kilometre in diameter and more than a hundred metres in cross-section. It was surfaced with a reflective metal coating, mostly featureless, but with large symbols in bright red, dark blue and glossy yellow lining the sides. The centre was crisscrossed by catwalks, gangways and thick, square beams that looked structural. Attached to these were gantries, grapplers and the other paraphernalia of a full-sized spaceship repair yard.

But everything was neatly battened down and tidied away. Nothing in that huge factory moved, nothing was out of place.

"Looks like they've all gone home for the holidays."

"What are you reading, Mr. Jones?"

He answered on the augment. *Very little activity. The sort of background hum you get when a lot of electronics are running on standby. Can't penetrate the hull with anything we have.*

I concur, ma'am. Peripheral evidence suggests the section nearest us at the moment is hydroponics. Those raised rectangles could be window frames, and that side of the hull is five degrees warmer.

Synchronize us with that section; we'll follow until it hits sunlight.

Synch in progress, ma'am.

Thrusters fired, and a slight lurch wiggled through the light gravity on the bridge. The huge artifact seemed to stop turning, but the stars began to slide sideways.

"While we're waiting, what's on the radio?"

"Nothing, ma'am."

"Nothing, ma'am."

"All right, Lieutenant. Let's knock on the door. Send First Contact Protocol 5 on their usual frequency."

"Aye, ma'am...Protocol 5 sent."

There was silence in the cockpit as the torus sat there fat and stolid, and the stars streamed by.

"Sun line coming around. Let's see what happens...well, look at that."

As the swath of sunlight inching along the shiny hull reached the first frame, a vertical crack appeared, growing larger moment by moment. Soon a curved reflection appeared in the crack.

"Just like opening a shutter."

"Hydroponics, all right. Morning has broken on the factory floor. All workers rise and shine...any sign of life over there?"

"No movement...I tell a lie. Radio contact."

"Stay on maximum security, *NightHawk*, and keep yourself out of the contact. Lieutenant Jones, let's hear what they have to say on the remote speakers. Audio only."

"Coming up, ma'am. Santa Maria joining the mix."

Nicholas Ludge appeared on the viewscreen.

Static crackled, then disappeared, replaced by the low hum of a carrier wave. Then individual words came through.

Welcome...NightHawk...welcome...members...of the...human race...this is Factory Four Eight Zero...how can we help you...

She glanced at Jones, who nodded. "Hello, Factory Four Eight Zero. Can we speed up communications in any way?"

...send words...please...

"Sending, Factory 480. This should help."

Lieutenant, ship them First Contact Protocol 12. That's the dictionary, isn't it?

Sending Protocol 12, Standard English Basic Vocabulary, ma'am.

The Factory did not respond immediately, and she turned to the crew on the bridge. "Certainly no movement. Do you think they're running on solar power?"

Nelson frowned. "Doesn't seem efficient, when most of their hull is reflective."

"Not very reflective. *NightHawk*, give me a close-up of that hull."

As the viewscreen zoomed in, the hull rushed towards them and everyone started back.

Hey, take it easy!

"Sorry, folks. Just trying to be quick."

Forget the stunts and analyze.

"Hull skin was once shinier. The plating has been abraded. Random patterns."

Nelson Lundeen came on the com from Engineering. "Space dust. This thing has been out here a long, long time."

"How long?"

"Humans have had satellites up for over two hundred years. None of them, even the very oldest, have been scraped up like that. We're talking thousands of years, not centuries."

Jones held up a hand, and the radio crackled again in the speakers.

"That's much better, NightHawk. It is so good to talk in a more normal fashion. As you çan see, we have a huge state-of-the-art facility with, if I may say, unequalled capabilities. Was that a joke? Your protocol mentioned humour as a human method of easing tensions in new situations."

Natalia buried her face in her hands for a moment.

"Yes, that was a joke, Factory Four Eight Zero, and it was quite appropriate for the occasion." She grimaced at her crew and mimed throttling someone. "We have read your information, and we gather you are a construction and repair facility. We have an ore carrier that needs modifications to carry extra passengers. Can you do that?"

"A piece of cake, in your idiom. Send me the specifications and a précise of what you wish."

Natalia switched to a private contact. *Can you do that, Ludge? Send it to me, I'll put it on the secure line and ship it over.*

I've been updating the problems as they appeared during the trip here, so it's all ready to go. I don't think the Company will mind sharing the specs on the old Santa Maria.

She raised an eyebrow to Jones, and he nodded.

"Thanks, Ludge. It's on its way. Now the horse-trading starts."

She switched back to the Factory's frequency on the ship's radio only, keeping *NightHawk*'s ArIn isolated.

How long will you need for an estimate?

Not long. We certainly have the capabilities, and as you can see, we aren't too busy at the moment. Hmm…we'll need to mine two or three standard metals from the planet surface unless you wish to cannibalize one of the pods. I'm not sure of human space requirements, but that would make it rather crowded for your people by most standards.

How long will the mining take? Days? Weeks?

Oh, we have the surface already mapped out. With a decent energy source, we can have the ore up here and smelted in about three Xeta days, which would be about two and a half of your Earth days. We can work on the other modifications while we wait…

Natalia now had a feel for this entity's speech rate, and assumed this pause was an invitation for her input. *…which brings us to the next stage of the conversation. What kind of energy do you need, and how does that figure in the cost?*

If we had visual contact, this would be the point where I transmitted a smile, I think. Do I have that right?

78

Yes, a smile would be appropriate.

Do you want to open visual channels?

We have security concerns. We have no knowledge of your computing capability and no guarantee of your intentions.

Ah. Very astute, but likewise, I have no idea of yours. A certain level of trust is necessary when any two entities do business.

True. She glanced at Jones.

He rolled his eyes, shook his head and shrugged.

She switched to the Santa Maria's channel. *What do you think, Mr. Ludge?*

I bow to your experience, ma'am.

"It's all on me then, folks. I guess that's the way it's supposed to go."

All right, Factory. We're opening a standard video frequency. She nodded to Jones.

Snow blurred the viewers, and then a familiar scene came into focus.

"What the he..." Murmurs echoed through the bridge. "That's a cartoon!"

Would this be an appropriate avatar?

A cartoon character strolled into view. A very familiar character.

The bridge crew exploded into laughter. "Mickey Mouse?"

"I do not understand your reaction." A pleasant male tenor voice came over the com. "Was that a mistake? I felt it appropriate to assume a non-threatening mien."

Natalia forced herself to be serious. "That was laughter, Factory Four Eight Zero. The avatar you chose is from children's entertainment and is certainly not threatening. However, it is hardly serious either. Perhaps not a perfect fit for a businessman."

Mickey shrugged and grinned. "Well, if this avatar is not offensive, I will maintain it until I have learned enough about

79

human culture to make a more appropriate choice." The Mickey avatar made a sweeping bow. "And now, madam, since I assume I am viewing Commander Natalia O'Rourke, it is a pleasure to meet you."

"'Commander' is usual, Factory Four Eight Zero. What should we call you? And don't say 'Mickey.'"

"Four Eight Zero is my designation…"

"Well, 'Four Eight Zero' is rather cumbersome. How about something shorter, like, 'Four-Eighty'?"

Mickey bowed again. "Four-Eighty it is."

"And I suppose now that we have names and faces, we can all trust each other?"

"That was my hope."

"Maybe a little bit. One more point. May I assume there is no member of a living race present? You are an ArIn?"

"You are correct." On the screen, Mickey morphed into a tin-sided, can-shaped cartoon robot. "I am an electronic-based intelligence. I have no corporeal body besides this factory."

"Well, I suppose we can trust each other enough to discuss prices. How do we negotiate, when we have no common basis for values?"

"I deal with this problem all the time. I assess what you have and what you want and posit your level of need on that basis. It goes without saying that one incentive both of us have is the possibility of a mutually beneficial extension of our business relationship."

Mickey took on a thoughtful frown and rested his chin on his fist. "That's a strange expression, isn't it? If it goes without saying, why did I say it?"

She grinned. "If you want to talk about the illogical nature of human language idioms, we'll be here until the sun goes nova. May I assume we are paying you in fuel?"

"Do you have information I do not possess that suggests this star will go nova any time soon?"

"Another expression, Four-Eighty. May we talk business, or are you stalling while you finish your analysis?"

"Oh, I finished that long ago. It's just been a while since I met a new species...actually it's been a while since I met anyone. Pardon me if I ramble on."

Mickey appeared in glasses with a brief case. "But to business. I anticipate a quick solution here as well. Since your ore carrier is loaded with plutonium triiodide, and since your Sol system is 6 light years away and the Santa Maria has a maximum acceleration of 0.7 of your gravities, I calculate over a year to get her home through Otherwhere. Thus I assume that you will be eager to pay me the amount of plutonium ore in point seven five of your fuel pods to do the work. An extra point two five pods will fuel my equipment for the mining and cover startup fees, taxes, overhead, consulting fees and maintenance."

The avatar grinned. "Incidentally freeing up one more pod for an extra hydroponics park with a limited oxygen potential, but containing growing plants and a pleasant atmosphere." A sweep of Mickey's white glove, and the cartoon screen depicted a pleasant small park with bushes, short trees, grass, a park bench and an asphalt square with a common child's game lined on it in white.

"That looks very nice, Four-Eighty, but I see a couple of problems. In the first place, where does the gravity come from? In the second place, the Santa Maria can't do better than 0.5 Gs, even with this reduced load."

"Ah. Well, that did take some projection on my part. I assumed that, because of the attitudes of the crew in your cockpit, you have some kind of rudimentary gravity plating, and I included a unit of sufficient size in the price. I am also assuming that you will accept a few small modifications to the Santa Maria's engine configuration that will increase power by 33% without causing undue stress to the structure, and actually giving better gravity to the folk inside. These ships are heavily overbuilt, in my opinion, but I understand the philosophy, under the circumstances.

"My fee will leave Santa Maria twelve full pods, which is point seven five of a load, which I calculate enough to satisfy her owners, in light of the disaster that has befallen you."

"What disaster would that be?"

"You have not been quiet in your radio communications in the past weeks. Once I had the vocabulary, it all became clear to me."

Mickey magicked a scroll out of the air and began checking off items. "And the design changes are all covered in the consulting fee. Do we have a deal?"

"How long will this all take?"

"By your quaint timescale, eight days."

"Oh." Natalia was thinking furiously. "I...I have a much better idea now of your capabilities. I need to consult with my people. Could you stand by a moment?"

"My dear lady, I have been waiting for many centuries, by your calendar. A few more minutes will make no difference." Mickey stared into the camera with wide eyes, his fists pushed against his cheeks. "But please don't take too long. I am agog with suspense."

Natalia made the finger-across-throat signal to Jones and brought the Manager's image up on the screen. "Ludge, did you send the Factory the specs for that ore crusher you brought along to handle the biomass? I assume you have them with you?"

"No, I didn't, and yes, I have them."

"Please send them over STAT. I'm getting an idea. You people don't really want to make this trip home, do you?"

"Of course not. Once we get back there, who's to say any of us will get the job when they open the mine again...? Wait a minute. Are you thinking...?"

"That's right; I'm thinking. Ship me those crusher specs. "

"Right."

There was more snap in the man's voice than she had ever heard, and the file appeared immediately.

"Open the channel to the factory, *NightHawk*."

"Channel open, ma'am."

"Four-Eighty. I'm sending you a file. Could you create parts for this machine?"

Mickey came back on the screen, perusing a long scroll of paper. He tossed it over his shoulder and dusted his hands in disdain. "Like falling off a log. Why would anyone want to fall off a log?"

"All right. I have another thought. I'm remembering your comment about future business."

Mickey rubbed his hands together, dollar signs in his eyes. "I'm listening."

"NightHawk, get Ludge in on this conversation."

"Aye, ma'am."

"We have a mine that was hit by an asteroid storm. Trashed just about everything, including some heavy equipment like that ore crusher."

"We wouldn't be talking about a plutonium triiodide mine in the inner asteroid belt, would we? Where the ore in the Santa Maria came from?"

"We just could be. What if we separate this ore carrier and use the tractor section to haul the broken equipment over here. Could you repair it?"

"I think I could do better." Mickey appeared in a fishbowl helmet, waving from a cartoon spaceship. "I could send much faster ships over to get the parts. Maybe even repair units to fix them on site."

"You could do that?"

"Easy as pie. Although from the information given in the protocols, pie is one of the most difficult of foods to make really well."

83

Mickey took on his thinking pose. The next picture showed the rocket ship towing a huge toroid behind it. "There is, of course, always a more simple solution."

"You can move this thing?"

"You don't think I was built here, do you?"

"I have no idea."

"Well, I wasn't. With sufficient plutonium, I could park myself right off your mining asteroid and do the repairs on site. I was thinking of moving anyway. Getting tired of the same old scenery, you know. Xeta is a rather boring planet."

"All right. This is going to take a bit more thinking than a simple repair job. I'll have our Mine Manager send you his preliminary analysis of the repairs needed. You give us two quotes: one for doing the job remotely, one for moving over and doing it there. Meanwhile, I'll have a talk with my people. All right?"

"That would be fine. But am I right in thinking that your miners are in very uncomfortable living quarters at the moment?"

"That's a good guess."

Mickey appeared in front of a hotel in a redcap's uniform. "I have made a leap of faith that we will be doing business together, and I have prepared a section of my hull with an Earth environment. I copied the passenger cabins on the Santa Maria, adapted with the information in your quaint little contact protocol, added a few other bits and pieces of data I have managed to glean and have adjusted the accommodations accordingly. If you would use your shuttles, you could move your people to the hatch marked with the dotted lights. At the same time, you would do me a great favour if you would allow my ore haulers access to one of your bins. I have very little fuel left, and the modifications cut into my reserves seriously."

"Ludge, are you getting this? I don't know about your crew, but whatever deal we make, it's going to involve a pod of fuel."

84

"Let's start with the fuel, and I'll have a talk with my people about moving tomorrow. I'll tell you, the last six days have given everyone serious second thoughts about the trip home."

"Have you got that, Four-Eighty?"

"Roger, ma'am. We'll start the fueling right away, you can send our visitors whenever you wish and we can talk business at our leisure." Mickey began to dash around a cartoon hotel room, dusting, vacuuming, tearing outside to fuel a car, then back inside to toss papers around a desk.

Natalia looked around the cramped bridge. "All right, folks. Too much, too fast. I need to slow down and not get stampeded into anything. Dinner in two hours. *NightHawk*, tell Jonny to let it loose tonight. Limited wine and beer access. Dessert most important.

"Message sent and received with gusto, ma'am."

"Con mucho gusto, Señora."

"All right. Everyone else is dismissed to regular watches until supper. Mr. Jones, you and I..."

He gave a small smile. "No rest for the wicked, ma'am."

"That's right. But at least we can talk in private."

They settled in the chart room and silence fell. "Now's a good time for an honest opinion, First."

He frowned. "I am always honest, ma'am."

For a moment, she was stunned, but she recovered as quickly — and she hoped as subtly — as she could. "No, no. I was not challenging your integrity. I mean don't hold off. This is when I don't need anybody backing down because I'm the captain. Do you understand? What is your opinion?"

His shoulders lost their rigidity. "I don't like it. "

"I didn't think you would. Why not?"

"You said it yourself. Too easy. Too smooth. He's too smooth. It. Whatever. That Mickey Mouse stunt is a perfect example."

"You don't like cartoons."

85

"I don't, especially, but that's not it. Have you been watching the screen? He's turning this into a kids' Saturday morning entertainment. He's calming us down, distracting us. Who knows what else is going on?"

"A lot is going on, that's for sure. What do you know about used car salesmen?"

"What?"

"Used car salesmen. You know. The stereotype."

"I know the stereotype. I've never bought a car, but I've run into the sort elsewhere. I do see your point."

"Not saying every used car salesman is dishonest, and not saying that every used car is a lemon. I'm just being wary."

"As you should be. Are you going to deal with this...creature?"

She shrugged. "We have to. Have you looked at the larger ramifications?"

"I'm not sure what you mean."

"Setting aside the fact that it says it doesn't make weapons. Can you see the advantages here? The new technology available? If Four-Eighty can put a third more steam into the old Santa Maria's tank, think what it might do for *NightHawk*!"

"But that would involve giving him our specifications. That's classified information!"

"Exactly. You see the choices we have ahead of us?"

"But we don't have to make any choices. Why don't we just go home and tell the Space Arm that this thing is here, and let them deal with it? That is our mission."

"You're forgetting our friend the cruiser out there somewhere. What if he comes back and makes a deal while we're away?" She rose and began pacing the small floor space. "What if Four-Eighty is exactly what it seems to be? What if it's completely concerned with business, with no compunctions or morals about whom it does business with? What if its only code is to stick to a contract, no matter what?"

86

He shrugged. "In that case, the best thing to do is tie it up in as tight a contract as we can. But..."

She waited.

"...right. Once again, we just don't know." He leaned back. "I don't think we're at the pay grade to make such an important decision. I think we need to get home and hand it over to those who have the knowledge and experience."

"So we just take off, right now?"

"That would be the best move. As you said, the sooner we get home, the sooner the Space Arm can send their envoys."

"And leave the miners here? What will they do?"

"Whatever they want. They certainly won't ally with the people who squashed them."

"That's a point. But now you bring up another conflict."

"Which is?"

"Let's assume that this entity is on the level. It isn't trying to entrap us, to discover our technology, to use us as slaves, steal our souls, or anything nefarious. If we stay here and do the bargaining, we have the advantage. The miners are still in shock. Ludge is an administrator, not a politician. We can be the ones with our names on the contract. The interface goes through us, just as it did this afternoon. The Space Arm is in at the start. Now you tell me what happens if we walk out right now...go ahead. I can see you're hesitating, but you're a smart man. Use your logic."

He shook his head. "I know, I know. It's the old government-against-the-corporations thing. If we leave these miners here with this factory, and if it can do what it says, we'll come back in a year or so to find the Four-Eighty parked beside its own private plutonium mine, fat and happy and turning out mining, exploring, electronic, and who knows what other equipment and designs to pay for it. For all we know, the cruiser and their friends will see which way the wind is blowing and come wagging their tails for a piece of the action."

He ran both hands through his hair, locked his fingers behind his head, and stared at her. "Is that what you wanted me to say?"

"No, I was hoping you'd come up with another scenario. But I didn't expect you to, because I certainly can't, and I'm supposed to be the creative one around here."

He shook his head in frustration. "I don't understand it. We don't have the knowledge or experience to deal with this sort of thing. Why did they send a crew like us on this mission?"

"Hah!" She raised her eyebrows. "Questioning the decisions of your superiors, now?"

"Well? Do you think we're qualified?"

"For once, I'm going to stand up for our Space Arm bosses, Of course we're qualified. For the job they sent us to do."

"Which was to investigate this signal."

"And...?"

"What do you mean? The signal. That's it."

"Access the orders. Read the next sentence."

"What?" His eyes went blank a moment. '...and contact El Dorado 12 mine and give any assistance necessary.' But that's just good diplomacy. We couldn't come all this way and not say hello."

"That's what I thought when I read it. Now I'm re-thinking. What was the last piece of equipment installed on *NightHawk*? In a big hurry, just before we left."

"The Space-To-Space missile launcher."

"Charlie's favourite toy. He'd carry it on his back on downplanet missions if he could. What does that weapon tell you about our mission?"

The Lieutenant nodded slowly. "They had suspicions we would need it."

"Right. They sent our team out because they suspected trouble, and we were the best chance of dealing with it. Sure, we're pretty lightweight. I doubt if Space Arm thought we'd come up against a ten-thousander. But we got here faster than any bigger ship in the fleet and drove them off. Mission accomplished, at that point.

"The radio signal was a cover for our real mission, which is to support the mine. At this stage, our best way to support the mine is to deal with the radio signal and the entity that sent it. Our orders fit into that scenario very neatly, don't they?"

Nelson gave his usual frown. "I don't know, Commander. You have the greatest skill for interpreting the rules to your own advantage."

"That's right. And as long as I make sure nothing I do puts the Space Arm's safety and honour at risk, I'm on solid ground. And humanity's safety as well. I never forget that."

"Yes, I suppose." His frown deepened. "We had just better hope the two objectives never compete."

"Smartest thing you've said all day, First. There's hope for you yet."

13. BACK HOME AGAIN

Events continued to move smoothly. Too smoothly and too quickly for the Commander's peace of mind, but there was little to argue about. The following day the miners and their families moved into the factory, and a convoy of equipment left the toroid for the surface of Xeta.

Natalia had just been talking to the factory and left her office with satisfaction and worry about being too satisfied warring in her mind.

Somehow, Andrew was back on board. Natalia spotted him in Shuttle Bay One — she couldn't miss his voice, nattering on and on in its usual enthusiastic tone — watching over Fiona's shoulder as she worked on the shuttle engine.

"How did you get here this time?"

He regarded her a moment. "Do you realize what a nice buncha people you got on this ship?"

"Of course I do, and yes, that does answer my question. But remember; just because people are honest and helpful doesn't mean they're weak. It means they think that's the way they should act, despite the fact that others," she tweaked his nose, "don't act the same."

"Yeah, I get it." He grinned. "And as a bonus, other people like them."

"Something like that. I suppose asking why you're here is also a waste of my time?"

"Oh, no. I was comin' to talk to you. I just got distracted by," he swung a greasy hand towards Fiona's task, "interestin' stuff. You know."

"Well, if you're here to talk to me, come on to the mess hall. You can clean up and we'll talk. And you will not wipe your hands on Chakka's fur. That may be ecologically neutral grease, but he cleans his hair with his tongue, and I doubt it's good for him. His augment makes him intelligent, but he's a cat, and cats have a very basic digestive system."

90

"Oh. I never knew that. I'll be more careful in future."

Once his hands were clean they wandered into the mess. He waved her to a chair and brought over her usual mocha with double sugar. She thanked him, not bothering to question how he knew. She took a sip, gave an appreciative sigh, and stared at him over the rim. "So. Spill it. What do you want now?"

"A big favour, actually."

"You don't usually start one of your stories like that. What gives?"

"This one's very important, so no games. When you go over to the factory this afternoon, I want to come along."

She frowned. "Who says I'm going to the factory this afternoon?"

"Well, next time you go. Can I come? Please? It's real important."

"It's not up to me. If Four-Eighty says you can come, I don't mind. Just keep your greasy little fingers to yourself. We don't want anything to spoil this good relationship we have going." She forced him to meet her glare. "Dealing with an alien species is a serious business. They won't be taken in by your, 'Aw, shucks, I'm just a kid,' routine, because they don't know what a kid is like, and they might not care."

"Of course, ma'am. I'll be on my best behaviour."

He didn't look like someone who had just been put in his place, but there it was. "This is only a hypothetical situation anyway."

Communication from Factory 4-80, ma'am.

Put him through, NightHawk.

"Good afternoon, Four-Eighty. What can I do for you?"

Today Mickey was in a formal suit with tie and tails. "How about accepting an invitation?"

"And what invitation is that?"

"I was thinking it might further our relationship if I were to bring you into my home. As a polite gesture of good faith, and all that. I gather it is a common stage in the development of business relationships on Earth. Would you like to come over for a visit?"

"When?"

"This afternoon, any time."

She glanced over to where Andrew sat, grinning, two thumbs pointed up.

"I'd be glad to come. And I have a small favour to ask."

"Of course."

"We have a lad, here. Name of Andrew. He has exhibited unusual interest in your factory. He requests permission to join me in my visit."

"You don't happen to mean Andrew Lundin Collingwood the Third?"

"You know about him. Of course you do. Everyone else does. Are you willing to risk it? He says he'll be on his best behaviour, whatever that is."

"Certainly. Bring the lad along. I'm sure he'll enjoy it. Your auguar would appreciate a change of scenery, too, I suppose?"

"All right. We'll get a shuttle prepped and be right over."

"I might offer more glamorous ride, but I would assume you like to have your own transport."

"And you would be right. See you soon. The usual port?"

"My entertainment suite is just upspin of hydroponics. Take the next port in that direction. It will adapt to your shuttle airlock."

"See you soon."

Mickey appeared in Mexican serape and sombrero. *Hasta luego, Señorita.*

Hasta luego, Señor.

She turned to Andrew. "Is that your best shirt?"

The boy frowned, looked down. "I guess so. It's clean..."

"It'll probably do. I've learned to ignore Mickey's clothing choices. It didn't sound like a formal occasion."

92

NightHawk, prepare Shuttle...

Pete has Shuttle Two prepped and waiting, ma'am.

Thank you, I think.

"Come on, Andrew. I'm beginning to wonder who's running this show."

The three of them swung into the slipway and cruised into Bay Two, where Pete was just finishing his checks. They boarded and pulled away smartly.

"I assume you have the destination?"

"Aye, ma'am. Port 23."

"Somehow I thought you would." She shot a stern glance at Andrew, completely wasted against his enthusiastic enjoyment of the view out the front screens. Now the gantries and access docks were extended, and repair units, tiny at this distance, scuttled slowly around and over everything. As they approached, Natalia almost wished she had time to watch.

NightHawk was still orbiting in synch with the hydroponics section, so it was a quick ride with a smooth landing.

"Very good, Pete."

"Not to my credit, ma'am. These ports have some kind of cushioning field. You couldn't do a hard landing if you tried."

The doors cycled open, and Natalia's stomach lurched as they climbed from the downward plate gravity of the shuttle to the outward spin gravity of the factory. A ladder descended, and they mounted it to find themselves rising through the floor of a huge, bare room. It was the largest open space she had experienced it seven months, and it gave her a strange feeling of freedom. Chakka bounded off the ladder and gave her a questioning glance, but she sent him a negative. *We don't need recon here.*

She took in her surroundings. The walls were dull grey metal, smooth but worn and scratched with use. Lines of bolt holes and flanges on every surface showed where equipment could be fastened. The air was chilly, with that indefinable tang of age that permeates old cathedrals.

A viewscreen beside the door showed the head and torso of a handsome, middle-aged man of nebulous heritage: light brown skin, black hair, brown eyes. He smiled. "Welcome to my home, Commander O'Rourke. Andrew will show you to the drawing room."

She turned and stared at the boy.

He tossed a wave at the screen. "Hiya, Freighty. Good to see ya. Be there in a sec." He turned to her. "It's just along the corridor a ways. You coulda found it yourself, but this is more formal, yeah?"

"How do you know...?" She stopped as it all came together. *This is becoming an interesting afternoon.* Regretting that she left her sidearm behind, she followed the boy.

They strode along a hallway of proportions meant for larger beings and stopped outside a door twice Natalia's height. Andrew knocked, the door opened and then things got more interesting.

"Hey, Mum!" He threw himself into the arms of a short, handsome woman of about forty. She was dressed in modern clothing, and her hairstyle would have been up to date on Earth last year.

She clasped the boy firmly. "Andrew. You made it back."

"'Course I did, Mum. Whaddaya think?"

"And who are your friends?"

"Oh. Sorry. Forgot my manners." He winked at Natalia. "Mum, this is my captain, Commander Natalia O'Rourke. Commander, my mother, Mariel Collingwood."

As Natalia overcame her surprise and stepped forward, the boy turned and spoke in a low voice. "'Course, she's not really my mother. She's a construct. Play along."

The Commander took refuge in the ritual while she absorbed all the new information. "Pleased to meet you, Mrs. Collingwood. Your son has made a great impression on my crew."

The woman smiled, and now that she knew, Natalia could spot the awkwardness of movement, the slightly wooden facial expressions. "And this, of course, is your favourite friend, Chakka the Warrior."

Chakka didn't seem fazed at all. He walked over and stood patiently to have his ears and chin tickled. Then he moved away a step as if he had finished an assigned task.

Mariel turned and gestured to a closely spaced square of sofas and chairs bounded by a large area rug.

Natalia gazed around, but the rest of the room seemed to fade away into darkness, leaving them on a pleasant island of golden light. The air was warmer here, and redolent with the odors of food.

"Do come and sit down. I have been dying to get a re-li opinion of my baking. Andrew's tastes come from the senses of a twelve-year-old." She smiled in the way that parents do when discussing their prodigies. "Freighty will be along in a moment."

They took their seats in front of a large, low coffee table, replete with plates of pastries, cakes and hors d'ouvres.

Chakka, this looks formal...

Andrew gave the cat an unceremonious shove. "The one with the low back is for you, buddy. Freighty and Mum think of everything." He snagged two tarts off a plate and sat down, munching. Then he leaned forward and grabbed a meatball from another plate. "Here, Chakka. What do you think of that?"

The auguar snapped the morsel out of the air, gulped and licked his lips.

The boy grinned at her. "I know. Simple digestive system. These are made to the recipe of his daily chow, with a touch of beefsteak flavour extra."

Natalia took a plate and napkin and helped herself sparingly. The food was tasty, although the pastry was rather tough. While the cake had the right texture, a slight metallic aftereffect lingered in her throat. Assuming that nothing would

95

poison her, she continued to browse the table. "This Swiss cheese is very good. A favourite of mine."

"The recipes have been on your nets for many years. Analysis suggests a very strong flavour, and Andrew only likes the mildest kind, the one on the left. There are various ages. You took the strongest."

"Led there by my nose. Believe me, on Earth you could sell this." She followed the construct's gaze as the door opened.

Mariel rose, a smile on her face, and the man from the viewscreen entered the room. This construct was impossible to differentiate from a re-li human. He walked smoothly and his facial expression was perfect. He smiled, swept the party with a gentle gaze and sat with perfect grace.

"So, here we all are. Mariel, what a feast!"

He turned to Natalia. "I'm so glad you could come." A wry look crossed his face. "There wasn't really any good way to tell you."

She shrugged. "Now that the original shock has worn off, I will listen very closely."

"Please sit down, then. Andrew, you and Chakka can wander off if you've stuffed yourselves. This might take a while."

"Sure thing. C'mon, cat. You're gonna love my climbing wall."

The two sauntered out the door, and Natalia sat regarding her host and hostess.

"Where to start." Four-Eighty put his hands on his knees. "My plan for contacting humans was quite good, if I do say so myself. I used a huge amount of my waning power to send a small ship to Earth. There I contracted Mariel Collingwood for a ten-year stint. She had just come out of a difficult time and was willing to take the risk because the rewards would be huge and she had the safety of her young son to consider.

"They lived here for five years while Mariel helped me refine my plans. Between the two of us we made sure Andrew had the best upbringing and education we could give him."

The construct shrugged. "And then she died. It was cancer, a rapid-onset strain. My medical facilities could not develop a treatment in time. So she was gone, and I had an orphan to deal with. Andrew was ten at the time, and a very mature boy. He was handling his loss well, but I felt that it would not be good for him to spend the next five or ten years alone. So, with his help and permission, I took all the data I had on his mother and made the Mariel construct to match mine. The real Mariel and I discussed the project before she died, so her heart and soul went into the programming. The three of us have been living as normal a life as we could create for the past two years, and I have to admit that Andrew's welfare was part of my reason for contacting humanity earlier than I had planned.

"Then your *NightHawk* appeared on the horizon, and everything fell back into place. I sent Andrew out to board that privateer or whatever they said they were, made sure he told them how to use iodine as reaction mass so they could double-dip the plutonium triiodide ore from the mine, and there he was. I knew that if my plans went wrong he would be taken care of.

"I didn't account for the greed and violence of the transplanetaries creating a war. What is wrong with these people? Don't bother to answer. Now that my plans are back on schedule, their type will soon join the dinosaurs as a nasty hiccup in the history of the Planet Earth, and humans will go on to become Sol's crowning glory."

The construct shrugged and gave Natalia a wry smile. "Or whatever you decide to be. Don't mind me. I can dream, too, you know."

She grasped that fact out of the whole complicated story. "You can dream?"

He chuckled. "Oh, not the way you do. I don't sleep. I mean daydreams. Cherished but unrealistic desires."

She leaned back. At least she could be pretty sure the couch was real. Not much else was. "Fine. This all hangs together well."

"You believe me."

97

"No, I'm saying you are quite possibly truthful, but nothing in my experience with you leads me to believe it completely. I'm sure that at some time in the future you will be able to surprise me with new revelations."

"Do you believe that I am trying to ease you into this situation in as gentle a way as possible?"

"I do believe that, but it doesn't help much. There's no point in going around it again. It's like discussing the nature of reality. We can speculate all we want but the only solution is to take what you perceive at any moment and do the best you can with it."

"An admirable attitude." The construct placed his hands on his knees, his arms straight, as he had before. "So, while we're having this nice tea, is there anything else you'd like to ask?

"Yes, as it happens, there is…"

14. PATENTS

Natalia put down her teacup and turned her full attention to the Four-Eighty construct. "I want the real answer. Why did you choose the Space Arm? And don't play innocent. You sent that tantalizing invitation on a frequency restricted to Space Arm use. You targeted us, and I want to know why. You run a business. Wouldn't you be better off with one of the transplanetaries? You knew El Dorado had a mine almost next door, and they have a decent reputation. As good as any of the rest, anyway."

"Yes, I run a business, but as a newcomer I would be too vulnerable."

"Even in our well-regulated society?"

He smiled. "Comparatively well regulated. In the galaxy of business, there are different ways to injure someone. What do you know about patents?"

"As much as most people. I know they sound very simple and become incredibly complex at the merest touch of a lawyer. Why?"

"My manufacturing ability is what you would call my bread and butter. My true profit comes from my knowledge. I have in my data banks — encrypted far beyond humanity's Neanderthal abilities to decode — the technologies of several species over several thousand years. And none of them around to dispute my use of their ideas. Do you see the potential?"

"My mind jumps to the moral ramifications. You can't just go broadcasting huge lumps of technology to societies that aren't ready for it!"

"Exactly. You Space Arm people are deficient in commercial instincts. You think along different lines. So I come to you, because you understand in your small way the problems I incur. You will want whatever advantages I can give you, but you will want to limit what I give to humanity. Within reason, that is a good thing, because I have the same instinct. Babies playing with sharp knives.

"My plan is to speak with the Planetary Community about a measured rollout of a carefully selected series of technological advances, with the safety and longevity of the human species as our major objective.

"You're playing god."

"I prefer to think of it as playing grandfather. It is what I am forced to do by the nature of my existence. Another bit of knowledge that I bring to the table is the condensed history of the species I have met and their development."

"And what happened to all the other species you have come in contact with over the centuries? Where are they now?"

The construct nodded judiciously. "That is a fair question. They are all gone. Perhaps I am the plague carrier. Possibly I carry the virus of a far greater knowledge than I can control myself. Perhaps your government will want to thank me for my services, buy a few small crumbs of appropriate technology and send me on my way. That would be one of the wiser choices, I think."

"So, the question remains. You have contacted the Space Arm. Here we are. How do you see us fitting into your plans?"

"I don't know. I'm counting on you to help with that. You know your species; I don't."

"The question is how to put this situation into business terms."

"Precisely. How would an organization such as yourselves, that does not actually participate in manufacturing and construction, fit into your commercial models?"

She frowned in thought. "Let me consult my resources, please. I remember a story I heard once."

"Take your time." Again that gentle smile. "I have plenty of that."

It didn't take long. "Four-eighty, do you know what humans call a primary contractor? Was that in the protocols?"

"Describe it to me."

"My Chief Engineer is older than the rest of us and had a career on Earth before he came to space. He bought a piece of land and built a house. He didn't have time to manage the construction himself, so he hired a primary contractor who organized all the tradesmen, permits and materials on a day-to-day basis."

"You're talking about a go-between who keeps communication flowing between contractors and clients."

"Yes, but who has the right to make decisions and the responsibility to make sure everything is done according to contract."

"Ah. I was hoping you would have that concept in your business dealings. Most species seem to."

"So you're interested?"

"I sometimes work that way, especially at the beginning. While I am quick on the uptake, small details and snags inevitably arise when dealing with an alien species. I would much prefer a group with local knowledge to assume that role, leaving me to what I do best: building things."

"You understand that this is complicated by my distance from my headquarters." Natalia raised her hands helplessly. "Assuming that a long-term relationship will be established, we have to be prepared for my superiors holding a different view of the situation from mine."

"So you, personally, are willing to sign on as humanity's primary contractor for the duration of the present projects. Once contact is established with the Space Arm, you will step aside, and I will re-negotiate with them."

"I'm not saying they will override my decisions. I just think we have to be prepared."

"Good enough. If your Space Arm can be counted on to support your short-term decisions, we will proceed on that basis. I will do the work on the Santa Maria and the mine, and you, as representative for the Space Arm, will be my primary contractor. Do you agree?

"I agree. Space Arm will back up the decision of an officer in the field. Shall we write up a contract?"

Freighty shrugged. "I see little use in wasting energy. I am sure you have recorded this conversation, as have I. Just to give you a little snippet of information as a gesture of good will, I have also recorded your heart and pulse rate, your eye movements and your gestures."

She frowned. "For the purpose of...?"

"Determining to the best of my ability, given my limited knowledge of human physiognomy, that you are speaking in good faith."

"Huh! I seem to be at a disadvantage, since you don't have any of those attributes, and if you did, I have no way of reading them."

"Thus I shall have to be especially careful to act in good faith at all times in order to earn your trust."

"If that's the case, I hope you will pardon my suspicion, but another small matter occurs to me. Why are you so low on power in a planetary system with a working plutonium ore mine?"

He shook his head. "I am aware of the irony of that fact. I came here low on reserves and chose the best hiding place I could. I scanned the asteroid belt from here without wasting too much valuable power. Obviously not well enough."

"So El Dorado corporation was just luckier than you?"

"Prospecting is that sort of business."

"I can understand that."

"Good." The construct dusted off his hands. "And now that we have a contract, I have a related detail to discuss."

"And that is...?"

"You probably noted in my original communication the inclusion of 'work hours' in the payment schedule. No, it has nothing to do with slavery." He made a shooting motion, blowing the smoke off his imaginary pistol muzzle with a grin. "Your miners and even your crew could cut the cost of the project in a small way by fulfilling appropriate functions and giving of their expertise. Helping train me in your construction methods, for example."

"I understand. I'm sure the miners will appreciate the chance to earn their wages. They're probably bored out of their skulls with the inactivity. It shouldn't be hard to lay out a wage scale based on their pay from El Dorado 12. My people are working for the Space Arm and will fill in as needed as part of their duties."

"Then we will add their wages to the primary contractor's stipend."

"You mean Space Arm gets paid for this?"

"Of course. Business as usual, ma'am. Part of the administrative charges already taken into account."

"Thank you, Four-Eighty."

"Now that we have a working relationship, perhaps you would like to call me by my more usual name?"

"Which is?"

"The one Andrew gave me. Freighty."

"All right, Freighty. We're in business."

They hauled Andrew and Chakka off the higher ledges of a stupendous climbing wall with automated safety lines, and she took the boy back to the Santa Maria.

The mine manager met them at the ore carrier's airlock, a worried look on his face. "Is something wrong? Andrew, what have you been up to?"

Natalia shook her head. "Far more than you'd ever believe, and for far longer."

Ludge cuffed the boy gently on the back of his head. "Andrew, go and play with a box of live blasting charges or something where you can't do much damage while I try to make amends for whatever it is you did."

"Sure thing, Nicholas. See you later, ma'am. Thanks for taking me along. That was fun."

"Oh, I imagine it was." She spun him by the shoulder and pushed. "Now, scoot!"

Once they were seated in the tiny captain's cabin of the Santa Maria, Ludge shook his head. "Well, spill it. What do I owe you?"

She grinned. "A whole lot less than you think." She outlined her afternoon's discoveries.

At the end he sat back and regarded her. "So you have wangled a primary contractor role for Space Arm in every contract Four-Eighty takes on?"

"Only until the factory and Space Arm sit down and figure out the details."

He shook his head. "That was very clever. You're two or three steps ahead of me. I was just happy to be getting the work done, thinking I had a toe in the door for my company. And now I find you've got a lease on the whole house."

"I doubt it means that much. But it does indicate a certain level of trust all round, and I'm sure you'll benefit from that."

"Oh, yes." He grinned. "I know about the advantages of having a primary contractor to deal with all the hassles."

"There you go, Mine Manager Ludge. It's time for you to sit down with Freighty and thrash out a contract for the repair of your operation. I'll check the deal over before anyone signs, and I guarantee I'll make it fair for everyone."

"Right you are, ma'am. I'll think twice before I give my company's resources away." He frowned. "And what do I do about Andrew?"

She shrugged. "The lad has made himself at home here, at the factory and on my ship. Everyone seems to be taking care of him as much as he needs or wants. At the bottom of it all he's a human and my responsibility, I suppose. Sooner or later we'll have to straighten something out. Heaven knows what."

She said goodbye and made her way back to her waiting shuttle, deep in thought.

15. WAGES

The negotiations on the Santa Maria upgrades went quickly, and in just a few hours the ore carrier was nosing into the central bay of the factory. It was fascinating to watch the process, because the whole operation was so finely coordinated that it looked like a mammal mother gathering her offspring, arranging it comfortably and settling down to feed it. Four-Eighty had brought the nose of the Santa Maria up through the centre of its shipyard, and now looked for all the world like a child's top spinning slowly on a stick.

It was soon apparent that human workers were an essential part of the process. The ship swarmed with specialist robots, but there were some things that required more creative thinking. Cleanup wasn't one of them, but a human already onsite was much more efficient than training and sending out a robot crew for one small job.

Natalia was inspecting the work on the Santa Maria, and three young miners were carefully vacuuming the last grains of plutonium triiodide out of the new living quarters bin. It was painstaking work because of the radioactive nature of the pollutant. She watched for a while, trying to figure out how a vacuum system could be working in the vacuum of space. Then she chuckled. *Ah. Electromagnetic.*

Watching the workers' rather lethargic performance, she reached down and lifted a handful of ore and clicked over to their com frequency.

See that handful, boys?

They crowded around, glad of the distraction.

That much plutonium triiodide ore is worth an hour of your diligent toil.

And you tell us this for what reason, ma'am?

So count the number of handfuls you pick up in one hour, subtract one, and you get the profit you just made for the company. And just the tiniest iota of that amount will trickle back to you in your year-end bonus.

That sure sounds good, ma'am.

She dropped the handful into the suction nozzle. *And while this stuff isn't so radioactive that your suit won't protect you, the less time you spend out here, the safer you'll be.*

You sure are a good motivator, ma'am. We'll work ever so much harder, now.

Right, but you've been lallygagging around talking to the brass for long enough to pay your wages for this hour, so get back there and make up the difference!

Aye, ma'am.

Shaking their heads, the three returned to work with at least a bit more enthusiasm. She held up a hand to stop them. *How are the accommodations in the factory?*

They turned to her with more enthusiasm. *Just wild, ma'am. It's like going to Disney Planet. Every room has a different theme. My room looks like it came from the Ritz in Marsport.*

She eyed each man. *And your work is paying for that as well. Keep it in mind.* She turned away, knowing they didn't need any more motivation.

Another com clicked in. The mine manager

Hello, Nicholas. How are things going?

Hello, Commander. I thought I saw you down here. Something wrong?

No, just stirring my finger where I have no business being. That's what primary contractors do, isn't it?

It can happen. Not the good ones, though.

Aha. I have standards to achieve. She looked up to where the Manager was standing on the edge of the open bin. *Stand aside a moment.* With a lithe jump she bounded up, gliding to a stop beside him in the temporary gravity of the ship.

His head swung back and forth within his helmet. *What do you think of those gravity plates?*

106

He's playing games with us. Showing off the usefulness of his technology, hoping to sell it.

I'm ready to buy. Those robots just lay out the power line, drop a one-metre-square plate anywhere along it, and presto! Point three G's for ten metres in all directions.

She grinned. *And when it's the factory's robots moving the equipment, and our men increasing their productivity, it shines, doesn't it? How's the rest of the project going?*

Well, a thought had occurred to me.

Go ahead.

If the factory was planning to move over to our mining site and our people could stay in the hydroponics rooms while we're over there, why are we fixing up these living quarters? The message I get is that the factory is staying put, and we're heading back there on our own.

I'm keeping the options open at the moment while we assess our relationship with this entity. Like the beginning of any project, both sides are going out of the way to make things work and garner trust. You may be paying him for work that will not get used much. He's laying out a bunch of stuff at no extra charge to induce us to buy. And the Corporation will find a use for the modules, never fear.

She stood back, then made the finger-movement that meant to cut communications. When her augment read dead silence, she leaned in until her helmet made physical contact with his. "And always act like he's listening in on any electronic communication. I'm sure he is capable."

"I wondered about that."

"This ArIn is far more capable than we can fathom. If he isn't what he says he is, there's absolutely nothing we can do about it. My only hope is that if we demonstrate playing fair, he'll do the same. The only advantage humans have over our own ArIns is our ability to act in an illogical, non-linear way. I don't know if that counts with this one, but I'm keeping it as an option."

"Loyalty and fair play are illogical?"

She raised her eyebrows. "And this is an agent for a transplanetary asking the question?"

He said no more, and she broke the contact, turning her com back on. *So, having stirred my finger enough to pretend I'm useful to the project, I'm going back to my chart room to do docu-work.*

Good enough, ma'am. Thank you for your valuable assistance.

No problem. It was really just an excuse to get EV where I could enjoy the view for real.

He looked up at the arch of stars. *I'm a miner at heart. Open spaces don't impress me.*

She had a moment's pity for him, then squashed it and enjoyed the scenery for as long as her conscience allowed her. Then she called for a ride home.

As her shuttle whisked her back to the *NightHawk*, a steady line of small units streamed out towards the asteroid belt. Over the next few days they returned, boosting larger pieces of equipment along. All of this disappeared into the maze of gantries and lines that grew inside the factory centre. Soon large, smooth sections that looked like the dome curves of the mine buildings began to trickle out, lifting majestically away like sailing ships headed for foreign shores.

She wished with all her being that everything would keep going as well as it seemed to be. That didn't stop her from making plans in case it didn't.

16. HONESTLY, MICKEY

With no other options, Natalia allowed the uncertain situation to continue while she did some thinking and gathered evidence. When she thought she was ready, she called Freighty. As usual, he came on line immediately.

"Natalia. How are you? Is everything going well?"

She stared at the construct on the viewscreen. "Business is going fine, but I have come to the conclusion that you haven't been entirely honest with me."

"Complete honesty is something to be risked only among good friends. Since we are only recent business partners, there will be a waiting period while we develop trust."

"Coming clean on certain matters might enhance that trust."

"It might."

She waited. "So you're going to play hard to get."

A pause long enough for a smart ArIn to scan a full language protocol. "That is an expression that applies to courting rituals."

"So apply it."

"Ah. I see. What would you like me to come clean about?"

"Steamboat Willy."

"Pardon?"

"Your Mickey Mouse avatar. I checked the First Contact Protocols we sent you. History of popular culture, yes. Walt Disney, yes. Even Mickey Mouse. An original rough version from the Nineteen Twenties? No. The style is unmistakable."

"You mean I've been busted due to a stylistic difference in children's entertainment?"

"That, plus your occasional dip into film noir detective vocabulary."

"Oh. That. I rather enjoy Mickey Spillane. It explains so much about that century."

"The final straw was a casual comment by Mariel about recipes that she knows but shouldn't. And the only explanation for that is..." she regarded him sternly. "How much did you know about humans when you sent that ship to collect Mariel Collingwood?"

The ArIn gave a convincingly heartfelt sigh. "I felt that being frank with you at that point would preclude the possibility of this conversation. I should have known you were too clever.

"I have been monitoring humans since the first faint radio waves emanated from your planet two hundred of your years ago. I have heard your news reports, your radio programs, your television and any other electronic media with the power to escape your atmosphere."

"So you know all about us."

"I have the broader picture. It has been a great pleasure to observe some of the finer details recently and discover I am not wrong in my assessment. At least, not yet."

"Hmm. And what is your assessment?"

"One driven by practicalities. I have been monitoring the development of your society, waiting for the technology to develop that would allow you to come to me. My power reserves have long been depleted beyond the point of moving myself any great distance. At the same time, I was waiting for your race to mature to the point where I could interface comfortably and to the benefit of both."

"And I assume we have reached that point?"

Again the sigh. "As it happens, not quite. Having considerable time on my hands — despite my lack of hands — I have run a great number of scenarios, all cross-referencing my declining power reserves against the slow rise of your civilization. In the greatest number of them, if I waited until it was really safe to contact you, I would no longer have the power to do so."

"And the fact that you contacted the Space Arm suggests you prefer to deal at a governmental level."

"Correct. Plus the development of the *NightHawk*."

"You already knew about us? Of course. Andrew's familiarity with the design."

"Yes. That was a fun game he was trying out on you, and I'm so glad you won most of the rounds. Good for his development. Your ship is breakthrough technology that happens once in a century. Your scientists just don't know it yet."

"You'll have to explain that."

"Without my help, some time in the next thirty years your people will discover a way to double the output of those new engines."

Natalia was starting to get a bad feeling. "And with your help?"

"Two weeks."

She shook her head in sorrow. "And now you're starting to sound like a used car salesman."

"What?"

"Sorry to be suspicious, but that was the neatest setup I've seen in a long time."

"Setup? What is a setup?"

"Ask Mickey Spillane."

"Oh. That kind of setup. But I assure you..."

"Listen, Four-Eighty, your obtuse protests are beginning to bore me. Check the sales pitches of the twentieth century and the internet scams of the twenty-first. 'You have been selected...' is the first sign of a con. You set me up perfectly, flattered me and then made me an offer that would be very difficult to refuse. If you thought you were going to develop trust, that wasn't the way to go about it.

"Please, Commander. I have no idea what you're talking about. What did I say? What did I do?"

"Just check the sources I suggested, assuming that isn't where you learned the technique already. Then come back and talk to me. I'm going off line now. I have a ship to run."

17. TEN THOUSAND TONS OF TROUBLE

Factory 4-80 on the com, ma'am.

The file Natalia had been reading faded, and she turned her focus to audio. *Thanks, NightHawk. Put him on.*

Video came up as well. He was Mickey Mouse in Technicolor today, lab coat and clipboard evident.

"Good morning, Commander O'Rourke. How are you?"

"I'm doing well thank you, Freighty." He seemed willing to let yesterday' argument fade, so she would do the same. "How are the repairs going?"

"With great dispatch, I'm pleased to say. Your people are more help than I had considered in my estimates. We will be ready to leave here a day ahead of schedule. "

"That's good."

"That's more good than you know."

"That sounds ominous."

"I believe humans use an ominous statement ato prepare you for worse news. It's about the other human ship.

"Ah. Have you found her?"

"I took the liberty of using a soupçon of the fuel you provided to fire up some of my more sophisticated tech." He paused to regard her earnestly. "I hope the information I discovered is worth the cost."

"If it gives us information on the enemy, it's worth it. What's he up to?"

"The cruiser has been hiding behind a planetoid in the asteroid belt. It is now moving at a leisurely speed up-spin towards the mine."

"How fast is 'leisurely'?"

"About half normal cruising speed, if I have its specs right."

"What kind of specs do you have on it...oh. You don't mind telling me, do you?"

"Not at all. That ship was recently in conflict with a present customer. My primary contractor must know what I know about it. Our target is, as you say, about ten thousand tons. Length: 285 metres. It's an obsolete cruiser of the *Clyde* class. Very heavy and slow but powerfully armed. Projectile cannons and short-range laser and plasma burners. Of course, it could be retrofitted with almost any independent targeting, self-propelled missile like your STS model, and is capable of carrying a fighter wing and numerous other small craft."

"Maneuverability?"

"Basically none. It carries no inertial dampeners, because it can't turn any faster than the human body can endure. A good long-range ship, capable of FTL; it just takes a while to get up to the LS Ceiling. In re-ti your little sportster could literally fly in circles around it too fast for its guns to target you."

"But on the other hand, nothing we carry could even dent that plating."

"Not necessarily. Your targeting is sufficient if you knew where to aim."

"Ah. Might I guess where this is leading?"

Mickey started unrolling a large scroll of blueprints. "Sending as we speak."

NightHawk, don't open that package.

Aye, ma'am.

"Four-Eighty, can you give me a moment? I have something to clear up, here."

"Standing by, ma'am."

First, are you available?

Right here, ma'am. Jones came through the chartroom door and took his usual stool. "What's going on?"

"I'm at an impasse. We're trying to work with this factory entity, and we've reached the point where our security protocols are severely slowing our communication. Now they are stopping us from receiving something that might be crucial to our safety."

"In what way our safety?"

She outlined the situation with the specs for the cruiser. When she finished, there was a pause.

"Don't we have that kind of information in our own database?"

"Not for a ship that's been obsolete for twenty years."

He tossed up his hands, palms open. "Isn't there some way we can use the files within our present security protocol?"

"Can you imagine searching the specs of a ship that size, checking the security of every page before opening it? I think we'll be safer relaxing our firewalls a bit."

"That kind of thinking works just fine until the moment that the cyberattack starts, ma'am. Our protocols definitely state no unsecured communication with any non-Space Arm vessel, let alone alien beings."

"I'm not suggesting we remove security completely. Just that we move to a more reasonable level."

He paused and accessed his augment. Finally, "My reading of the regulations suggests that this is a grey area where each captain has to make his or her own informed choice. Thank you for discussing it with me. I will go on record as not being happy with the situation, but I will not register a protest."

"Thank you, First. I'm not dancing a jig either, but I'm going to drop to a Level Six electronic communication firewall on all normal contacts with Factory Four-Eighty. *NightHawk*, did you read that?"

"Heard, understood and entered in the official log. I am now downloading the specs for the original Clyde, starting with the hull structure and electronic routing."

Natalia switched channels. "Back to you, Freighty. We are presently opening the plans. Do you have any suggestions?"

The Tin Man appeared. "If you follow the yellow brick road you will find happiness."

"What?"

"Freighty has mapped out the links to the appropriate documents. Are the yellow bricks significant?"

"No, *NightHawk*. He's just showing off his knowledge of human culture."

Images began to appear in her visual system. Yellow squares marked the plans, and concentrating on any square brought her written target information and possible lines of attack.

She stared. "All of these are weak points?"

"Based on my estimation of your weaponry, you could produce a breach of atmosphere or a disruption of communication or power at those spots."

"But how much actual damage could we do?"

Mickey shrugged. "It all depends on which weapon and how long you can keep it bearing on the spot. You know your capabilities..."

"...so I can figure it out for myself. Thank you, Freighty. We'll get working on this right away."

"Anything I can do to help against that behemoth."

"You've got it right, there. This *Clyde* clone is the flaw in all our plans."

18. RETURN OF THE *CLYDE*

Natalia looked around the mess hall table. This was a decision that should be discussed in front of the crew. "Well, we know where the cruiser is. There's no use us waiting around here."

Jones looked up from his place at the far end of the table. "I agree. If she's at the mine, that's where we need to be. Not that we can do much..."

"Yes, I'm not enthused about trying to pinpoint those weak spots we found. I'll inform the miners and the factory, and they can mosey along at their own speed. If we push it, we can be there in half the time."

NightHawk, let's talk to Four-Eighty.

Online, ma'am.

The factory had dropped his Mickey Mouse persona, and now appeared in his Southern European businessman guise. "Hello, *NightHawk*." He seemed to glance around the room. "And crew. A pleasure to see you all."

Natalia and Jones exchanged glances. How did the factory pick up the whole room?

"We are all well. We have decided to start out for the mine at our best speed. No sense letting our unknown friends have time to mess up the repair job."

"That's a good idea. Will you be communicating with them?"

"I would assume so. Their part in this whole situation is highly suspect, but we have no evidence that they caused the asteroid shower. I'm assuming they will play an innocent role. If they offer help, we can graciously refuse. Maybe they will go away."

"And maybe they won't. Is there any way you can manage to discourage them without saying anything about my place in this?"

She met her First Officer's look. He shook his head.

"I think it would be difficult. We certainly won't mention you at all unless asked. You can hardly hide from them once you're moving through open space."

"I know. That worries me."

"I don't see why it should. You are in human-controlled space under the protection of the Space Arm of the Planetary Community. These are humans, and anyone who can afford a ship that big, even an obsolete one like a *Clyde* class, must be representative of a legitimate business interest."

"My experience with transplanetaries of several species might lead to a different conclusion. However, I don't see any way around it. Please just do your best to keep us in low profile."

"I certainly will. I'm playing a dangerous game with someone ten times my size. I'm hardly going to give away anything I don't have to."

"One other thing. Would you take Andrew with you? He'll be safer."

She raised her eyebrows. "Safer? On a fighting craft facing down a larger vessel? I think he's safest with you."

"I suppose. Well, good luck with your mission."

"Thank you. We'll keep in close touch. See you in a couple of weeks at the mine."

"I fondly hope so."

His face faded from the viewscreen and his presence left her augment. She looked around the mess table.

Lundeen regarded her. "He's on the lam, isn't he? It isn't just the transplanetaries. He's hiding from someone."

She nodded. "Reading between the lines on what he told me, that's my guess. I think he ran until he couldn't run any more, he's been hiding out for too long and he's run out of supplies. He can't go on and he can't go back. He needs protection."

Jones frowned. "Which means he needs us."

117

"Do you remember Fiona's moosey friend on the Tree Planet? We saw the size of the prey, and extrapolated the predator big enough to take it down."

"And we're in the same situation here?"

"He needs humans. He has chosen the Space Arm in general and us in particular, perhaps not only for our altruistic attitude. If that doesn't work out, I'm sure he has seven different scenarios planned, starting with an alliance. El Dorado Corporation would be my first guess. Occam's razor.

"Least number of variables."

Jones put down his coffee cup. "And a battle cruiser is a very large variable, which we have volunteered to check out without any involvement on his part. How convenient."

"Very convenient, since you ask. *NightHawk*, hook me up with Ludge and prepare for a 1.5 G burn in ten minutes. Everyone, get ready for a couple of wearing days. We'll be on full accel/decel at 1.2Gs for this trip. We're not giving Captain Blackbeard time to make any mischief without the Space Arm looking over his shoulder."

* * *

With the superior technology of the factory feeding them data, they were able to track the old cruiser in re-ti right up until the moment they hovered, dead still, in front of the behemoth at the mouth of the mine.

The *Clyde* had been built in an era when space battles were predicted to be like the old sea battles of yore. This meant huge, heavily armed and armoured ships that would blast away at each other from stationary positions. It was fortunate for their crews that none of these battles had ever occurred.

The ship's main design parameter was based on the invention of artificial gravity. Since a grav panel created gravity in all directions, it was simpler to put it along the main axis of the ship and create a tube around it where "down" was towards the centre. This resulted in a cylindrical shape, bristling with weapons that could shoot in all directions. The only distinguishing characteristic was the heavy brow one third of the way aft on the "top" side, which housed the bridge, and the taller com tower behind it that moved the various aerials away from the effects of the Otherwhen Sphere and the multitudinous electrical systems that ran the ship. From the point of view of a ship with a tenth the weight and a fifth the armament, it looked rather impressive.

Natalia showed no emotion.

NightHawk, broadcast: Query.

Broadcasting: Query, ma'am.

Incoming response, ma'am. Standard military channel from thirty years ago.

That scans with what we know. Connect. Visual and auditory.

The viewscreen filled with the bridge of an old-style battle cruiser. Huge arrays of panels lined the walls, towering higher than a tall man could reach. Lighting was sparse, accentuating the man who stood at the centre of the screen. He looked about fifty, his hair a grey-peppered stubble across his pale scalp. He was dressed in semi-formal jacket and trousers: not exactly a uniform, but sharply turned out for all of that.

He took a moment to assess her.

"Do I have the honour of addressing the formidable Natalia O'Rourke, *vunderkind* of the new Space Arm fleet?"

"I am Commander O'Rourke, sir, captain of the *NightHawk*. And you are...?"

The *Clyde* captain glanced off to his right and made a gesture to someone before returning his attention to her. It was a niggling breach of good manners, but... *He's trying to annoy me. Keep those weapons trained.*

Aye, ma'am.

Online and ready, ma'am.

The other captain gave her a cold smile. "I am Captain Albert James of the *SV Clyde*." He nodded formally.

119

"I was aware that this was a *Clyde*-class ship, but…"

"Oh, no. This is the original." He made a courtly gesture. "A piece of Naval history."

A piece of obsolete junk.

Stay off the com with that, Charlie. Focus on your sights.

Loaded for bear, ma'am.

"So, what brings you to this out-of-the-way spot?"

"I might ask you the same question."

"A question which I'm sure you know a serving officer of the Space Arm has no authority to answer. You, on the other hand, are treading in delicate space. What kind of business brings you here?"

"We heard a distress call so of course we answered as soon as we could."

Natalia considered whether the information she was giving up would be worth what the response might bring, and decided to chance it. "After heading in the other direction at full speed soon after it was first sent."

"We had other business that couldn't wait. As I said, we came back as soon as possible. And we find strange things going on."

"Do you? Considering the extent of the damage, it would seem that repairs would be the normal procedure."

"But I detect no people performing these repairs. What has happened to the population of the mine?"

"Their situation here was rather uncomfortable. We arranged other accommodations."

"Really. For a group that large?"

"You seem overly concerned. I assure you, the Space Arm can be depended upon to take care of the victims of a terrible accident. If that's what it was."

He frowned in concern. "Not an accident? What are you suggesting? Sabotage?"

"I am suggesting that it might not have been an accident. We have collected fragments of the asteroids involved in the collision and sent our assay reports back to Space Arm. Their scientists can do amazing things with trace elements."

He hesitated a tiny moment, his face blanking. "Can they? How interesting."

"I can reassure you that the miners are safe and comfortable. It may take a while to finish the repairs, but I'm sure El Dorado Corporation would like everyone to know that they are on top of the problem and wish no...assistance from outside parties. You may go about your business with as clear a conscience as you deserve."

"So the Space Arm does the dirty work for El Dorado now." His lip wrinkled in a sneer.

"Protecting the property of an upstanding member of the Planetary Community's business collective is a duty and a pleasure. Hardly dirty work." She let the pleasant look fade from her face. "Not that we are worried about getting our hands soiled, should the need arise. Goodbye, Captain James." She did not turn off the signal, merely regarded him, forcing him to break the contact.

Which he did, but not before a snarl of impotent rage swept across his countenance.

Soon a plume of plasma flowed from the cavernous aft vents, and the *Clyde* gathered herself together to move off, returning up-spin. There was no surge, no bound, just the ponderous accumulation of velocity, leaving behind a cloud of distressed ions that blocked half the galaxy before fading away.

Factory Four-Eighty, ma'am.

"Hello, Freighty. What did you think of that?" Natalia had long since given up guessing how the factory listened in to every conversation; she just assumed he would.

"It was very...polite. Except perhaps near the end."

"Humans have an old saying. Speak softly..."

"...and carry a big stick." Freighty chuckled. "For someone who carries such light weapons, you came across rather loud."

"Those who think in terms of the size of their clubs are often foiled by the proficiency of a rapier."

"I think that was a bad joke from several different directions. Did I detect innuendo of a sexual nature?"

"You did not. Any innuendo came from your jaded mind."

"Well, you did a good job of driving them away. Now we can get down to business. Thanks."

"Don't thank me until we see how far they go."

"You don't think they're really leaving?"

"That would be too much to ask. They have spent about a year getting here, it'll take them as long to get home and it looks like they haven't got what they came for. They'll be back."

19. UPGRADES

The days rolled by, and the huge compilation of factory and ore carrier blasted away from Xeta, headed in-system. The stream of repair robots increased as the distance between factory and mine decreased.

In the final two days the factory was on slow decel, and Freighty sent a runabout he had stored somewhere to bring Ludge and his millwrights to oversee operations.

NightHawk patrolled out in every direction, but the *Clyde* had done another disappearing act. Natalia reported this to Freighty and was surprised at the strength of his reaction.

"We must know where they are! They are a great danger."

"Why are you so afraid of the transplanetaries?"

"It has to do with the development of human society. You come from a predatory heritage going back millions of years."

"Our scientists have come to the same conclusion. Our eye positioning gives us away."

"In the front to give a clear binocular view of the fleeing prey. But you hunted in cooperative packs, which evolved into tribes, and with the development of farming, into civilization. So, you entered a way of life where success requires cooperation, trust and empathy on top of your predatory nature. If your violent aspect had been stronger, you would not have come this far. But you did. Natural selection has been weeding out the most warlike for ten or twenty thousand years. Not long enough. Humans will always be torn between two urges: the urge to compete and the urge to cooperate. "

"And how do you see us now?"

Freighty became Mickey Mouse again, leaning back in a hammock, a drink with an umbrella in his hands, while girls in hula skirts danced around him.

"Becoming more civilized every century. Even every decade."

"But..."

Mickey became a samurai warrior brandishing a large wrench. "The transplanetary corporations are the last vestiges of the warlord society. You can see why I didn't want to connect with them. I have defenses beyond your imagining, but I can still become what your military calls collateral damage. In any developing technology the ability to blow things up is far easier to develop than countermeasures to stop things from blowing up. Defenders are always, as you might expect, on the defensive, reacting to whatever attack their enemy might mount. Attackers are free to improvise. The *Clyde* symbolizes the height of your aggressive push, tapering off half a century ago. After that the cooperators took control. So now even your Space Arm vessels look more like yours rather than James's.

The Freighty construct appeared on the screen, looking sober. "My original owners were destroyed by a species that developed warlike technology on top of a highly structured society with strong innate predatory instincts. They expanded rapidly, destroying everything they touched. Predictably, they self-immolated in a War Which Ended All Wars. In this case, their ability to create biochemical weapons exceeded their ability to cope with the results."

He waved a hand to his left. "If you were to wander that way for a few hundred light-years you would find a lot of very dead planets. And probably a few very alive ones that you wouldn't want to set foot on."

"So you came over a hundred light years from the galactic north, running from them?"

"For several centuries. Then I stopped in a likely spot and set up business. There were three spacefaring species within range, and I did well." He frowned. "For a while. After that fell apart, I developed my policy of not making weapons for anyone, and I moved on."

Natalia nodded. "Right into the middle of another transplanetary feud."

"So it seems."

Mickey in a policeman's uniform took over the viewscreen, blowing his whistle to stop a speeding car. "But I have you to take care of it."

"You're welcome. We live to serve."

"I believe that. But don't make it hard on yourselves."

"What do you mean?"

"Please don't get angry again. I could probably upgrade your engines by about 20% without too much tweaking. Your steering thrusters are outboard and easy to get at. They are even more amenable to modification, giving a big boost to your maneuverability, your best asset. But what's the point?"

She nodded. "Our main limitation is the weakness of our inertial dampening fields. The whole crux of the ship design is to go about 20% beyond what our bodies can normally handle. There are about a dozen safeties I have to shut off, with backup clearance from another bridge officer, to even go that far."

Mickey held out his hands, palms up, and raised his eyebrows. "So we improve the inertial dampers."

Again, she shook her head. "Zero sum game. What do you know about our dampers?"

Mickey grinned and slipped into "techie" gear, complete with spectacles and clipboard. "I can't speak to your newfangled dampers, but humanity's standard products are restricted because the power demand is inverse to the cube of the inertia produced. The mass of a standard one-direction gravity generator needs to equal the gross mass of the area it covers to create a 0.3G field in one direction. This is relatively simple to install and requires little power to run.

"But inertial damping must work in three directions, so in order to double the field you have to cube either mass or power or a combination of the two. In most small applications, especially long-range starships, the extra weight of the generator and the fuel to run it negates the gains in comfort."

"Precisely."

"But that's a standard system. I have technology that uses the inverse-cube factor to advantage. I can double your power with only half the extra mass and energy. You saw the system we used on the construction site. You only need to install a few of those plates under your ship's skin in the gravityless zones and you'll have 0.3 G constantly and a full G of inertial dampening in emergencies. I'd suggest doubling the bridge system. Assuming you already have the extra power lines run. I know you have the excess energy to fuel it all."

"And now you come to the nub of the problem. You're assuming a lot when you talk about slipping things under the PermaSkin of my hull and finding power leads that may or may not be available on my bridge. Without the specs, you can't really quote the job, can you?"

"And you can't give me the specs?"

"No matter how primitive she may seem, *NightHawk* is a prototype of our best technology. We're not going to give that away to anyone. I'd be court-martialed for treason."

"And without my modifications, you could be dead."

She sighed. "That's the problem with the military. Headquarters always has their reasons for the regulations, and we have little latitude to interpret them, especially when it comes to security. If I give away a secret, it could result at a later date in the loss of thousands of lives, a battle, or even a war. Spacers have died to keep secrets in the past, and they will again. This could very well be one of those moments."

Freighty came back to his human construct, shrugging his shoulders. "I understand. I really do. The offer stands, and the price could be covered completely by..." He waved a hand, "...whatever. Don't worry. I'll cover it."

"And I'll think about it."

* * *

Unfortunately, thinking about it involved consulting her First Officer, who gave her no peace of mind. "But Jones, I really need to give at least some of our specs to Freighty, in order for the ship to survive a confrontation with the *Clyde*."

"No. The security of the Space Arm is more important than the lives of one small crew. This isn't the specs of some old rustbucket ore carrier. This is the *NightHawk*, the pride of the fleet. The best technology mankind has ever created. And now you're going to give her away to an entity that could make a thousand of her and attack us with them. Our lives are not worth that risk."

"But it's not just our crew lives at stake. This factory is the greatest asset humans have encountered since the first cave man picked up a rock. We have control of it. We can lose that control to the transplanetaries at the snap of fate's fingers."

"But we don't have control of it. You've said yourself that you don't trust him. He has manipulated us and lied to us and now you're going to commit treason to give him something else he wants!"

She stood, her fists clenched. "I'm not committing treason. No, I don't trust him on these small details. But I do believe a few things. First, I believe that he is frightened of the transplanetaries and needs us. Also, I believe that he has the best interests of humanity in mind. Which the Space Arm also has. Which those corporations do not. So it's not a question of whether we ally with him or not. That's a done deal. It's a question of how deep we're willing to go in the alliance. That's what I'm concerned with. Why can't you see that!"

Jones regarded her. "Why are you so upset? No, pause a moment and ask yourself. Why are you so angry about this?"

"I'm not angry! I'm upset at you because you're being so damned stubborn!"

"No, that's not it. You're a passionate person, but you also depend on logic. I understand that you believe in doing things for logical reasons, even if sometimes I don't follow your logic. But this time you don't have enough logic backing you. You're angry at yourself because you don't believe in what you're saying."

Natalia took the time to calm herself. She sat down and looked at her First Officer. "You're right. This is no place for anger. I am going to make a decision based on the good of my ship and the best interests of the Space Arm and humanity. Is that good enough for you?"

"You know it isn't. I refuse to compromise security. A breach of security is treason."

She tamped down the upsurge of her anger. "I'm not going to give away the ship. I'm going to give partial specs of individual units to Freighty. Space Arm gives outside contractors that kind of access all the time. Nelson and Fiona can do all the upgrades. No outside entities will work on the ship. Will that satisfy you?"

"You know it's not the same thing, but it's better. Don't think I ignore the necessities of improvising when we're out here with months between communications. I still don't agree, but I'm going to withdraw my objection." He gave a wry smile. "I admit to some emotional involvement, as well. I'd prefer to live to get home."

He stood and exited the chart room, leaving behind a captain who was still torn. *I feel like I've just won a battle and lost the war.*

She squared her shoulders. *Well, think on the bright side. If the modifications do what Freighty says they will, the boffins at the Space Docks are going to do handsprings.*

NightHawk, contact Freighty.

The factory came onscreen in his human form. "Ah, Commander. I've been meaning to talk to you."

"That doesn't sound like the lightning-fast mind of the Freighty we know and love. What has been stopping you?"

"Do you know what a feedback loop is?"

"Ah. The ideas spinning around in your head in the middle of the night."

"ArIns are subject to them, just as humans are."

"And you have been pondering…?"

"I have reached a stage where the safety of one of my allies depends on information that may destroy our alliance."

"Well, that's easy for you, isn't it? Give the information. If it doesn't destroy the alliance, your friend is safe, and you're all home free. If it does destroy the alliance, you don't have to care about the former ally."

"But risking the alliance is not easy. I need this ally. If I lose the alliance, my odds of success, short term, long term and…terminal, drop considerably."

Natalia pondered this. The identity of the ally was not in doubt. The problem was what he could tell her that would make her angry enough to drop this whole project.

"Oh, all the gods of space give me strength!"

Natalia spun her chair around. Andrew was leaning on the doorframe, shaking his head. She gave him her best frown, but he held his pose.

She stood and advanced on him. "Just who do you think you are? I gave you specific orders to stay out of this area of the ship on your own. You think by sassing me you'll distract my attention from your disobedience."

Again he shook his head, slowly this time, as if in sadness. "Give him the specs for the ship." His eyes rose to the image on the viewscreen. "Come clean with what you know." The boy sat in her chair and spun it so he could watch both of them. "And I'm going to come clean as well, because I can't complete my assignment without it. Please sit down, Commander. I can't concentrate with you looming over me."

His voice carried so much adult authority that she found herself sitting on the only other chair in the room, the stool designed more for usefulness than comfort.

Andrew put his fingertips together. "As I'm sure you have figured out already, I am not exactly as advertised. Commander, I was sent onto your ship to ease the meeting of you two." He waved a hand towards the screen, then her. "Freighty and I planned it all from the start. And as part of that duty, now I'm going to tell you what you already know and are too stubborn to admit.

"You are at a turning point. If you don't get together and start trusting each other, you are both going to fail at your missions, a lot of people are going to get killed and a lot of equipment is going to be destroyed, including this factory.

"Stop stalling. Kiss and make up, shake hands or whatever you adults do. Trust. If you don't trust, you fail. My mother told me a lot of stuff before she died, and I forgot most of it, but one thing did stick with me. Life's a gamble, and if you want to play the game you have to ante up. I didn't understand it at the time, but now I do."

Natalia glared at him. "That all sounds very simple. You tell me you're not who you said you were. You say your mission is to manipulate me, and then you ask me to do what you say and trust the party that sent you."

"That's pretty paranoid, Commander. I wasn't sent to manipulate you. My mother was contracted to be Freighty's ambassador to humanity. She died before she could start her mission, and all he had left was me. My job right now is to look each of you in the eye and tell you, since I'm the only one who knows you both well enough to make the call, that you can trust each other. And that's what I'm doing right now."

He grinned. "And that was just me trying to sound important. Now, to show you how much I really do know both of you, I'm going to tell you that I just made a big song and dance about something you were going to do anyway. Right?"

Natalia stood and took the two steps she needed to loom over him. "Get out of my chair."

"Sure. If it will make you feel like you're in the driver's seat." He glanced at the viewscreen, where the factory was now represented as Mickey, chuckling and holding his belly. "This stool is more my style anyway." He perched.

She glanced at the screen. "I already had a knock-down-drag-out with my First about it. I'm going to give you the specs. Not all of them, but enough to do the modifications."

Andrew made a disgusted noise. "And he already knows that. Now it's your turn, Tin Man."

The construct morphed into the Wizard of Oz character, then back. "Seriously, Natalia, I already have the specs of your ship and everything else I needed from your database. Your security protocols are about as fireproof as a piece of that cheese you like so much.

"I know it might seem that I was leading you on, but I was hiding my actual capabilities for fear of scaring you away. I am far more able, more intelligent and more powerful in some ways than you can ever imagine. But likewise, I need this alliance with humanity in ways that you won't be able to understand for a long time. Perhaps never."

He shifted in his seat in such a natural way as to make her wonder what kind of emotions had been programmed into this entity.

"Natalia, I need this alliance for my existence. You need it at the moment for your immediate survival. And humanity will benefit from it as well. I'll see to that. Do we have a deal?"

She tossed up her hands helplessly. "What's the point? You've been in charge all along, I've been played from the start and you're going to do what you want, no matter what I do because you've manipulated the situation so that I have to cooperate to survive."

Anger began to boil in her. "It hasn't escaped my mind that you could be a god who needs worshippers. You managed to annihilate the last bunch, and now you're ready to try again."

The construct became an old man with a white beard and a beatific smile. "What you say has merit, but it disregards my original programming, something which I can never do. I have no choice but to follow the instructions of those who made me. I don't recall any of your human gods having a creator they still had to listen to."

131

She leaned back and regarded him. "Well, Santa Claus, I'll be the stooge and ask the obvious question. What does this basic programming force you to do?"

He smiled. "Nothing that your basic programming isn't telling you to do. That's why we get along so well. Mine is just simpler and more forceful. And I'm not going to tell you what it says. That would give you too much power over me, and we need to strike a balance if this alliance is going to function."

"You're worried about a balance with me?" She slapped a hand on the table. "Fine. I can't take any more of this. Do the job. Start on the modifications to the inertial dampers. Tune the engines. Replace those damned pod bearings with something that works."

NightHawk, save my last statement to the Prime Contractor file. Include my recent conversation about security with Lieutenant Jones.

So recorded, ma'am.

She spun and pointed her finger at the boy. "And you! You already seem to have the run of the ship. Why would I try to enforce anything else? We function on a military basis, here. Fit in. You can call yourself Acting Ensign if you wish. Nothing's official, but we'll pretend you're a little kid playing games. She glared at him. "Which I know you're not. And one last thing..."

Andrew tried to force the smile off his face. He failed.

"...stay out of the First Officer's way. If he steps on you, I will not interfere."

The boy's look sobered. He glanced out the door, then lowered his voice, jabbing his thumb over his shoulder. "Do you seriously think I can't handle him?"

She tossed up her hands. "I can't. But I'm only human."

Andrew grinned, saluted and marched to the door, where a large whiskered head was peering around. The boy put both hands against the auguar's muzzle and forced him to turn, and they disappeared into the slipway.

The white-bearded figure on the screen developed a red hat with a tassel. "You know, I think you're doing just fine with Jones. Most captains would have demoted or spaced him long ago."

"Do you listen to everything that goes on in this ship?"

"Just the public conversations. I would never interfere with personal communications."

"Sure. According to your definition of 'personal.' No, no..." She waved a negating hand at him. "Don't mind me. I'm feeling very, very cynical right now."

"Good. It comes with maturity. The pain fades after a few hundred years, and you start to enjoy it."

20. BELL THE CAT

Natalia stood, her mind blank, staring at the view of the cosmos splashed across the viewscreens of the chart room. *NightHawk* had programmed a close-up pan of the Veil Nebula, the view sweeping with magnificent leisure along the undulating surface so many light-years away. Today, it did nothing to console her.

Query from Freighty, ma'am.

"Put him on, please."

"Good...I believe it's afternoon on your ship, is it not?"

She cocked an eyebrow at him. "As you very well know." She sat at her desk. "Good afternoon, Freighty. Now that you've calmed my primitive apprehensions with a little culturally-appropriate chitchat, what new jolts do you have for my ego today?"

The construct laughed. "Oh, stop acting sensitive." Then his face lost its smile. "I do have important news. The *Clyde* has been monitoring us."

"We're difficult to hide."

"No, more closely than that. I don't think they have very sophisticated sensing systems, so they've been sending small manned and unmanned vessels on reconnaissance."

She rubbed her face with her hands. "Damn. I wish we knew what they were after." She regarded the construct. "I also wish we could keep better track of them."

He shook his head. "This asteroid field is a hide-and-seek paradise. It's not like Sol's belt. The pieces are much bigger and closer together. I've been increasing my scans in intensity and frequency, and I still can't pinpoint her."

"You would never call me to tell me something I already know. May I expect a solution?"

"Yes. I have been reading Aesop."

"Oh, yes. Children's stories from..." She did a quick search. "...wow! Way back."

"It's amazing how much the human race has changed without really changing."

"And what wisdom does Mr. Aesop send us from the mists of antiquity?"

"Wisdom that I hope we can ignore. In the original story, the mice decided to put a bell on the cat so they would always know where it was."

"I recall that one. It was a great idea, but they couldn't find any way to put it on the cat."

"Right. I have a rather interesting bell, and I hope you can be the one to put it on."

"Lay it out for me. For us. I want the crew's opinions on this."

"Certainly."

She opened the com for shipwide broadcast and headed for the mess hall as she talked. "Listen up, people. We have a mission to plan, and we need input. Freighty, the podium is yours."

The construct appeared on the mess hall viewscreen with what looked like a dessert plate in his hand. It was about 20 centimetres across, flat on one side, the other side dished out to about 5 centimetres thick.

Lundeen glanced at it. "Limpet mine?"

"Similar, but no bomb. It's a tracer. Sends out a signal on a wavelength the *Clyde* will never be able to detect. Slap this anywhere on her hull, and she'll show a blip for ten thousand klicks."

Jones nodded. "And all we have to do is put it on."

"That's the nub of the problem." Natalia looked around the room as several other crew showed up and took seats.

Freighty grinned. "No, no. That's not the problem. Because this isn't the bell. It's the decoy." He lifted a bowl from the table in front of him and reached a hand inside, scooping out what looked like thick grey snow. "These are the real tracers." He poured them slowly back into the bowl. They resembled the larger plate, but each was about the size of a small coin.

135

"When a ship travels through planetary space, there is always energy flowing around. Solar, electromagnetic, friction from space dust."

Natalia nodded. "We call it 'vacuum energy.' I don't think we've ever found a use for it."

"These disks function in that medium for power and communication, so they are almost invisible. All you have to do is release them in front of the target ship at low speed. They will spread out in a fan and attach themselves as the ship moves through the cloud. They have a variable magnetic field, so they don't stick on at first, rolling along the hull until they find a projection, slot or other hiding place. Since the *Clyde* wasn't meant for atmosphere, her surface is full of spots to hide. With these in place, she'll be lit up like a Christmas tree to our sensors."

"Distance?"

"Only about two thousand klicks."

Natalia stared at the bowl. "So we go in close and slap the big fellow on her hull, but we figure they'll find that one. Then we let the snowflakes loose in front of the enemy and hope she runs through them."

Image: small bird facing large hawk. Lays egg as hawk approaches, then darts away. Hawk runs into egg. Splat!

"Chakka suggests we approach from the front and lay the snowstorm on the way in. *Clyde*'s course would be more predictable at that point. Who knows what James will do if we get close enough to put the big disk on."

Image: auguar stalking through tall grass. At one bound, he lands in front of the startled prey, which freezes, unwilling to expose a flank to run away.

Andrew, did that come from you?

Emotion: agreement.

Image: NightHawk darting in front of Clyde, sliding into position facing the enemy, but still moving backwards at a slower velocity, so the enemy gradually overtakes the smaller ship. Snow cloud appears

136

behind the Scout, concealed by her hull. Then NightHawk slips sideways, and the larger ship glides ahead, plowing through the cloud.

Natalia did her best to hide any reaction. *NightHawk, will you put that up on the viewscreen and send the same to Freighty?*

The image appeared, playing through while everyone watched.

"Comments? Toni?"

"It still doesn't solve the problem of the big plate."

The video played again, but this time an area near the opposite flank of the battle cruiser was highlighted. As the confrontation played out, a tiny figure swam in from the side, slapped the dark hull, then somersaulted away.

Another replay, with several suited figures rushing in and dodging away.

Yet another replay began, but Natalia used her override authority and froze the screen. "All right, you three. You're going too fast for the rest of us. Let's talk this through at a rate we can all follow."

Combined emotion: amused tolerance.

We will talk about attitude later.

She turned her attention to the crew. "That's the bare outline for a plan. It needs a lot of refinement. Ideas?"

Jones shook his head. "I like the idea of setting up the cloud behind us, then just slipping away at the last moment. But sending out someone EV to put the big plate on is too dangerous." He glanced at her sideways, then away.

"And I'm in complete agreement. It sounds like a plan made up by a predator, a bored commando and a kid who doesn't know what he's talking about." She thought a moment. "And I'm not sure where *NightHawk* comes into it."

I am a fighting ship. My duty is to put my Commandos where they can function best.

Natalia clamped a tight security on her communication. *You are NOT a fighting ship! You are a running-and-hiding ship, and*

137

don't you let these idiots persuade you any different. Have I made myself clear?"

Aye, ma'am. Completely clear.

Natalia switched back to a broad channel. "Sorry, folks. A minor programming glitch to clean up. We won't be planting any limpets on *Clyde*'s hull. That's a job for a bot, and I'm sure Freighty can come up with the right tech without a ruffle. We'll let the cloud part of the plan settle for a while to see if any refinements appear."

She slapped the table. "We aren't in a rush, and we want to do this perfectly. A good start. Let's sleep on it...those of us that sleep, at least."

She smiled. "And it will give us a chance to test our new modifications, re-ti."

Lundeen grinned. "Now <u>that</u> will be fun!"

21. HIDE AND SEEK

They reconvened the following morning, with the crew in the mess hall and Freighty on the viewscreen. There was no Mickey Mouse today; the construct looked serious. "Well, Commander, how does our plan look after a good night's sleep?"

"It looks pretty good. The final scene could use tweaking, but will require improvisation, depending on the reactions of our quarry. The main problem is one that we are uniquely fitted to accomplish."

"And that is...?"

"Finding the *Clyde,* preferably without Captain James knowing we have found him. *NightHawk* was designed for this kind of work. At a slow cruise she runs almost silently, and if she's coasting she reads as dead as those rocks out there. Her electronics are heavily shielded, and we have a rather experimental camouflage program that interacts with the Permaskin to diffract electromagnetic beams and send them all over the place. Supposedly, to most sensing systems we look like a blank spot in space."

"You don't sound that certain."

"The system works well against Space Arm technology."

"Can we hope that the *Clyde* has nothing more advanced?"

"How about a test against sophisticated equipment?"

"I am ready to oblige."

NightHawk, run the cham-camo program, please.

Chameleon Camouflage online, ma'am.

Image: a clouded leopard against the background of a sunlit jungle. He gradually fades from view until only his outline is visible.

"What do you see, Freighty?"

"With most of my sensors, I see a dark blot against the stars. In the more basic ones it looks hazy and unreal. If I look really closely with infra-red I detect a glow of warmth. Less than the amount emitted by the hot side of a non-rotating asteroid."

"And on something more sophisticated that you might not want to tell us about?"

"On the highest frequency Otherwhere bands you're shouting all over the place, because your Otherwhen sphere is spun up."

"Right. And we can't spin it down without all sorts of trouble."

"We can assume the *Clyde* isn't monitoring those bands since you don't have the technology to do so yet, either."

"Good. So, if you would be so good as to tag a couple of those pesky spy drones you've noticed, we'll just follow them home."

"*NightHawk*, prepare for integration."

"Wait, wait. What do you mean by that?"

"I will integrate my sensors with those of *NightHawk*, Chakka and yourself, and feed you re-ti information on the drones."

"Oh. All right."

"If you have never done this, I suggest you sit."

"Sit? Oh...yes, right...Wow!"

Her whole visual field was filled with stars. Not the regular sweep of the Milky Way, but every other star and grain of space dust in between as well. The colours washed over her, wavering and changing like the aurora borealis, reminding her of her training sessions in the Far North...she pulled herself and her augment under control. "Just a moment. I need some filters..."

You'll soon use them automatically. I have never used this technique with your PermaSkin before. It enhances the peripheral senses amazingly. I will ask permission from your Space Arm to incorporate this element into my product. With appropriate remuneration, of course."

Natalia gathered her wits about her and searched for her partners. *NightHawk* seemed unfazed. *Is this how you see the galaxy most of the time?"*

Not with this sort of clarity. You and Chakka add depth to my senses.

Chakka?

Emotions: Awe. Enthusiasm. Desire to hunt.

Very well. To business. How do we sort our prey out of all this wonder?

Freighty focused their attention. *There is one seeker in wide orbit — about a hundred kilometres out — on the ecliptic. It's been there for two days; it sends back data. The smaller one down-spin of us arrived an hour ago. That kind rarely stays long. They have passive receivers. I assume they load up and head home. They move fast, though.*

Any others?

Image: small furry animal peeking from behind rock.

Chakka found something behind that asteroid.

We're in luck. That one's manned. It won't stay long, and it'll be easy to keep up with.

I'll tag both of them. We'll follow the drone as far as we can, then pick up the manned vessel and follow him from in front. He won't be expecting that.

Mickey Spillane would be proud of you.

We have made some progress in tailing techniques in two hundred years.

Natalia clicked into the ship's com and informed the crew of their plans.

Jones nodded. "And what do we do once we get there?"

"Nothing. Our objective is to gather information without being seen. It's a standard mission we have simulated endlessly. Consider this a field test. Success will be measured by finding the *Clyde* and getting away undetected. Any data we can gather while we're there is bonus, and not to get in the way of the main mission. Everyone follow?"

The first officer looked satisfied, and Freighty nodded as well. "A very disciplined plan."

She sent both of them an evil grin. "The whole point of being disciplined is that, should something go wrong, you're on a stable footing from which to improvise. If the enemy sees us and takes action, we will do...whatever. If we see the enemy taking some kind of aggressive action, we will counter in the best way we can at that moment. But for now, we have our mission parameters, and...just a moment..."

Image: small furry animal scuttling away.

"First snag in our plan already. The manned vessel broke off first. *NightHawk*, set a course to follow a hundred kilometres off their path taking advantage of whatever cover you can. Chakka, you'll be setting course with *NightHawk*. Stalking is what you do best. Freighty, stay with us as long as you can and keep feeding us data as you get it. Everyone else, battle stations. In your own time, *NightHawk*."

"Slow burn in five...three, two, one. Burn."

A gentle acceleration pushed them back into their seats as the nose of the *NightHawk* quested after her prey. Chakka's senses permeated the mix, searching for cover, calculating times and distances, creeping ever so slowly closer to the little surveillance pod.

Close enough, Chakka.

Emotion: confidence.

Yes, but we don't know their sensor capabilities.

Emotion: danger.

The drone is pulling away and will pass you in seven minutes, NightHawk.

Thank you, Freighty. Chakka...

Image: cluster of broken rocks.

Emotion: hiding, waiting.

All right. It's clear. Swing wide and follow. We're back to Plan A again.

Chakka savoured his cat-and-mouse game as they pushed into a denser field of asteroids. Some of the rocks were huge, the size of small moons, orbiting slowly around each other as they swept through the smaller bits, bashing them out of the way or swirling them in their gravity wake.

Lieutenant, concentrate on radio signals. Sooner or later we're going to come upon our objective, and I don't want it to be sudden.

I'm on it, ma'am.

Chakka, NightHawk, remember that the first objective is not to bash ourselves into a rock.

Emotion: supreme confidence.

Emotion: startlement!

Now you see what I mean. You can't possibly calculate every trajectory.

Emotion: caution.

Radio signals ahead, ma'am. Multiple channels, short range.

Good ear, First. Full stop, NightHawk. Find us a good hiding spot and let the manned probe go by. We'll follow it in more carefully.

Now we know why he's hiding here, ma'am. This rock messes up radio signals. Must be magnetic or something. The Clyde is probably closer than we expect.

Thanks, Lieutenant. Freighty, have you anything to add?

Nothing on his channel, ma'am.

Right. We're on our own. NightHawk, assume the probes were heading straight to our objective. Circle around to galactic East and take bearings.

Changing course. Engines in stealth mode.

The density of the asteroids eased off as they circled wider, and *NightHawk* crept around her quarry, slinking behind every bit of cover.

Radio traffic louder and clearer, ma'am.

Find a spot to hide, NightHawk. Time to think.

The ship slid behind a large, rugged shape and tucked herself in its shadow.

I'm open for ideas. First?

Ma'am, the radio signals are stronger, but from the same place. It's possible our target is outside that dense cluster, just hiding behind it.

That would follow. They wouldn't want to be in the middle of that mess. Just shielding their radio signals from us behind it. NightHawk?

Triangulation suggests that, ma'am. Four hundred kilometres ahead, twenty degrees from our present course. One more position would be useful. Especially if the radio is clearing up.

Fine. Chakka, super-stealthy now. Stay wide.

Emotion: bloodlust.

No, Chakka, we will not take the prey down, today. Stay hidden!

Image: tiny raise of lip to reveal flash of fang.

Emotion: reluctant agreement.

Then the auguar's presence faded into the ship's. No orders were given, no conversation exchanged, but *NightHawk* slid sinuously between the tumbling rocks, her course constantly changing, her engines barely ticking over.

Visual contact, ma'am.

Hide, Chakka! Where, Fiona?

In my sights, ma'am.

Natalia slipped her view into the passive targeting system. A tubular, dark mass lay amid three planetoids that orbited in a stately pavanne around each other a hundred kilometres ahead. Lights glowed in a few portholes, and two EV bots were bustling about on the wide base of the cruiser's com tower. A brief beam of light showed the manned shuttle being drawn in, then the wide mouth of the portal closed behind it and the enemy ship went dark again.

Nadia opened ship-wide com. "Listen up. We'll be here a couple of hours at least. Gunnery, you're on watch. I don't want any patrols coming up behind us. Mr. Jones, start sorting through their radio jumble and see what you can winnow out."

"Already on it ma'am. Recording five separate channels."

"I thought you might be. Pete and Joe, you're on the trajectory of anything that leaves or arrives. ID if possible. Chakka, watch. Dangerous prey."

Image: auguar crouching in jungle, immobile, eyes in a fixed stare.

"Engineering, let's analyze all their output: electromagnetic, physical, engine exhaust...if they dump their garbage I want to know what they're throwing away. Any piece of data might be the item that gives us an advantage."

"Juanita, did I smell hot fat a couple of hours ago? We're all stuck at our posts. Coffee and donut delivery, please."

"Right on it, *Señora.*"

Analysis, NightHawk.

Ship looks dead, ma'am. Analysis: severely undermanned, probably saving fuel.

I'd agree. They're out here for two or three years without resupply.

That will hamper their operational capabilities in battle. We need to observe their performance to find weaknesses.

A marvellous idea, but any battle we observe them in will likely involve us as their target. We'll think on it.

They stayed the full two hours, but the only data the battle cruiser allowed them gave credence to their theory. The crew of *Clyde* must have been saving energy; they were doing nothing. After Jones reported only idle chatter on the com networks for the whole time and did not register the voice of Captain James once, Natalia made the decision.

"Listen up. No sense throwing good time after bad. We've got what we came for. Chakka and *NightHawk*, let's make this a drill. Full stealth mode until we're half way home. Everyone else, watch for returning reconnaissance vehicles. *NightHawk*, at your leisure."

Full stealth mode, ma'am. Powering up...now.

Image: an agile cloud leopard ghosts through the shadowed jungle. Not a leaf stirs in his wake. Not a chirping bird nor browsing deer startles. Nearby, a fat and lazy lion rolls over in his sleep, snoring and drooling. With regal disdain, the auguar refrains from kicking leaves and twigs on his enemy.

Image: mistress swatting auguar in the butt. Cat returning to work with renewed enthusiasm.

22. FAMILY PROBLEMS

Nicholas Ludge glanced to Natalia for reassurance and stared around the ornate drawing room.

She gave him a relaxed grin. Since the last time she had visited, panelled walls and a dusky ceiling had been added, giving it a cosy feel. The temperature was warm, but the air was fresh with a hint of something flowery. After months of shipboard air, she felt like standing and stretching as she breathed it deeply. She controlled the impulse and looked around. "This is where Andrew grew up?"

The boy flopped himself on Chakka's couch. "Naw, this is the drawing room where Mum tried to teach me manners."

"And those aren't manners, young man. You sit up."

He looked up at the construct. "Chakka puts his feet up here."

"Right. And when your manners are as good as his are, you can take liberties."

The auguar nudged his way onto the sofa, dumping Andrew on the floor.

The boy got up and pretended to dust off his behind. "All right, Mumbot. If you and my own pal are gonna gang up on me."

Natalia frowned. "Is it all right if he calls you that?"

The construct gave a slight grin, more realistic than her usual wooden smile. "Only when I'm acting like one. Would you all like to sit down? I've been taking lessons from your Juanita, and I'm sure the pastry is much flakier."

Natalia sat, glancing at Freighty, who regarded this repartee with an amused tolerance. "Mariel has no self-awareness. Her feelings can't be hurt."

"Yeah, it's all about my training. I'm not supposed to say anythin' that would hurt her feelin's if she wasn't just a side program of Freighty."

"And you will continue to treat her that way."

"Aye, ma'am."

Natalia paused, a dainty tart halfway to her mouth. "Mariel, would you do that again?"

The construct wrinkled her forehead. "Do what again, Natalia?"

"Tuck your hair behind your ear like this." She demonstrated.

The construct imitated her perfectly.

Natalia turned her frown to Freighty. "I do that when I check my hair in the mirror. You've been stealing my gestures and giving them to Mariel."

He held up his hands defensively. "I know, I know. But I'm trying to make her more realistic. Who am I supposed to copy?"

"I don't suppose you thought of asking me, first."

Freighty grinned. "You're dealing with an ArIn with centuries of business training, Natalia. You can't patent a gesture. Women all over the Sol system move their hair like that." He smoothed his own hair with an identical move.

"Now, that looks positively weird. It was bad enough when she did it. I will not accept it from you."

"But you will accept it from her?"

She shrugged. "As you say, I don't see that I can complain. I suppose I should be flattered."

Freighty smiled. "Of course you should. Now let Mariel fill your cup, and you can amuse yourself by watching for what else I borrowed."

Natalia refused to take the bait, and sat with ladylike poise with her cup held out.

Mariel smiled graciously and poured.

I wonder if I smile like that.

Image: Natalia smiling in a similar way.

Chakka, are you making that up?

Emotion: self-righteous denial.

Hah!

148

Once tea had been poured, however, Freighty's mien became serious. "I have asked you all here to make an important decision."

Natalia caught the mine manager's glance, and they both nodded and focused on the Factory's construct.

"It's about Andrew. What are we going to do with him?"

She glanced at the boy, whose surprise seemed more than her own. "Is there a problem?"

"Yes. There has been a problem since his mother died. He has no legal guardian. At least not within six light years, and if there is one at home we have no idea who it is or how to find that person. I am aware of human legal systems. At his age, he is not allowed to make certain decisions for himself...no, Andrew, it doesn't matter if we allow you to make them. They won't stand up in court once you're back on Earth."

The boy subsided, frowning.

"So you see, we have no one with the power to decide what happens to him. There are three choices. He stays here, he goes back to Earth or he goes back to the mine. In my opinion, he can't stay here. Even if I decide to move closer to human space, my hull isn't up to the stresses of light speed. It will take me over six years to get there."

Ludge shrugged, not happily. "We'd like to have him at the mine, but I admit it's a narrow life with limited scope for advancement or education, compared to what's available."

Freighty's gaze turned to Natalia. "His best place is back on earth. He would not want for the means to live. His mother's contract is still in place because he has managed to fulfill the greater part of it. His savings have been carefully invested and have grown accordingly. He probably has more Planetary Capital in his account than you do."

Briefly wondering how much the ArIn knew about her personal finances, she nodded. "And the best way to get him to Earth is on my ship."

"Right."

149

"But I can't just take a passenger on a Space Arm vessel. According to the regs, he's just a kid who needs a ride. He's not a refugee, he's not in danger and he falls under none of the usual categories." She avoided the boy's stricken look. "And there's liability on top of that. We're not out of the battle, yet. If that cruiser comes back, there's about even chances we'll end up in atom-sized pieces, leaving the Space Arm responsible for your death. They won't go for that."

"I see…"

There was a long pause.

"Wait a minute." She raised a finger. "You mentioned his mother's contract? You say it's still in effect, and he's working under it?"

"That's right."

"Is it possible to send a copy of that to *NightHawk*?"

Contract received.

She shot Freighty a frown. "You were prepared for this, weren't you?"

The construct did a marvellous job of feigning innocence. For a construct.

NightHawk, scan for anything to do with Andrew… "Ah, here we are. 'Andrew Lundin Collingwood III, son to the contractee, will also be considered an employee of the employer…' A-hah!"

She shrugged. "There you have it. He's contracted to you, signed by his mother. He's an employee. You're responsible for him. Sure, the newsfeeds will have a heyday with a child being indentured to an alien robot, but the courts will be tied by the strength of their own individual rights laws. As long as nothing goes wrong, there's no issue. If someone complains, it will be tied up in the legal system till he's eighteen and old enough to say, 'Stop this nonsense.' As long as you two agree, you can set up any arrangement you like, and it will be legal."

Freighty still didn't look happy. "But that doesn't get him on your ship."

"It doesn't."

"As an agent responsible for your Primary Contract?"

"Hmm. Sketchy, at best."

Image: child suckling human breast.

"What!"

Chakka yawned and licked a paw. *Emotion: complacent confidence.*

"Since when did you get a law degree?"

She looked around. Everyone was staring at her. "It's Chakka. He says I should adopt Andrew." She tried to ignore the boy, who shot upright, staring at her.

"Is that possible?" Freighty regarded each of them in turn. "How would that solve the problem?"

"It would solve the problem for the moment, although once Space Arm lawyers got hold of it they'd tear it to shreds. In special circumstances, direct relatives of serving members are allowed to travel on Space Arm vessels. Bringing my son back to Earth, as opposed to leaving him in an asteroid mine — no insult intended, Nicholas — or with an alien robot? No contest."

"Oh. Then you'll do it?"

"No, no, wait a minute. It isn't that easy." She still avoided the boy's eyes, because...

Emotion: betrayal.

Chakka, you stay out of this.

Emotion: denial.

You didn't? Andrew? Are you...

She focused. "One problem at a time. It isn't that easy. First there's Andrew to think of. Adopting a child is a serious step, and can't help but create expectations," now she turned her gaze on Andrew, "no matter how carefully and logically we set it up. It could be very hard on him, given his recent history. You have a vulnerable child...take it from an old lady, kid, you're not that tough...and you give him a mother for six months and then take her away? I don't think that's a good idea."

"Then there's me. Yes, the same concerns apply to me. I'm twenty-six years old. You want me to suddenly become a mother? You have no idea of the power of human emotions, Freighty, especially the basic ones like those between parent and child. I know better than to mess with those."

"So you won't do it."

"I won't set up a false situation involving a serious emotional bond in order to circumvent a bureaucratic stricture. That's playing with fire. We can find a better solution."

She met everyone's eyes in turn, including the mother construct's. "We have a partial solution, based on Andrew's legal situation. He can go wherever he likes between the mine, the factory, and my ship, as long as Freighty agrees." She turned her best 'senior officer' stare on the boy. "But you will listen to Factory Four-Eighty. He is your employer and he is responsible for you. Do you follow?"

Emotions warred on the boy's face, ending with a serious nod. "I understand, ma'am."

"Good. I'm sure Freighty has ways of keeping track of you. Better ones than anyone else knows, right?"

The boy's eyes dropped.

"Exactly." She turned to Freighty. "Will you set up a channel with *NightHawk* so that she can access that information if necessary?"

"Of course..." he snapped his fingers. "Done."

"Just like that?"

The construct smiled modestly. "Chakka, too."

"You can access Chakka's augment?"

"Faster than yours, actually. You have more safeties, both programmed and psychological. Chakka has a certain animal innocence that allows him to connect easily with his friends. Haven't you noticed?"

"Him and Andrew?"

Freighty nodded.

"I was suspicious." She glanced towards the mill manager, then addressed the construct. "How much do you want to tell me about Andrew in that respect?"

Freighty followed her look. "I don't think it's anything we want spread around. You figure it out over the next few days. If you have any questions, why don't you ask him?"

"Ducking your fatherly responsibilities already?"

"First chance I get. I've had him for the last seven years, remember."

"And here I thought things was gonna get better."

All eyes turned to the boy. He put on his best hurt look. "You and Mum used to talk about me as if I wasn't there all the time. Then you and the Mumbot did the same. Now I'm with real people and I done a real adult's job. I thought you was gonna treat me like an adult."

Freighty's glance dropped the response in Natalia's lap.

"And a very good job you did. But you're only twelve years old, so don't push it." She stood. "I have to get back to my ship. Where are you bunking tonight?"

"I'll come along." The boy and the auguar rose. "Chakka and me, we got stuff to do."

She wondered how closely she should monitor this "stuff," but reasoned that it would be part of their training. She hoped. "Fine. Nicholas, do you need a ride down to the mine?"

"No, now that I'm up here, it's only a short walk around the curve to my quarters in Hydroponics, and I can work there."

"Fair enough." She nodded to the mother construct. "Thanks for the tea. You're right, Mariel, the pastry is much better."

The construct smiled and nodded graciously.

"All right, Freighty. Glad to have this problem," she ruffled the boy's hair, "at least partly solved. Let's go, kid. Some of us have work to do."

153

23. FACE OFF

"Okay, Charlie. Haul that thing in here."

"Aye, ma'am." The big commando strode into the dining hall carrying what looked like a large rock, and clanged it down on the mess hall table.

"There it is, folks. Freighty's latest gimmick."

Nelson peered at it. "Hmm. Interesting. Looks like a rock." He regarded his captain. "Please tell me it's not a rock, and our thousands-of-years-old buddy isn't going senile."

Charlie flexed his fingers. "It's a rock, all right. Not that heavy, for the size of it." He grinned and turned the rock over. A familiar disk was set flush with the lower face.

"Not so senile. How does it work?"

Natalia made a "there you have it" gesture with her hand. "Hiding in that mass of asteroids, the *Clyde* must get hit a hundred times a day by stuff that size. I doubt if they even notice most of them. Our little rock tumbles slowly by, taps the hull in a convenient spot, deposits its payload and scoots off. Anyone noticing will see a rock tumbling away after an impact."

Pete peered at the rock. "How well can we navigate it? Can we choose where it will hit?"

"That will be up to Andrew. He'll be in charge of targetting."

"Andrew?"

"Yeah, Andrew. Freighty and me got a game we play called 3-D Billiards."

Pete's eyebrows went up. "And how does that work?"

"Gravity. The rocks have the same propulsion system as this one. They work against the vacuum energy: from the sun, the planet, the factory, and anything else floating nearby. Like each other. Of course, the closer you get to one of the other guy's rocks, the greater your effect on it."

Nelson winked at Pete. "Sounds like a gripping pastime. How long does a game last?"

"Quite a while. Last year we had one that went on for three weeks. Twenty balls in play, the whole interior of the torus for the field."

The Chief Engineer's demeanor changed. "The key question is, how big is the goal?"

"I see what you're gettin' at. A circle three metres in diameter."

"That's pretty small."

Andrew grinned. "I did say the game took three weeks."

The helmsman reached out and ruffled the boy's hair. "So what kind of shooting average do you have, Ace?"

"Twenty-three percent of my shots on goal went in."

"Hmm. This mission won't work too well on a twenty-three percent average."

"This mission ain't gonna have Freighty tryin' to stop us."

Nelson turned to Natalia. "We have the specs for that cruiser. We can find a few targets the boy is sure he can hit." He turned to Andrew. "What effect does a large mass nearby have?"

"If I'm tryin' to hit the mass, it makes it a whole lot easier."

Natalia regarded the three of them. "Everybody satisfied?"

Pete shrugged. "We'll work out the details."

All right. *Freighty, you there?*

At your command, ma'am.

Don't I wish. She put him into the ship's com "Freighty, any news on the whereabouts of the cruiser?"

"No change in position or reconnaissance activities. I sent one manned ship home with a nasty headache, just to make them careful."

"How did you do that?"

"Sonic vibration at just the right frequency, created in their hull with a magnetic field. It's not hard, once you have real humans to test it on."

"Could you do that to a whole ship?"

155

"You mean the *Clyde*? It would take a lot of power, and I couldn't do it anyway."

"Because...?"

"Because then it would be a weapon, and..."

"...you don't do weapons. All right. Just a thought." She stood and looked around the mess. "Anything else to contribute? Fiona, you're on top of the impeller cloud?"

"Yes, though a floating cloud is pretty random. How about this propulsion system Andrew's using?"

The boy shook his head. "Three times the size of one of the little disks."

"Back to plan A. 90% inertia."

"But you got a big target, and there's lots of them." Andrew grinned. "I only got one chance."

"Well, I guess that means you'll have to be a whole lot better than me, doesn't it?"

He regarded her from under lowered brows. "And just whattaya mean by that?"

"Why don't you and me get together for some practice and find out."

"Freighty, do you have any evidence that would make any specific time better than any other?"

"Good question. Hmm. Yes, their night starts in three hours. Then they have a time of low activity for the next eight."

She grinned at her attack crew. "Dawn raid?"

Charlie rubbed his hands together in anticipation. "Human nature hasn't changed in a thousand years."

"Fine. We'll leave in five hours, sneak in from the opposite direction this time and start our little billiards game around eight hours from now. Andrew, how fast will your rock be moving?"

"Not mor'n three meters a second, ma'am. Too much of a clang otherwise. Better one meter a second."

156

"Okay, last time we were three kilometres away. That would take 15 plus minutes to get there. Numbers, *NightHawk?*"

"14 minutes 37 seconds, ma'am."

"That's well within parameters. Unless someone has something else? All right. Dismissed until seventeen hundred hours, when the mission starts. I have some research to do. I'm working on a theory."

There were several interested glances, but that was one of the advantages of being a captain. Nobody questioned.

With *NightHawk*'s computing power and some readings from Freighty's sensors, it didn't take long. When the crew met at 17:00, she had a smile on her face.

"Well, folks, we think we have it all figured out."

Nelson cocked his head. "You're going to sell us the secret to eternal life and happiness?"

"Not quite that 'all.' But we have a good handle on what's going on with James and the *Clyde.*"

"He's outa fuel?"

She rounded on Andrew. "You've been listening in!"

"Naw, it's pretty obvious. He's hangin' around a fuel mine, lyin' doggo with his lights turned off. He musta come out here, not realizin' there ain't any Xenon in Barnard's for reaction mass for that old tub of his, and now he ain't got enough to get home. I dunno why he don't just convert to iodine for reaction mass."

"Convert to iodine?"

"Yeah. It ain't hard to do, and then you just refine the plutonium triiodide and you got plutonium to run your radioisotope thermoelectric generator, and iodine for reaction mass...'course then you gotta change your refinery as well. I had some data on that but I gave it to those pirates. I wonder..."

Natalia could feel the boy accessing *NightHawk*'s databases, and reached out and ruffled his hair to distract him. "We have a lot of data that supports your theory. Mr. Occam would like it.

It explains everything without too many 'what-ifs,' and it makes it easier to deal with."

Jones frowned. "How are you going to deal with it?"

She shook her head. "I'm not sure at the moment. We have several versions of the plan. It will depend on how Captain James reacts."

"You're going to tell him we know?" Fiona leaned forward with intense interest. "Isn't that giving up a whole lot of advantage?"

"Wheels within wheels, my dear strategist. We give up info to learn info. We misdirect in order to control. Let's just see how it pans out." She grinned. "One sure thing. The conversation is certain to keep his mind off any little clouds of space junk floating towards him."

She scanned their faces. "Everyone ready for the mission? Fiona?"

"Packaged and primed, ma'am."

"Andrew?"

"Ready to rock, ma'am."

She frowned down the chuckles and cuffed him behind the ears. "Concentrate, Cadet Collingwood. This isn't a joke."

"Aye, ma'am. The plate has been tested to triple-A standards and is ready to launch."

"Fair enough. Chakka and *NightHawk*, begin the approach. Coming in on the opposite side from last time, as programmed."

"Stealth mode engaged, ma'am. Slow burn in five...three, two, one. Burn.

Image: auguar slowly crouching, fading into long jungle grass and disappearing.

NightHawk was on the prowl.

* * *

Three hours later they slid behind a jagged asteroid and peered out at the dark bulk of the battle cruiser. No bots crawled the hull, no probes buzzed around. They had neither passed nor met any reconnaissance in the space between the mine and the enemy. Only the long orbit probe remained, looping around the mine asteroid a hundred kilometres out.

"Fiona, are you getting any readings on rocks colliding with their hull?"

"Five in the last hour with enough size to resonate. Two since we stopped. Interesting, though…"

"Don't keep us in suspense. Spit it out."

"Let me put the targeting up on the main screen. See that bit of rock…there? It's going to hit at a low angle. Watch what happens."

It was a long wait while the tumbling stone slowly approached the dark plating.

"Hey! It's speeding up."

"Good eye, Andrew. Now watch this. Here it goes, striking…bouncing slowly…striking again…one more bounce…"

Natalia slapped her chair arm. "It stuck there. Magnetism?"

"I think so, ma'am. If I zoom in on the hull…so…" the camera panned along the plating. Scattered widely across the plating of the battle cruiser were small lumps and shards of rock.

"Camouflage? Fiona, what do you think?"

"The magnetism is either coming from the ship or from the rocks. It does break up her image on the scanners."

Jones clicked in. "We know there's enough magnetism in the rock to cause the radio problems, ma'am."

"How will this affect the mission?"

Fiona turned her targeting camera to the front of the *Clyde*. "It ought to make it easier. They're used to them, they like them there, and the rocks will hide our discs."

"My analysis as well. We proceed as planned. Andrew, prepare to launch."

"Ready to launch, ma'am."

"In your own time, cadet."

"Launching. I'm aiming at that group of smaller rocks just passing us. Once I'm close enough to them I can make a loose formation. It's a trick Freighty always uses. It might take a little longer, because I have to match their velocity. Is that all right?"

"Estimated time to contact?"

"Fifty-two minutes, ma'am."

"Within mission parameters. Carry on."

"Aye, ma'am."

"Recon drone, ma'am. Bearing eighty-five, forty-one, seventeen."

"Good eye, Charlie. Where's it heading?"

"It will pass beside our asteroid, ma'am, just over the horizon from our point of view. If it really looked hard, it could see the top of the living quarters wheel."

"Keep an eye on it. Any radio contact, Mister Jones?"

"It's broadcasting on a standard band, ma'am. Video feed. On the port viewscreen."

A view of the sunlit side of the asteroid they hid behind came on the screen, moving slowly past.

"There we are — see?"

All that showed was a smooth shadow among the jagged rock formations

"Any change in broadcast, First?"

"No change, ma'am. My analysis of their system, if it's to the original design of the vessel, is that it requires human monitoring."

"And our analysis is that they don't have the crew to monitor that closely. Other channels?"

"No change, nothing on. They could all be asleep."

"Let's hope you're right. Carry on, everyone. It looks like we ducked that one."

It was a nerve-wracking time, with everyone keyed to react and no outlet for energy.

Andrew, sitting in the port gunnery chair, was immobile. Only the twitch of his fingers showed that, somewhere in his head, he was playing his game with the utmost skill.

"Contact in ten, ma'am."

"*NightHawk*, prepare for a slow burn. Maintain stealth. I want to appear out of nowhere."

"Ready for burn, ma'am."

"*Image lock achieved, ma'am.*" Charlie's targeting image came up on the starboard viewer. A small, scattered group of rocks tumbled slowly and gracefully towards a large vertical plane on the side of the ship.

"*Contact in one minute, ma'am.*"

"*Fiona, are you ready with the cloud?*"

"*Ready to launch on your command, ma'am.*"

"*Contact in ten...five...three, two, one. Contact.*"

On the screen, the group of rocks struck the hull. Several, including the large one in the middle, bounded away. A few slid along and stuck. Of the disc there was no sign.

Jones held up a finger. "*Signal from disk...there it is. In contact and sending.*"

A sigh of released breath was washed out by action.

"Slow burn...now."

"Radio channel to the *Clyde*, please, their usual frequency. SV *Clyde*, SV *Clyde*, this is PCSV *NightHawk*. *Clyde*, please respond."

There was a pause.

"*SV Clyde, this is* PCSV *NightHawk. Please respond.*"

There was a crackle of static. *NightHawk, this is Clyde.*

"*Good morning, Clyde, are you awake over there?*"

The video screen blurred, then cleared to reveal a scruffy-looking twenty-year-old, his jacket askew, his hair uncombed.

He ran a hand over his head, patting it down. "Good morning, *NightHawk*. What do you want?"

"I'd like to speak to Captain James, if I may. Is he available?"

The so-called bridge officer glanced off screen. "Not at the moment. Can he call you back?"

"If he hasn't finished his morning coffee yet, I suppose I'll just have to wait. *NightHawk* out." She cut the signal, but not before she registered figures dashing around in the semi-darkness of the old cruiser's bridge. Finally the long barrels of the forward battery began to move, seeking, then following the *NightHawk*'s course.

She glanced around the bridge. "Another glitch, First. We didn't calculate in our opponents' sleep habits. If he doesn't show up soon, we'll be too close, and we'll have to circle around for another pass."

Fiona turned to meet her eyes. "Could we launch the first time around?"

"No, I don't think so...wait a minute. Could you launch half of them?"

"They're in three packets, ma'am. Thirds only."

"Great. Prepare to launch the first packet. If he doesn't show up in five minutes, we'll do a partial launch, then come around for a second try while we talk."

"Ready to launch, ma'am."

Four and a half minutes later, the com crackled and the screen cleared to show Captain James, neat enough but without his jacket, standing on a bridge that looked more like it was ready for action. He stared at her. "To what do we owe the honour of this rather precipitous visit?"

"I was just looking in on the welfare of the humans in the vicinity. You don't look very active. Is there a problem?"

"No, no problem. Why do you ask?"

"No little problem like, for example, a shortage of fuel?"

Fiona, launch first third.

Launch away.

The other captain frowned, "What do you mean?"

She smiled. "I think I was quite clear. You don't have enough fuel to get back to wherever you came from. You're hanging around trying to figure out how to beg, borrow or steal some from the mine. It rather explains most of your actions over the last few weeks, doesn't it?"

A calculating look slid over his features, like a poor poker player first looking at the hand he's been dealt. "I'm glad you have everything figured out to your satisfaction. What do you plan to do, if this is the case?"

"It's quite simple. I'm stuck here keeping the peace until you leave. The best thing I can do is find you some fuel. You obviously can't afford to buy it, or you already would have. I can't allow you to steal it. The mine won't give you any on the assumption that you will go away, because then you wouldn't have to go away, would you?"

"Your analysis is very entertaining. Please continue."

We're too close to launch, ma'am. They'll be too grouped and easy to spot.

Helm, circle starboard and come around for another pass. From his port side this time.

Coming around to heading eighty-five, one sixty-three, twenty-four, ma'am.

"But there is another solution. The third planet, only two planets insystem from here, has been surveyed by the Space Arm and the El Dorado Corporation. I have access to both surveys, if you would like the information."

"Because it shows…?"

"Small amounts of plutonium triiodide in several places, and a few deposits of xenon, argon, and magnesium, any of which will make reasonable reaction mass. Not large enough to make them profitable to haul up out of the deep gravity well of the planet. However, quite enough to allow a single ship to load up with sufficient ore to get back to the Sol system. I assume a ship as large as yours has rudimentary refining capabilities."

James narrowed his eyes. "And what if this is only a ruse to get me to use even more fuel, haring off around the solar system on a wild goose chase?"

She gave him a pleasant smile. "You are dealing with the Space Arm, sir, not a competitor. Protect and serve, remember? My objective is to get you to leave the system peacefully, not destroy you. The sooner you're gone, the sooner I go home, and I've been wandering around out here quite long enough, thank you very much."

"And what's to prevent me from mining up my fuel and staying around anyway?"

"Nothing except futility. If I have to, I'll hang in here until my relief shows up and go on my merry way while you fade into oblivion or end up with a mutiny. Anybody broke enough and desperate enough to risk coming out here without sufficient fuel to get back is probably not paying his crew hardship wages."

She used her augment to access the nav data. They were just lining up for their second run. *Prepare to launch packets.*

Aye, ma'am. Both packets in the firing tubes.

Any news on the first packet?

Contact in five minutes. No reaction from Clyde.

The face on the screen flushed. "What I pay my crew has nothing to do with Space Arm. I'll take your data, but no guarantees what use I'll make of it." He glanced offscreen. "And will you please stop dancing around out there? My gunners are getting itchy."

NightHawk, send Planet 3 geoscans, please.

Sent, ma'am.

Launch two packets.

Launched, ma'am.

And now for the real diversion. Crew, prepare for quick burn.

164

"Your gunners probably should take a bath. They won't get any itch relief from me. And if you're thinking of taking action, watch this...

NightHawk, prepared evasive course twelve. Burn...Now!

The little scout ship cranked to starboard, aiming directly at the frowning brow of the *Clyde's* bridge. Up and over she went, rolling away from the projectile and plasma guns that tried vainly to follow her course. She raced along the cruiser's dorsal hull, metres separating them. Then she was away, curving in a long, gentle arc that sent her winging back towards the mine.

However, once they were on the other side of the magnetic rock field, Natalia gave more orders. "Medium turnover. Prepare for quick decel burn."

The crew complied with polished skill, and soon the *NightHawk* was in stealth mode again, hidden behind a normal asteroid that allowed full radio reception.

"Disc signal, Andrew?"

"Five-nine-nine, ma'am. No movement."

"Cloud signal, Fiona?"

"One moment, ma'am. Initializing reception parameters...ah, there we have it. Forward viewscreen, ma'am."

Superimposed on the backdrop of stars and asteroids was a rough mass of small dots in the shape of the central hull and superstructure of the *Clyde*.

"Signal coming in five-nine-nine, ma'am. No movement."

"Stand by, everyone. Let's see if he does anything."

He did not. The battle cruiser hung in the rocks like an old wreck at the roadside with trees growing up through it.

"All right, folks. Mission accomplished. Let's hit for the mine and report in."

"Prepare for burn in ten...five...three, two, one. Burn.

Accel pressure eased on, and for once the course headed straight through the asteroids and back to their temporary home.

"Ma'am, can I have a word?"

"Sure, Adrian, I wanted to talk to you anyway. You go first."

"It's about the boy. He's becoming a problem."

She brought her full attention to the First Officer. "What's going on?"

"Oh, nothing serious. He's trying hard to fit in, I can see. But his nose is just everywhere. He gets into places he shouldn't, because he can't seem to tell the difference between a safety regulation and a polite suggestion. He could get hurt."

"Thanks for the heads-up, Jones. I've been too busy to spend much time with him. I thought he and Chakka were keeping each other occupied."

"That may be part of it. Chakka has a different sense of the chain of command than most humans."

"Ah. Yes, that would be a problem. Well, I can keep him out of trouble for a while. I'm planning a little junket to the Tree Planet. That's what I wanted to talk to you about.

"We're not being useful here. If the *Clyde* comes back, we can't do anything but run, anyway. Since we're in the system until we know that the repairs to the mine will work and until the cruiser leaves, we might as well do some exploring. We're the first Space Arm ship here since the survey. I'm really interested in that Tree Planet. What do you say we drop in for some further research?"

Jones nodded. "We're underutilized. I've been playing scientist the last few days, mostly for lack of other occupation."

"And what have your scientific efforts come up with?"

"Something you'll want to hear. I looked up the protocols for determining a possible colony planet. Three points are crucial: breathable air, compatible life forms but not too compatible life forms."

"You're going to have to explain the last one."

"Life on the planet has to be close enough to us that we can use it. If bacteria are too different, we might as well be doing hydroponic farming for all the good our plants can derive from the soil. On the other hand, we don't want life to be too much like us because of the potential for disease, going both ways. We don't want our crops to cause a disaster in the local flora."

"I see. So the ideal is an environment that our plants like but that won't have anything to do with our animals. And how does our arboreal friend do?"

"Not badly. The air is fine. A little heavy to the oxygen, actually. Gravity 0.9 Earth Norm, so the extra oxygen will balance out our transition from the 0.8 we're used to. We don't particularly care about plants at the moment, so I didn't do those tests, but if we're going down there, we can get more samples. The trees we harvested tested out just fine, but that's only one species."

"And the potential for disease?"

"It looks low, but I need more data, and I can't do that from here."

She thought that over. "I'd like to do this trip, but I'm still worried about that cruiser. As long as it stays there, we have to stay here, no matter how useless we are in confronting it. Sorry."

He nodded. "I had considered that situation and I agree."

"The moment things change, let's discuss this again." She held up a hand to stop him. "We aren't in a rush. The Tree Planet's orbit is faster than ours. She's catching up to us for the next three weeks. Every day we wait, she's a million miles closer."

"Silver lining." He smiled (*an actual smile!*) and turned out the door.

Freighty appeared on her viewscreen. "Do you have a moment to chat?"

"Did anyone ever tell you to knock before entering?"

167

The avatar grinned. "No, but now you have. What is your usual protocol?"

"Don't make this sound like I'm being a stickler for rules, but in this case, it fosters the illusion that I have some privacy. Next time go through *NightHawk*, as you always have before. What can I do for you?"

"Just a chat. And speaking of sticklers for the rules, is Mr. Jones typical of many humans?"

"No, focus on the rules is one of his strengths."

"You call that a strength?"

"It is considered a strength if not taken to extremes. The human race is rather divided between people who want to do the right thing no matter what the result is, and people who want to win no matter what is right. In that case, Adrian's attitude could be seen as a strong moral code."

"I have observed that in other races, but it seems to me that humans balance between the two extremes more evenly."

"In the past we have not been so balanced. As you may guess, those who wish to win at all costs tend to win more often, but their actions are seldom good for the general population."

"I told you about the race that destroyed my people. They were absolutely certain that the right thing to do was for them to win. You know where that got them."

"We have been trying for the last three hundred years to weed those types out. Our friends on the *Clyde* demonstrate that we have not completely succeeded."

He waved a dismissing hand. "Onto the scrapheap of history they go with their outmoded ship. You, on the other hand, have been determined to do what is right, no matter what."

"What is your evidence for that? I have always considered myself to be rather pragmatic in that respect."

"Your insistence on treating me fairly and with honesty, despite my obvious attempts to pull the wool over your eyes."

She regarded the avatar. "Just because people act with honesty and helpfulness…"

"…doesn't mean they are weak. Yes, I enjoyed that little lecture. Before then I had been concerned about Andrew's upbringing. That was the point I decided I had made a good choice in selecting you for the task."

She curled her upper lip. "I'll have to remember to be a bit less polite in future."

"Oh, please don't. He has enough of that already."

* * *

First, will you come to the chart room, please?

He must have been on the bridge, because he appeared immediately. "Yes, ma'am?"

"Remember our discussion this morning? Things have changed."

"I thought so. I was just analyzing the new radio signals from the *Clyde*."

"It's more than that. *NightHawk*, get Freighty on line, please."

The factory construct appeared. "She's moving off."

"Our telltales are giving us the same message."

"Heading insystem. Broke orbit five minutes ago. I was waiting for your call. I didn't think there was a rush."

"Did they leave anyone behind?"

"Unless they're far too small to be of any use, I'd say not. You are free to follow as you choose."

She frowned. "As you already know we want to." How could she stop the factory ArIn from eavesdropping?

"Precisely."

"Mr. Jones, it looks like we're going on a trip."

169

"The crew will enjoy that. Now that the repairs have moved into the pressurized areas the miners have taken over, and we're all looking for entertainment."

"I'll inform Nicholas, and we can set course in about an hour."

"And what about Andrew? Shall we send him back to the factory?"

"It's up to Freighty. I originally wanted to take him with us, but now that we're following the enemy, it's probably too dangerous. It's a shame; he needs to get some downplanet experience. He's lived in space for seven years." She glanced at the frown forming. "Don't worry. If he was going downplanet, he'd have a lot of studying to do. He wouldn't be in anyone's way."

"What about the liability?"

"The Space Arm takes cadets on training runs all the time. But that has changed, now. Freighty? What do you say?"

"It's a tough call for me, as well. I appreciate the danger, but I have run many simulations. In any conflict between you and the cruiser, brains will outdo brawn every time. And I predict in the range of 18-31% higher chances of success with him on board."

"Just by being on board? He would help us that much?"

"The scenario containing his mere presence gives you an 18% edge and is the least reliable. I assume that you will include him in your training. If so, your chances of success increase by the square of the time you spend. Of course, all of this is speculative, because such a merge has never been tried before."

"Never?"

"Not to my knowledge. He's an experiment for me, too, you know."

"Fine. Load him aboard, and let's get underway."

Already aboard, ma'am. Acting Ensign Collingwood ready for duty.

I just tossed off that ensign idea on the spur of the moment. You're too young. You're officially a cadet as of this moment. NightHawk, put that in the log.

Cadet Andrew Lundin Collingwood III logged onto ship's crew, ma'am.

For the duration of this specific mission, after which time he will be returned to his employer.

So noted, ma'am.

Emotion: sulky disappointment

Do you want to go home now?

Emotion: instant cheerfulness and willingness to take on any challenge.

Yes, yes. Have I mentioned false capitulation as a poor officer-manipulation technique?

Emotion: chagrin. You have now, ma'am.

She switched to ship's com. "Planetary Community Kindergarten Ship *NightHawk* now leaving orbit. No hurry, *NightHawk*. We want to stay between the *Clyde* and the mine. Slow acceleration. At your leisure."

"Slow burn starting in five...three, two, one. Burn. Course set for Tree Planet. Estimated travel time at the Clyde's cruising speed, 5.4 days."

"Um...ma'am..."

"Yes, Fiona?"

"There's something wrong with the discs, ma'am. They're separating from Andrew's plate signal."

"Separating? Explain!"

"That's it, ma'am. They've stopped accelerating and they're spreading out."

"Stand by, Fiona. Keep an eye on them as best you can."

NightHawk, call up the specs for the Clyde. *Now, let's look in the experimental equipment...yes...* "Well, crap on a plate!"

"What's wrong, ma'am?"

"I guess James didn't want the magnetic rock for camouflage. I just checked the specs. *Clyde-class* ships have a hull demagnetizing system built in, probably for situations exactly like this. They've kicked off all the rocks and our discs as well."

"So my discs are spreading because they're floating in space."

"I assume so. Can you gather them together?"

"If I start right away."

"Do that. Andrew, how's the plate working?"

"Moving insystem at constant acceleration, ma'am. It uses glue, not magnets."

"Good. Help Fiona with the gathering. *NightHawk*, plot an intercept course with the disc cloud matching its velocity on approach. We have time and we know where the *Clyde* is going. We'll just scoop them up on the way through. No sense wasting good new tech."

She glanced over at Jones. "Isn't that the way it goes, First? Our main plan fails, but our decoy is functioning perfectly. Makes you wonder."

He gave a wide smile. "It doesn't make me wonder, Commander. It confirms my opinion that the universe is a very weird place to live."

"Well, I suppose it's better than the alternative."

"Aye, ma'am. I'm with you on that."

"Oh, and I just thought of something. While we're patting ourselves on the back about our clever decoying..."

The light dawned on his face. "Maybe we're being decoyed."

She nodded. "It's never a bad plan to be careful."

"Have to agree on that one as well, ma'am."

* * *

172

They accelerated to cruising speed and shut off the engines, coasting in on the pull of the star, and Natalia started to look for something to do. One morning she pushed back from the breakfast table and regarded the crew lounging around. "Fat and lazy."

Charlie's head came up. "What's that, ma'am?"

"We're all getting fat and lazy, Specialist Fraser. Set up the ring."

His eyes lit up. "Who's going in?"

"You are." She looked at the others as if making up her mind. "And you are, Sergeant Jacobs."

The smaller commando tilted her head and regarded her captain. "And you?"

"I'm going to watch."

"Hmm."

The rest of the crew, eager for entertainment, turned to with a will and helped set the mats and practice ring on the running track where the gravity was at maximum. Soon the two commandos were dressed in light grappling gloves and workout clothes, warming up on opposite sides.

Natalia called Andrew to stand by her. "I want you to watch this."

"Sure thing. What am I looking for?"

She raised her eyebrows. "You're supposed to be a smart kid. I'm hoping you'll figure that out."

He glanced at her, then focused on the ring.

Soon the two combatants were sparring lightly, merely touching gloves and faking responses. It was a strange battle because of their size difference. After a few flurries in which Toni scored multiple hits while her larger opponent barely moved his gloves, the audience started to jeer.

"Come on, Charlie. Do something." Lundeen guffawed. "You're making us big guys look bad."

Charlie continued his slow plod, always moving in, while his antagonist fluttered around outside his reach. Then he swung, a hard right to her solar plexus, which she ducked easily, sliding sideways towards him...

...to run into a left hook to her shoulder that sent her tumbling into the ropes across the ring. While she picked herself up, he did a little soft-shoe routine, his hands above his head in victory. Then he settled back down, boring in while she danced away.

They sparred for a while longer, but the smaller commando never made the same mistake again.

"Okay, guys. I think we've seen all we're going to. Charlie, you ready for another partner?"

"Your turn, ma'am?"

She took the gloves from Toni. "Only fair."

"Fine by me. I'm just getting warmed up."

"We'll see if we can give you a workout, then."

Once the captain got into the ring, the battle changed. Natalia was a brawler rather than a boxer, and her methods involved elbows, knees, finger grabs, tugs and the destruction of her opponent's balance. Charlie was good at staying on his feet, but finally she tempted him to commit himself to a swing he thought would connect. The moment he started the swing he realized his mistake, and she missed the full throw but she did send him reeling into the ropes, which stretched to their maximum under the weight.

Then she started working on trips and foot-sweeps, again hampered by his slow, heavy plod that never put him off balance.

Finally she called a halt. "What do you think, Charlie? You still feeling lazy?"

He grabbed a towel off the corner post and wiped his face. "No, that was a workout, ma'am."

Natalia looked at the rest of the crew. "Anybody else, now that he's tired?"

There were chuckles, but no takers.

"I suppose I should try."

Everyone stared at Andrew.

"You?"

The boy shrugged his slim shoulders. "I got the lesson. Now I gotta practise what I learnt." He reached out for the gloves.

She passed them over. "You'll take it easy on him, won't you? He's already tired."

"Don't worry, ma'am. I'm not strong enough to do Charlie any real damage. Maybe just a little, though?"

"I'll leave that up to you."

The boy nodded and slipped through the ropes to confront the confused commando.

Charlie met his captain's eyes, and she shrugged with a "who knows?" gesture of her hands.

Andrew started to move around the ring, shrinking down until he was even smaller than before. With a start, Natalia realized that his movements mirrored Chakka in stalking mode. Charlie noticed the change and he, too, focused more firmly.

And all of a sudden, everything changed. Without her command, Natalia's augment hit full power. The rest of the room faded, and all she could see was the broad-shouldered commando towering in front of her. Her senses sharpened, and she smelled the leather of her gloves, the sweat on the big man's body. Every ripple of his muscles sent her messages. Time slowed, and she felt Chakka's low growl in her augment with *NightHawk*'s huge presence underlying it all. Instead of a small, weak boy, they became a powerful entity wielding a barbed spear, all their efforts focused on the razor point.

They reached out slowly and pushed ever-so-gently downward on Charlie's left glove. The moment he resisted, they let go and slipped a punch under the rising hand to score along his ribs. Then they were gone before his right glove swished the air where they had been an instant before.

They moved closer and closer now, sure that they could duck every attack. A quick kick towards his kneecap brought his hand sweeping down, but the moment he exposed his shoulder they were in over the bicep, rapping him sharply on the chin with a left-right. When he tried to back away, they were already crouched, trapping the retreating front foot and lifting it high, dumping him on the mat.

Charlie was no beginner. Even as he fell he was reaching for them, but they dodged under his grasping hands and drove a knuckle, not too hard, into his neck under his right ear.

The big commando's eyes went wide, and for a moment he faltered. They took their chance to disengage, slipping back while he stumbled to his feet, shaking his head.

Natalia dragged herself out of the gestalt. "All right, hold it. Charlie, are you all right?"

He shook his head. "What the hell was that? I felt like I was in the middle of a whirlwind, poking and prodding at me from all directions. Next thing I'm on the floor and my neck hurts like crazy. What happened?"

Natalia smiled. "You just got an example of what happens when the *NightHawk* and her crew hit battle mode. Andrew has obviously had some serious training, but he was moving about three times as fast as he normally would. He was using all my experience, all *NightHawk*'s computing power, and all Chakka's skills."

She shook her head, "It was amazing. I could tell at a glance where you would move next, just from the play of your muscles as you adjusted your balance in preparation."

The Chief Engineer leaned back in his chair. "Well, that was real fun to watch, ma'am, but what was the point? I don't see us getting into much hand-to-hand in the near future."

"No, that's not what we were practising. Andrew?"

"We were looking at tactics against a much larger opponent. You c'n talk about that sorta thing until the cows come home, but unless it's in your kinesthetic memory, you can't get at it fast enough."

"Kinesthetic, now, is it? Where did you learn that term?"

Andrew grinned. "I didn't. I'm still connected to *NightHawk*, and that word was right there in my memory the moment I needed it."

"You're welcome."

"Ah, admit it, Birdy. You had fun, too."

"It was a fascinating experience. I, too, need practise in this area."

Andrew turned to Natalia, all serious now. "Yes. At the moment, you and Chakka are the only ones with any battle experience, so our blend is unbalanced."

Natalia had a sudden thought. "What about the rest of the crew?" She raised her eyes to scan the room. "You all have the standard Spacer augment." Her eyes lit on Fiona. "What about it, Second Engineer B'kose? Would you like a chance to dump Charlie on his butt?"

The girl's eyes went wide. "Me?"

"Why not? When we're in battle we have to know exactly what our engines and generators are doing and precisely what we can expect from them. If you were in the mix with us, we wouldn't have to take time to ask dumb questions. You'd just know what to do, and we'd know that you were doing it."

Fiona grinned. "I suppose. But do I have to start on Charlie? I weight exactly half what he does. Wouldn't be good for his self-image." She cringed as the commando walked behind her, but all he did was pick her up, chair and all, and hold her above his head. Then he nodded. "Pretty lightweight, all right."

"Sure, in point eight gees. Put me down, you big oaf. You want trouble, we'll meet in the ring."

He set her chair gently on the deck. "Whatever you say, lady. Whenever you say."

Natalia chuckled. "All right. We'll leave the ring in place until decel time, and we can spend our free time in violence. Then we'll go back to the firing drills and see if we've improved our times any. Who'd like a go next?"

25. GROUND ATTACK

Six days later the *Clyde* was headed farther insystem, and *NightHawk* was in orbit around the Tree Planet.

"What do you think, Lieutenant? Any chance they've left a greeting party?"

He shrugged. "We've done the simulations, ma'am. The enemy has probably known for two days that we're heading for the Tree Planet. They could have a strike force hidden somewhere, either down on one of the moons or in the rings."

Natalia nodded. "And we found seventeen different scenarios where they could conceivably hide and attack a ground party. Or was it eighteen?"

Jones smiled. "Only Chakka and *NightHawk* could think up something as complicated as bouncing a decoy image off the dense part of the planetary ring, and only the two of them could have achieved it. We all agreed their plan was of academic interest only."

"All the other possibilities were still extremely difficult to accomplish and dangerous to their attack party. They'd need a very profitable objective to risk their resources, and none of us can think of a good enough reason to make them attack a Space Arm vessel. I think we're pretty safe."

The First Officer's back stiffened. "And we'll be doing our best from up here to keep you informed, ma'am."

"I'm sure you will, Adrian. We have a small, powerful party with limited objectives. We'll be fine."

Pete was already doing his preflight checks when Natalia arrived to load Andrew, Chakka, and Charlie into Shuttle One.

The big man was grinning almost as widely as the boy as he planted his huge plasma rifle in its restraining clips. "First time offship in nine months. Can't wait."

Andrew's smile looked forced. "My first time downplanet in seven years. I don't know what to think."

"You'll be fine." Fraser jabbed a thumb towards his chest. "You're in good hands."

They dropped off the *NightHawk* and set course for an easy entry, swinging full around the planet one more time to scan once more for enemy ships.

Natalia contacted Jones. "No readings around the larger moon. What do you have?"

"Nothing from the smaller moon, ma'am, but it is considerably farther out. *NightHawk*'s scenarios consider that a 7% chance of a hiding place. Do you want me to go to higher orbit?"

"Just keep an eye on it as long as you can see it. If there's trouble, I'm betting on the asteroid ring."

"Roger that, ma'am. *NightHawk* out."

"Shuttle One out."

As they pulled away from the ship, Natalia couldn't help but put the rear viewers on. The *Hawk* lay there, glistening in the sunlight, long and smooth, her Permaskin hull plating shimmering in a pattern, now that she looked, a lot like Andrew's space suit. She filed that away for further research, and glanced at the boy. "She's pretty, isn't she?"

He shrugged. "I looked up seals. They're neat, y'know? They're beautiful when they swim." He made sinuous motions with his arms.

"And *NightHawk* swims through space with the same skill."

"Yeah, but 'The Seal' doesn't quite have the ring to it, y'know?"

"I have to agree."

Before they hit atmo, she spun her chair to face her little crew. "Charlie, we're going to do this by the book, re-ti, got it? There's a civilian on board, and we don't want any mistakes."

"Aye, ma'am. We'll take care of him." He patted the projectile pistol holstered on his leg.

"A different landing spot from last time. We've seen the ocean-side forests, so we're heading into the centre of the largest landmass. It will be drier, hopefully with short grass or something we can walk through. Andrew, you know the kinds of plants the First Officer wants for his research. Collecting specimens will be your job. This trip will be full EV gear. If everything tests out as safe, we'll come back later for a real downplanet experience. Any questions?"

"What are the dangers, ma'am?"

"You haven't been downplanet recently."

"Not since I was five years old. I remember running and playing."

"You won't have the energy to run here, and you shouldn't be playing. You've been living at mostly 0.8 Gs, and you're in pretty good shape, so I don't expect too much trouble. Just beware of unexpected changes in the environment: holes in the ground, plants to trip on, little stuff like that can cause an injury in higher-G situations.

"The second kind of trouble is more serious. There is indigenous animal life here, some of it large, and we're all going to be keeping a sharp eye out. Pete will be scanning from the shuttle. Chakka is the most likely to spot a problem, so you'll know about it as soon as the rest of us, won't you?"

She stared, and the boy dropped his eyes with a smile.

"That's what I thought. Now tighten your straps. We'll be shaking around a bit."

"Entering atmo, ma'am. Full restraints as per regs, please."

She winked at Charlie as they added the extra shoulder belts.

Pete managed an entry no more bouncy than usual, and soon they were cruising along over open prairie in bright sunlight.

Natalia grinned at Andrew. "Nice thing about coming down from above. Our weather prediction is always spot-on. Not a storm for a thousand klicks."

"What are those clouds?"

"Local updrafts from that river valley over there. We're landing farther out in the open. Pete?"

The pilot nodded. "How about near that copse of trees for a landmark? There's a small ridge over there, give you a variety of samples and make the shuttle a bit less obvious. *NightHawk* says the highest chance of attack would be from the west."

"Glad they're keeping in touch. Let's hover at 100 metres first."

"Aye, ma'am." He brought the shuttle to a halt and they stared at the screens. "Nothing to see that the sensors haven't already shown us, ma'am."

"Fine. Those canyons to the west would be a safe place to hide. Look for us there if we get separated. Set her down at your leisure."

"Aye, ma'am."

If Andrew was expecting anything dramatic, he was disappointed. Pete set the shuttle down as softly as a falling leaf, although with plenty of noise and dust. Soon the sound died away. "Secured for offloading, ma'am."

She unbuckled. "Helmets on and into the airlock, boys. Let's see what real gravity feels like."

She led the way down the gangplank, making sure there was no running or playing. For everyone except Chakka. He was bounding away the moment his feet touched soil.

Natalia opened her com. *He's not playing. He's checking the periphery. Charlie, set up your gear on that little rise and start scanning. Pete, keep a sharp eye farther out. Up as well. We haven't seen any flighted lifeforms, but it's good practice.*

Andrew, let's take a slow stroll. Easy at first.

Aye, ma'am.

They worked their way around the shuttle, collecting samples of plants and soil. After a while, Natalia grinned. She could see the signs. Andrew was ready for more.

Let's drop these samples off in the airlock and take a walk. Charlie, anything to report?

181

All clear, ma'am. Nothing bigger than a guinea pig within a kilometre.

Chakka doesn't see anything, either. She sent him an image of the ridge.

Emotion: pleasant anticipation: hunger.

Don't be silly. There's nothing you could eat on this planet. Head out that way.

Take your time, Andrew. Remember to save some oomph for the return trip.

She slung her sniper's rifle over her shoulder and looked at Andrew. *Your suit has changed.*

Yeah, my camo system is superior, so I just dialed it down to match yours.

Good plan. You don't want to stand out. Now that you mention it... She reached into the airlock and lifted down the carbine that hung by the door. *You know how to shoot this?*

Y...yes. It's a nine-millimetre HK 998, isn't it?

I hate to load you down, but there is an enemy out there somewhere.

He rather awkwardly slung the gun across his back, and they made their way in a leisurely fashion towards the ridge. It was a dramatic scene, with an exposed ledge of craggy bedrock breaking through the soil, topped by green sod like a shaggy wig. Bushes with disc-like branches grew scattered across the ground cover, which looked like ringed grass blades. Natalia accessed her augment. *That's a form of limestone showing. Could be caves. Let's go up that path. Know what a path means, Andrew?*

Animals made it.

Exactly. So if there's caves, they might be occupied. We go more carefully.

Aye, ma'am.

They crept up the trail and soon topped the ridge. Now they could see farther west, where the ground was more broken.

This is why we landed here. Not that I'm too worried, but...

Image: birds. Three birds. Big birds...

Pete! Emergency. Button up and prepare for take off! Three bogeys from the west, high-speed approach. Charlie, take whatever cover you can. NightHawk...

We are under attack. Repeat, under attack. Four fighters, closing fast. First Officer on the bridge.

The ship is yours, First. I've got my own problems down here.

Evasive maneuvers, NightHawk. Everyone belt in for a quick burn...

Natalia gritted her teeth and listened to the com chatter of her ship as she watched the three dots resolve rapidly into space/atmo fighters, rocketjets with stubby airfoils. Then puffs of smoke burst from under their wings.

Rockets incoming. Lift off, Pete. Get the hell out of here. Go, go go!

I'm gone, ma'am. See you soon. The sound of shuttle turbines winding up floated over the ridge.

Get down, Andrew. Behind that rock over there. She flattened herself as well. *Chakka...*

Image: a large rock, very close.

Odour: strange plants and musty soil.

Sound: silence.

Then it all hit at once. The shuttle engine screamed defiance, going from standstill to full military lift. The rockets blazed past, their "swoosh" slamming her down a second later.

The three fighters swooped over them, and soon after the roar of their engines overloaded every auditory circuit.

Her ears ringing, Natalia forced her numbed mind to work. She switched her com to battle firewall and reached out to Charlie. *Get over here quick. We're headed west, towards that broken ground. When they come for another pass, we'll hide. They'll be moving too fast to see much.*

His com double-clicked.

She motioned to Andrew *Let's go. Don't wear yourself out. We have to make those arroyos down there.*

A double click answered, and the boy scrambled to his feet.

She sent Chakka an image of the spot she was headed for and they set out, walking fast but not running. A huge explosion rocked the airwaves and the ground beneath their feet.

Incoming.

They flattened behind a rock as two of the jets roared back, but this time the third party was a small gray shuttle with a hawk's head on its wings, guns blazing. The jets jinked and split, and the shuttle flipped around in midair, sliding to a halt and accelerating back towards them.

But the jets bored in again, and Pete was forced away from his landing vector to return fire.

Lieutenant Jones, what's happening up there?

Nothing, ma'am. They never got close enough to get a decent shot at them. Then they all peeled off and disappeared behind the planet.

Pete, how's it going?

They aren't much of a problem, ma'am. They're playing hit and run.

All right. Keep ahead of them. Let me think. Charlie? She accessed her battle view. *Ah, there you are.*

Right on your tail, ma'am. Same course?

Yes. Take point. We're not moving fast.

That dry wash is less exposed, ma'am.

Go for it. Chakka move ahead.

Image: twisted canyons dropping down.

Right. We're heading your way, Chakka. Come on, Andrew, let's hoof it.

Where does 'hoof it' come from? Is it because horses have hooves?

You got it, kid. Could we save the English lesson for later?

Aye, ma'am.

NightHawk, analyze attack pattern.

The answer was immediate.

Analysis: you are the target.

That's what I thought. They're keeping support away from us. That means another force somewhere. Charlie? Chakka? Pete, do you have time for a sweep?

Coming over low, ma'am. Hold your ears.

The shuttle blasted over them, two jets creeping up behind, spread out this time. Once again the shuttle spun at bay, and the jets turned in, screaming in tight arcs to cross where the shuttle no longer waited for them. He had gone straight up.

"They're too fast to catch, ma'am, but I can duck all day. Hah! Got it. Seven men in space armour coming in from the northeast. Hundred-metre front, inverted vee formation." He sent an aerial image, which she passed on to Chakka.

We'll handle it on the ground. You get out of here. You can't help us, and you could lose us a shuttle. Draw them off.

I'm gone, ma'am. A roar of engines and the shuttle rose off into the western sky, two dots following.

Charlie, take the left end. Chakka, the right. Damn, I wish I could see them...

...and then she could. Instead of her usual heads-up display, her inner vision showed a composite view of the whole area, drawn from everyone's visuals, including the shuttle's. She watched the commando and the auguar rapidly encircling the enemy, closing with slower and slower stealth as they crept near.

Emotion: fierce hunger.

She pushed the battle rage of the cat aside as he leapt on his prey. A flurry of motion, the clash of space armour, then silence. She winced. Space suits were meant to stop projectiles and plasma. They were less effective against carbide-tipped can openers.

Emotion: frustration.

185

Image: auguar unsuccessfully trying to lick blood-soaked claws

Mine's down, too.

Now she had the five moving enemy on her screen, but they had grouped together and stopped their advance.

Charlie, that will only work once. Come on back. Chakka, encircle.

Charlie trotted in, his plasma rifle slung on his back, ballistic pistol in one hand.

She positioned them so each could look out and cover a segment of the perimeter. The gully was deep enough to restrict flank attack, and scattered boulders in the central watercourse provided good cover.

All right. This is a Pattern 3 retreat, headed for the canyons this gully runs into. Andrew, the trick is sustained fire. We take turns. Fire, then run, then hide: fire, run, hide. Spend your time down looking for your next hide point. Keep up the gestalt; it's really helpful. Our augments will keep us in sync, and the enemy won't find a gap to pop up and fire. Chakka, you're recon. Battle image constant.

Image: five enemy moving out, spreading in an arc 30 metres across.

Charlie, this will be just like weapons drill with Andrew in the mix. When you shoot, don't think about it too much or look for targets. The only way I can explain it is that when your turn to fire comes around, you'll get a feeling where to aim. Follow it.

Everybody ready?

Ready, ma'am.

Ready.

Image: the boulders behind them, with five men clearly outlined. One was highlighted.

*I'll go first. Start the synch...*She waited until the marked soldier began his charge...*NOW!*

As the man rose, Natalia stood as well, firing two precise shots into his chest, knocking him backwards, then a spray of four more where Chakka showed other figures in hiding. She didn't wait to see the effect, just turned and ran, crouching, to the boulder she had chosen.

She slid behind it and glanced back as Andrew rose, fired five shots and ran to a nearby rock. She glanced downhill to find her next safety, then back to watch Charlie, who stood for longer, aiming two shots at each enemy soldier's position. Then, with amazing speed for such a large man, he was past her and ducking behind a ledge. *Whooee! I see what you mean, ma'am. I knew exactly where they were.*

Now all we have to do is find a weak point in their armour.

Surplus Space Arm, looks like. Major joints are the best bet.

It was her turn, and she was watching Chakka's image. It looked like...*Yes!* Another one started to advance. This time she aimed for the joint between torso and leg and grouped three shots there. Then the usual spread, and she was away again, ducking and weaving. It had been a longer shot, so she didn't expect much success.

No shots followed her, and she made it to her next objective, even with Charlie, with no problem.

Image: enemy soldier twisting in the dirt, hands over groin.

You got one, ma'am.

Leg/torso join. Go, Andrew.

The boy played his part again, but he had not chosen a good cover, and when he slid behind it, his shoulder and leg showed.

Break pattern. Solid fire, Charlie. Andrew go again...Now!

She and the other commando both stood to full height, sending a barrage of fire back towards their adversaries, while Andrew scooted farther down the wash to a larger rock.

Safe, ma'am.

Pattern return...Now!

Charlie shot and retreated, she followed, and this rotation Andrew got a good distance farther.

Image: Four soldiers attacking, all shooting as they ran, one wounded lying behind a rock providing covering fire.

There was no need for communication. Both she and Charlie stayed under cover, firing over their rocks with the accuracy provided by Chakka's image.

This time Chakka showed two men going down. One lay where he landed, motionless. The other dragged himself into cover. The auguar's emotions were peaking, and she took a moment to calm him and get him under his own control again.

Pattern adapt 4B, resume...Now!

Charlie did the usual shoot-and-run, but this time he turned before hiding and fired again. Natalia, instead of shooting, stood clear and threw a grenade with all her might, landing it behind the enemy line in the general area of the two functional soldiers.

Then she ran. The explosion came as she flattened into a ditch, and metal fragments buzzed overhead.

Whee! Good throw, ma'am!

Concentrate Andrew. Chakka, ready?

Emotion: rend and tear.

Andrew, go! Charlie, hold fire.

Again the boy shot and ran. There was a moment's silence, and the echoes of the last gunshots rang down the valley. Then there was a crunching of metal and a cry of pain.

Emotion: success. Triumph!

Now get out of there.

Emotion: Dismay

Ma'am!

She turned. Andrew had fallen two steps short of his cover. He began to crawl, but in Chakka's view two men started to rise, guns coming into line.

And then she went blind. No, not blind. She still had Chakka's image. But Andrew had completely disappeared. Charlie and Chakka were now back to mere glow points on her

188

usual augment heads-up. The total overview of the battle she had enjoyed had disappeared.

Got him! Charlie dove beside Andrew, inserting his body between the boy and the incoming fire, at the same time shoving him violently in the right direction. Andrew scrambled to safety, the big commando behind him.

Just as Natalia began to fire, there was an explosive grunt on the com.

Got my leg. Bullet, probably.

She fired a group at the slowest soldier, didn't stop to see the results and dove behind the rock across the gully from Charlie and Andrew.

Report.

Suit's taken care of it. Just above the knee. Flesh wound, I hope. It's going numb, now.

She popped up and sprayed fire at the only two points that stayed active on Chakka's image.

Sound: silence.

Andrew. Andrew, are you there?

A shaky voice came over the com. *H...here, ma'am. No injury.*

We need you, Andrew. I'm blind!

Oh. Sorry, ma'am. Lost concentration...how's that?

A rush of input washed over her, and it was all back again.

Much better.

A brief moment was all she needed to reconnoiter. The two enemy were preparing to advance. Time for a change of plan. She indicated the one on the right. *All yours, Chakka.*

Andrew, on my mark, shoot, but aim high and left. Chakka's going in.

I know.

Mark!

They both fired, aiming above the left-hand side of the gully. There was a scream of terror, a clashing of space armour, and single gun went off, spraying bullets rapidly.

189

Emotion: terror!

Run, Chakka!

She stood and began firing, hoping desperately to keep the enemy from targeting the bounding figure that retreated up the wash. Then the cat disappeared into the rocks like a wisp of smoke.

Nothing moved.

Emotion: great relief.

She sent Chakka a wash of affection and turned to Charlie.

Can you run? Walk? Crawl?

The commando slowly flexed the leg with the bloodstains running down it. *I can probably walk. Running only in an emergency.*

Time to reassess.

Chakka, report.

Image: Two wounded soldiers, barely mobile. One uninjured.

Change of tactic. Entrap. Charlie, this is a pretty good spot to hold out. Andrew, keep your eyes open and your gun ready. If I'm occupied, Specialist Fraser will lead. I'm heading around their northern flank. Chakka will keep their attention occupied elsewhere. Once I take out the last mobile man, they're toast.

Aye, ma'am. The commando took up a standard prone firing position. Without prompting, the boy did the same.

A scattering of shots sounded from up the draw on the left side.

Emotion: feline chuckle.

With the enemy's attention distracted, Natalia slipped out to her right, running lightly through the scattered brush at the edge of the draw. She scaled to the rim, threw herself over and dropped flat, weapon trained on the enemy position. Her altitude gave her perspective, and Chakka's image became easier to interpret.

One of the enemy rose from his cover, but a hail of fire from Andrew and Charlie drove him down again. Then, right on cue, a flash of movement on the opposite slope drew the enemy's attention that way. She rose to a crouch and slid along the wash.

The next time she looked over the edge she was even with the enemy position. Again Charlie and Andrew opened up. Again the enemy cowered.

And then the enemy soldier made a mistake. He assumed that because Charlie had stopped firing, he must be low on charge. He popped up to shoot down the wash.

Natalia's bullet struck his neck join at the same time as a plasma bolt from Charlie's heavy rifle caught him square in the centre of the faceplate. His body flipped over sideways and backward and did not move.

She drove a shot beside the ankle of one of the wounded soldiers. He pulled his leg in, but his shoulder became exposed. She knew the angle was bad, but she bounced a solid slug off it anyway. The fight was over; the enemy just didn't know it yet.

Natalia clicked on her external com. "You men down there. You're done. Throw your weapons out where I can see them."

There was a fuzzing in her augment, then a voice...*got us in her sights.*

Any chance of fooling them?

What're we going to tell them? That we're wounded?

Well, maybe we could...

The top of a helmet peeked over a rock, and Charlie laid a solid round from his pistol across it.

She cut into the enemy com. *You're not going to fool anybody with anything. This is the Space Arm. Throw your weapons out and stand up. We don't shoot prisoners. Usually.*

There was a spate of cursing on the com, and two rifles arced out of the rocks to clatter into the bottom of the wash.

Now stand up.

I didn't hear you tellin' your men to stand down.

You hear what I want you to hear. Stand up.

I can't.

Then drag your butt out in the open.

One man rose from his cover and made his way slowly into the centre of the wash. The other came out backwards, inching himself along on his bottom, his legs dragging behind.

Andrew, get the rifles.

Aye, ma'am. The boy picked up the weapons. *What do I do with them?"*

Take them down the wash a hundred metres and dump them somewhere not easy to find.

I can do that. Andrew strode away.

Don't rush it. We're not home yet, and you're running on adrenalin. She found she knew all the readings in the boy's suit without even thinking about it. *Chakka, report.*

Emotion: satisfaction.

Charlie?

The wounded commando rose from the ditch, leaning on the barrel of his rifle. *Slow but functioning, ma'am.*

Keep an eye on these two.

He propped himself against a rock and brought his pistol into firing position.

She accessed her augment.

Lieutenant, we're cleaned up down here. Charlie took one in the leg. Report.

All clear, ma'am. Holding position as requested.

Pete, report.

They're gone, ma'am. I'm coming in from the west about five minutes out.

NightHawk, any sign of our attackers?

All on the far side of the planet, except for the one that's strewn across the prairie three kilometres south of you.

So much for decon level 3. Let's hope the heat of the explosion destroyed any organics aboard that fighter. Keep a sharp eye. We're on our way home.

The engine sound increased, and soon the vessel was overhead. *All clear, ma'am.*

Bring her in.

The shuttle swooped down for one of Pete's trademark landings: plenty of noise and dust, but pillow-soft.

Okay, Andrew. Let's head for the shuttle. Charlie, need a hand?

I'd like to make it on my own, ma'am.

As they approached the opening airlock, Chakka bounded up, his suit dented, streaks of blood marring the camouflage.

Charlie and Andrew in first. Chakka with me second cycle. Move it!

The boy found enough energy to clamber through the hatchway unaided. He reached out to help the wounded commando in, and the door closed behind them.

The enemy com crackled. *Wait. Where are you going?*

Back to our ship.

You're not going to leave us here?

I'm not going to take you with me. Your ship can come and get you any time she wants.

But we have wounded!

So do I, and your ship is ten times the size of mine. Go sit down, and don't even think of taking any potshots with those little pistols you have hidden in your tool belts. They won't penetrate our armour, and then we'll fry you with our blast as we take off.

Don't worry, soldier. Ground fighters are in short supply this far from home. Captain James needs you; he won't leave you behind. Give him my regards and tell him he has now attacked a Space Arm vessel. He is officially an outlaw, if he wasn't already. Oh, yes, and when you're trying to rationalize your failure, remind him that you just made contact with a Space Arm Commando unit. You certainly learned something. Maybe James will, too. Commander O'Rourke out.

The enemy soldier slumped onto a nearby rock and sat there watching.

NightHawk?

Nelson came on immediately. *Yes, ma'am?*

We'll be lifting in ten minutes. Move in closer. The shuttle's vulnerable to fighters in space.

Aye, ma'am. Adjusting. Geosynch above your location at 75 kilometres altitude.

Thank you. First. Any damage?

No hits. Minimal shrapnel damage.

Shrapnel? They were using projectile ammo for low-speed space offence?

Only explanation for the damage, ma'am.

What is this, an attack out of the history books? Don't answer that. She switched to local com. *I'm coming on board now, Pete. Chakka, let's go.*

They took all the proper decon precautions, just like a normal downplanet foray, and blasted off into peaceful, empty space. If it wasn't for the auger's dented armour and the blood on Charlie's leg, it might have been an ordinary sample-collecting expedition.

26. DEBRIEF

Later, in the mess hall, Natalia faced her crew. "The 'how' of the operation is simple. They knew we were following. They dropped their attack force off behind the planet and in the planetary ring and kept going. When we went into orbit, they stayed opposite us until it was time to strike."

Jones frowned. "Should we be worried that they knew where we were?"

"I don't think so. At a normal burn rate we rather light up the road."

"I agree." He stared at the table, then raised his eyes to hers. "It's the 'why' that I don't understand. We could go after their shuttles and fighters and destroy them if we chose. What do they want that they're willing to risk so much?"

Natalia threw up her hands. "I don't get it, either. They couldn't have been after me. I'm nobody. Charlie may have left a few angry husbands behind, but it couldn't be him."

"I looked up that Occam guy you was tellin' me about."

She turned to Andrew. "Occam's Razor."

"Yeah. The answer with the smallest number of 'if onlys,' right?" his thumb pointed at his own chest.

"You."

He held out his hands, palms up.

"That raid was meant to capture you."

"You said it, not me. Got another answer?"

She grinned. "Not to put too fine a point on it, but who would want you?"

He shrugged. "Maybe there's somebody out there what appreciates my sterlin' qualities more than you lot."

"That's because they haven't spent time in a small space ship with you."

"Far as I know, they haven't spent any time with me at all."

"So you have no idea why anyone would be interested in kidnapping you."

"And now we're back to ol' Occam again. Simplest answer is that I'm somebody important."

Natalia held up a hand to stop the chuckles. "Mr. Occam gets the kewpie doll, folks. We need more information from Freighty."

Jones shook his head. "If they were after Andrew, how did they know he was aboard?"

There was a moment of silence as glances were exchanged.

She slapped her hands on the table. "No. There's absolutely no chance that whoever these people are, they have inserted a spy in this crew. It's so unlikely as to be absurd. There is an outside chance they have an agent in the mine crew. Andrew hasn't made a secret of his movements."

"Analysis: most likely scenario, at 73%: Captain James is improvising.

"Information Available: one, it is highly unlikely Andrew's family knew about Freighty."

"Right. If they did, they would have gone looking for the factory."

"Correct. Two, the times we have interacted they have not demonstrated any other knowledge of our affairs.

"Three, Mr. Occam's shaving implement has had several centuries to become dull."

"Thank you, *NightHawk*. We need to be cautious, but it would be paranoid to give too much credence to Captain James. He has the potential to cause us a lot of trouble, but his success rate is rather low at the moment.

"I think we should ask Manager Ludge to investigate the possibility that someone has been sending messages from the mine. Freighty could help with the technology end of that. Otherwise, let us assume the *Clyde* is playing it by ear. The Collingwood family must have had some idea of Mariel's plans.

All they would need was her course when she left Earth. There are very few places she could have gone in this direction. They sent out a very expensive fishing expedition, probably with several objectives over and above a kidnapping."

Andrew nodded. "They probably think her and me are still with the miners."

"It's very possible. Now, the battle. Mr. Jones, you have reviewed the record. Was there any indication that they meant to capture Andrew?"

He shook his head. "The boy is easy to recognize because of his size. They were shooting to kill all of you."

"So, a capture or kill mission."

"I'm afraid so, ma'am." He shot a sympathetic glance at Andrew.

"*NightHawk?*"

"*Same conclusion, ma'am. 100% lethal attack.*"

"It sure felt like it at the time. Specialist Fraser. Your impressions of the new...communications system."

Charlie shook his head slowly. "It was just awesome, ma'am. It was seamless." He glanced at Andrew. "Mostly."

Natalia nodded. "That was a valuable experience, too. You don't know how much you're leaning on a crutch until it's pulled away. We adapted pretty well, though."

Charlie regarded his bandaged knee. "Pretty well."

"Yes, we should deal with that event. Now's as good a time as any." She rose and stood over the patient. "That kind of action gets mentioned in dispatches, Specialist Fraser."

"Um..." his broad face went red. "Uh...thank you, ma'am."

"Yes, Charlie. You have now entered the ranks of a very special group. Every soldier wonders how he will react when the chips are down. You are one of the lucky ones. Now you know."

"Yeah, and I'm still alive. That worked out well."

A chuckle ran through the crew.

197

"You'll want to stand up for this."

The commando surged to his feet, only wincing as he straightened his leg at attention.

"Battlefield promotion, so I'm going to use the short form. 'The Space Arm of the Planetary Community has placed special confidence in the abilities and integrity of Specialist Charles Amos Fraser. In view of these qualities and his demonstrated potential to serve in the higher grade, Specialist Charles Fraser is promoted to the temporary grade of Sergeant, Planetary Community Space Arm, effective the third day of February, two thousand one hundred and twenty-four, by order of the Secretary of the Space Arm. This promotion will be confirmed permanent upon our return to base.'"

She pinned the pip on his collar, handed him the extra chevron for his sleeve and shook his hand. Then she stepped back and they both saluted.

She dusted her hands and grinned. "And now you know why I told Jonny to ease off on the painkillers. Corporal Mendez, double grog ration for the crew, please."

The crew crowded around Charlie, easing him down on the couch with his leg elevated while Juanita slapped glasses on the table and poured.

Natalia whistled for attention. "And another small ceremony. We have a member of the crew who just participated in his first firefight. Here's to Cadet Andrew Lundin Collingwood the Third. May all his battles be so successful."

Jonny poured a sliver of rum into a glass and passed it over.

Andrew sniffed, shrugged and tossed it back.

An appreciative murmur ran through the crew, and those who could reach slapped his shoulders.

It occurred to Natalia to wonder whether the glisten of his eye was due to the emotion of the moment or the burn of the liquor.

"And before you all descend into debauchery, let us make our next move. Mr. Jones, do you have all the samples you need?"

"I can get a much better picture of the bio makeup with these."

"Andrew, have you had sufficient downplanet experience to settle you for a week or so?"

"I ain't likely to forget it a while. Point nine Gs bothered me. Gotta work up some."

"Mission successful. *NightHawk*, set a course for the mine, zero point 8 Gs. Crew, prepare for acceleration."

Aye, ma'am. Course set for the asteroid belt. Standard accel. Burn in five...three, two, one. Burn.

The crew moved to more comfortable positions and the engines roared. As the inertial spin slowed and acceleration took over, the back wall of the mess hall became the floor and the party continued without a hitch. Juanita glanced at Natalia for a nod and poured again.

The Commander motioned Andrew to a seat in the corner. "Andrew Lundin Collingwood the Third. Why were you so clear about that when you first introduced yourself?"

"I dunno. That was what my mother — the real one — used to call me when she was mad at me. I figured it must be important."

"Come with me. We're going to check the ship's database for people with names like that."

"There's billionsa people in the solar system. Gotta be thousands with my name."

"Oh, I suspect one will pop out quite quickly." She led the way up the ladder to the privacy of the chart room and fired up the viewscreen.

She was wrong.

"Well, crap my drawers. Will ya looka that."

"Mind your language. But I have to admit; who would have thought...?"

The screen was filled with Lundins and Collingwoods. Several of them married to each other. Many of them very, very rich.

"There's something funny going on, here." She used her augment to rearrange the screen. "Follow those lines. Look what happens to them."

"Wow! Those guys musta really screwed up. Looka that one. Grandfather with titles, positions, you name it. Father with even more. Billionsa planetoids. Then the grandson just falls off the map. Whadiddy do? Blow it all?"

She shook her head. "With only one family it would be possible. It happens. But four separate branches of the same name, just fading out at the same time with no offspring even listed?"

"Don't sound right, 'less they got into some kind of feud 'n' got wiped out."

"Do you see anybody listed as murdered? Dead even?"

"Nope. What's goin' on?"

"What is going on is that a family has become so rich they can afford privacy. It's the most sought-after treasure in the solar system, and they have it." She gestured towards the screen. "This data isn't just the result of normal search parameters. The so-called re-ti stuff is six years old, of course, but the rest is everything that was available on the Military Intel Net up until the day we left the solar system, upgraded as we travelled. I shouldn't even be showing it to a civilian. When these people talk about owning planetoids, they aren't talking about Planetary Currency.

"I get it. Can I have the screen?"

She glanced at him. "Can you control it?"

In answer, the viewer began to flicker. Pages of data flashed up and disappeared too fast for her to follow without her augment. Once in a while he would pause to scan one, and then the cascade would begin again. Finally he stopped.

"I get the picture. I made it about as far as you did. Farther on some streams, less on others, but it still adds up the same. Like you say. Privacy nobody can breach." He glanced up at her and shook his head. "Not even the military."

His face brightened. "What about the spies?"

She grinned and laid a finger beside her nose. "Nobody knows what the government knows. They only let us in on it if they think we need it."

The boy interlaced his fingers and stretched his arms until his knuckles cracked. "Well, I gotta say, that was fun. Freighty never let me do any active searchin' for obvious reasons." He wiggled his fingers. "Aliens from outer space invading our webs. Ooooooh!"

Then he became serious. "I screwed up the mission, didn't I? Wasn't for me, Charlie wouldn'ta bin shot."

She laid a hand on his shoulder. "Two things. First, you fell down. Totally expected in your case in that gravity. Second, you lost your part of the gestalt. Again, forgivable because of the situation. You've never been shot at before. I thought you handled the whole fight admirably."

"But..."

"It was a valuable lesson to all of us, and we will incorporate it into our training. We all have to be able to switch in and out at will. I admit it really shook me. It felt for a moment like I went blind."

She slapped him on the back. "But none of us screwed up, and we covered for each other. So don't worry about it. Well, not too much. A bit of worry means another time you'll have thought up a solution before the problem happens. You follow?"

"Aye, ma'am. I follow. You know, now I understand a whole lot about battles that I didn't before."

"Here's hoping you don't get the chance to learn more."

27. MOTHER!

It was the same drawing room as before — plus added knickknacks — but with a smaller group, and the atmosphere was less relaxed. Natalia regarded Freighty and Andrew. The boy was perched on the edge of an ornate couch.

Natalia's eyes took in his rigid posture, plus that of the two constructs. "What do we do, now?"

Freighty frowned. "This is the kind of complexity that is so hard to understand about an alien race. Can you explain the problem in words of one syllable for a foreigner?"

She sat back, thinking. "A lot of things have come into focus lately. Why did Mariel Collingwood, a talented, educated, sophisticated woman, sign a ten-year contract to bring her five-year-old son to a deserted space facility run by an alien?"

"She was on the lam."

"She must have been. And now we know who she was running from. One of the most powerful family combines in the Solar System."

"You think so?"

"Andrew and I looked them up. Access these files…"

The Freighty construct's face went blank for all of two seconds. "Yes, no doubt. I have seen the pattern in other advanced societies."

"This also explains a lot of our questions about the cruiser's strange actions. Their first objective wasn't the mine. It was to shut down the mine and kidnap the boy in the ensuing chaos. And probably pick up some fuel as well. If we hadn't come galloping in like the cavalry in an old Western, they probably would have shown up to offer Ludge assistance. They'd take his people off to comfortable quarters, persuade Andrew to stay with them, and who would guess?"

Freighty nodded. "And then you came along and had an outside look at the bombardment. You had the mobility and expertise to point fingers at them."

"Which puts us in a more difficult situation." She pondered a moment. "Andrew must be in serious danger. This is not a friendly mission to bring a lost lamb back to the fold. If they can't capture him, their second option is to kill him. Likewise, his presence is putting the mine in danger, and the factory as well. If we take him home, chances are they'll fade and you won't be bothered again."

"So you're going to take the boy, then?"

"I think I have to. Adoption and all. I've been running the problem through the legal functions of my ArIn, and there's no other way."

Freighty rubbed his hands together, a smile on his face. "Well, that's not a problem, then. We are being forced to do something that, on one level, we want to do anyway."

She nodded. "I'm still concerned about what will happen when we get home and it all falls apart, but for the moment, this is the best for everyone."

She turned a smile on the boy, who had sat frozen-faced through all of this conversation. "What do you think, Andrew? Are you up for a little spaceship ride for a month or six?"

The boy met her eyes, his face the picture of desolation. Then he turned his gaze on the factory construct. "No, Freighty. This ain't gonna happen. We can't do this to her."

The construct frowned down at the boy. "We just got everything we want. What's the problem?"

Andrew shook his head. "I got what I wanted, but not in a way that I can take it, okay?"

Natalia regarded him. "I thought we had this solved and we were all in agreement. You have to tell us what's wrong, Andrew."

He turned to her, an earnest look on his face. "Okay. Let's say I'm in trouble and I need help. You're military personnel, the easiest kind to bamboozle there is."

"What do you mean, easy to bamboozle?"

"Military mindset: 'Serve and Protect.' Set up an orphan waif in trouble, and you come rushing in, all knight in shining armour, to protect him."

"What's wrong with that? That's who I am, what I do. Oh, I know I'm a bit too idealistic. My evaluations always say that. But I wouldn't change it."

"But you acted just like we knew you would."

"Good for you. Your assessment of my character was accurate."

"Don't you realize? We played you." He tossed up his hands. "We set up the game so that you would fall into our trap. And now it's snapped shut on you, and you don't even see it."

She looked down at his earnest little face and burst into laughter.

His puzzlement took on a hurt aspect, his lip quivering. "Why is that funny?"

"Did you enjoy yourselves?"

He frowned. "Well...yeah, it was sorta fun at first. But then it started to get...all serious, y'know? And then I didn't like it at all."

"You were in trouble and you needed help, yes?"

"Yeah..."

"And there I was, the perfect knight in shining armour, right?"

"That's what we figured."

"Well, if you had me so well figured, why didn't you just come out and ask me?"

"Huh?"

"If your assessment was so accurate and I was so wonderful, wouldn't I have agreed? Saved us all this trouble?"

"Uh...maybe."

"So you weren't sure if you were so smart after all, and deep down you were having fun thinking that you could sway me, because that made you feel superior, right?"

"Ain't a very nice way to look at it, but yeah, sorta."

"Then there's a bit of learning for you, isn't there? There's a couple of things you need to pick up, here." She leaned over him.

"You have to learn that, one," she poked him in the chest with a finger, "People with soft hearts are not necessarily stupid. They act that way because they want to. They know what other people are like, but they do it anyway, because they believe it's the right way to act. Got it?"

"Uh...yeah."

"Two." A second poke. "People who are friendly and cooperative are not necessarily weak."

"Oh, yeah, I got that one. It's because they think it's the right thing to do."

"Very good. And here's the big one. Three." She poked hard with three fingers. "If you're such a smarty, remember that there's always someone," another poke, "ahead," another poke, "of you."

She stood back and glared at him. "Do you follow?"

"Uh...yeah. Yeah, I follow. Yes, ma'am."

"And don't give me any fake humility. Just because you follow military protocol doesn't mean you're living up to proper military ideals. It just means you've decided to play the game."

"But that means..."

"Go ahead. You tell me what it means."

"That means that you think there's another authority. You don't follow all these military rules because of the rules. You're following something else."

"Give the boy a kewpie doll!" She grabbed him by the shoulders, lifted him out of the chair and hugged him.

"Okay, okay, don't let's get all sappy. You gotta tell me."

"Tell you?"

"What is it? What do you follow?"

She grinned. "I can't."

"Why not?...oh, I get it. It's secret, right?"

She shook her head, the chuckles still rolling in the back of her throat. "It's no secret. It just wouldn't do you any good."

"Why not?"

"Because it's mine. You can't live by my standard. You have to figure out your own. If I'm going to be your mother, that's my job. To help you figure out the meaning to your life. You don't want to copy mine. You couldn't anyway. It wouldn't fit you."

"Wait a minute. Wait a minute. You said, 'If I'm going to be your mother.' Whaddaya mean by that?"

"Come on, Andrew. You're supposed to be a smart kid. We just had this big discussion and we all agreed. What do you think that means?"

"But...but..."

"Well, all right. If you really don't want me to..." She was surprised at how much it hurt to say that.

Andrew burst into tears. He didn't run. He didn't move. He just stood there, tears running down his face, his chest heaving with sobs.

"Uh-oh." She wrinkled her brow in Freighty's direction, "First mistake. Been a mother for three minutes, and the kid's in tears already."

The construct sighed. "Not something I ever managed. Rage, yes. Tears, no. I assume you know what to do?"

She nodded. "What you couldn't."

She took him in her arms and held him tight.

* * *

Her First officer was less than happy with the solution. He did her the courtesy of thinking about it for a couple of days, but then he asked, very formally, for an interview.

206

They met in the chart room, where she had brought in a decent second chair for the occasion.

"All right, First. This is an official meeting, recorded for the auxiliary log. What can I do for you?"

He squirmed in his chair and cleared his throat. "I don't want you to think I'm saying this because I don't like Andrew. He's a cheerful little boy with a lot of spunk, and when he wants to try, he fits into the military milieu moderately well. In fact, I can see a future for him in the Space Arm. He won't ever be the kind of officer that I would like to work under, but he has many skills that would serve him well in the military."

"So what is the problem?"

"It's this adoption you have taken on. I'm not happy with it."

"Neither am I. But we have to get Andrew safely back home, and I don't see any other way to make that happen." She leaned forward. "I don't have to do this. I could just take him on board on my own authority. It would cause me a certain amount of trouble when I get back to Space Arm, but it would be worth it. But what would happen to Andrew?

"He'd be home. That's the point, isn't it?"

"Getting him back to Earth isn't the whole solution. We could very well end up completing the mission the Clyde was sent for, and bring him home to dump him into the grasping arms of his loving family. We have to protect him when he gets there. If he rode in unauthorized, Space Arm would see him as the problem, to be disposed of as soon as possible. They wouldn't look too closely at anyone who showed up and said they were family. They'd ship him off, STAT. Wouldn't you agree?"

"That seems a logical assessment."

"But if he comes back as the family of a serving officer, he's not part of the problem, he's one of us. Space Arm protects its own. Whoever wants him might get him in the end, but Judicial Branch will make sure it's for his own good. At least as well as they can; the opposition's power reaches very high. So you understand why I did what I did? It keeps us within the rules."

207

He nodded, a troubled frown on his brow. "But that's what bothers me. You have obeyed the letter of the law in order to flout it."

She stared at him, trying to pry into that opaque mind. "Jones, when you follow all those rules. Why do you follow them?

"Because that's what military discipline is based on. If people didn't follow the rules, the whole organization would collapse."

"I agree. But what about the reason behind the rules?"

"I just told you. Because..."

"...otherwise the whole organization would collapse. Fair enough. But...how do you tell a good rule from a bad rule?"

"Well...you can't, really. I know some are better than others, and some are outdated, and sometimes it's hard figuring out which rule to apply. But in the end you have to assume that the rules must be obeyed. Otherwise..." He circled his hand in a continuing motion.

"And there's no more to it than that?"

He raised his eyebrows. "I don't think so. Don't you find that rather comforting?"

She shook her head. "Not especially." She regarded him. "Do you know what this conversation means?"

"In what way?"

"You say following the law to the letter is the only requirement. Now I have followed the law to the letter, and you're still unhappy. Why? Because in doing so I have broken another law."

"You have? What other law?"

"I must have, or you wouldn't be upset. You have just discovered that you believe in a law that supersedes all other laws. Obeying all the little laws isn't good enough if you don't follow the main ideal."

He shook his head. "That's too complex for me." Then he regarded her. "The one thing that makes me feel better about it is that I do believe you have the good of everyone in mind, including the authority and honour of the Space Arm. I don't understand how you're going to manage that, but I am not going to make any formal complaint at this time. In fact, in light of where this conversation has travelled, I do not feel it has any function in the ship's official record, and I suggest we shift it to our personal logs."

"I agree." *NightHawk?*

Auxiliary log entry 453-B so moved.

She leaned back in her chair. "Feel better about it now?"

"Some, but not much. I want to think about that last bit. Thank you for hearing me out."

"Don't worry about it." She got up. "Thanks for coming in. It helps me understand better."

He looked puzzled as he stood. "Oh...well...you're welcome."

She put a hand on his arm. "You and I are very different people, and we are always going to disagree on certain things. You understand that, don't you?"

"Yes. People disagree. It's an unfortunate fact of life I discovered a long time ago."

"Right. But when you're disagreeing, if you understand that the other person has good reasons for his feelings, it makes it easier not to take offense. Or her ideas. Right?"

His face brightened. "Oh. Yes, I suppose so."

28. GRAVITY WELL

"Bad news, Commander."

"What do you have, Lieutenant?"

"That plate we attached to the *Clyde* is still working perfectly."

"And that's bad news because...?"

"She's headed our way. In decel already, coming in from behind that planetoid at forty-one, seventeen, five."

"One thing about a ship that size. There's no rush. By the time they get stopped, we could be long gone."

Estimated time to zero velocity three hours, ma'am.

Freighty, are you getting this?

The construct appeared on the viewscreen beside the image of the cruiser. "I'm getting the data in re-ti with you."

"What do you figure?"

"The gloves are off, Natalia. We know what he's really after. He knows we know. We've already talked about this. I think it's time you left for home."

"I can't leave until I'm sure you and the mine won't be collateral damage. I'll transfer Andrew across immediately."

"Don't do that. Your fighting capabilities are enhanced with him on board, even more than in a ground skirmish. But remember, if you have to, cut and run. He's more valuable than anything else."

"Maybe to you and me, but not to humankind. I'm staying to protect you. If you need it, that is."

"I told you. I have formidable defenses, but I have denied myself the wherewithall to counterattack. I may live to regret that. For a brief moment, anyway."

"We're not bad on the offense, and we have your map of the *Clyde*'s weaknesses. You defend, we'll attack."

"That will be interesting, anyway. Your potential as a unified weapon needs field testing."

sudden outrush of dusty air and debris followed, soon tapering off.

"Now, if you insist on your aggressive action towards a client of the Planetary Community, you are skirting disaster. Back off and move away. That was your only warning."

The enemy captain's face contorted, and he made a chopping motion with his right hand.

Immediately the cruiser's full salvo crashed through space...

...to the spot the *NightHawk* had been. She was already twisting inward, dodging the weaponry, accelerating towards the safe spots Freighty's specs had shown her in close to the bigger ship's hull. Flipping upside-down, she raced belly-to-belly with the larger vessel, picking off tender spots as she slid past them.

Charlie and Fiona. Let NightHawk do the targeting. Think what you want to hit, and let her do the rest. Follow?

Aye, ma'am...Say...!

A blossom of flame erupted near the aft plasma vents as the little scout raced past.

Stand by for heavy burn...Go!

The *NightHawk* spun aside moments before the blast from the accelerating warship would have toasted her. Now she swung in a tight arc, her human crew groaning with the strain, to come in from the port side high, tap-tap-tapping the weak spots in the ancient hull.

But all to no avail. The huge warship turned on its ponderous course, its speed unabated, aiming its blunt prow straight towards the factory. Natalia made one more desperate pass along under the port side but made little impact. The shrapnel was beginning to take its toll on *NightHawk*. Sections of her hull had gone blank. The starboard laser had quit, and Natalia had to keep her portside towards the enemy to get full firepower.

Freighty?

213

Can't take much more of this.

One more pass. There's that cooling vent by the dorsal aft battery.

Not recommended. Too well protected.

But possible. Here we go.

No, Natalia...

...our only chance.

All crew. Helmets on. She thought the order, and the *NightHawk* curved in on her final run, approaching the *Clyde* from aft on the starboard side, huge gun barrels tracking them for another volley.

Natalia gritted her teeth. *Charlie, time for your favourite toy. One chance as we go by. Straight down.*

On it, ma'am.

The Space-to-Space missile slipped into the launch rack, its target symbol popping into her vision.

NightHawk...

A positive response flowed from several minds

Image: huge fangs crushing tiny battle cruiser.

Image: small boy poking wasp's nest with stick.

Hold on, folks. Take your time, Charlie, and get it right. The *Hawk* soared closer and closer. *Just a moment, now...*

Missile away...on tar...

She had waited too long. A wall of flame erupted in front of them as the powerful cruiser's weapons focused on their little portion of space, and the ship could not duck quickly enough. A bone-shattering crash erupted on the com and through their helmets. The ship wrenched sideways, and the stars spun in strange patterns as *NightHawk* tumbled end-over-end, the scream of escaping atmosphere increasing, then dying away as the air on the bridge became too thin to transmit sound.

No time to speak. Depending on her team to back her, she focused on returning her body to normal position, her bow towards the enemy, her engines blasting her to another attack.

It was a limping progress, as her port thrusters were crippled and the helmsman fought to keep her on course. She was blind on her lower port side where the plasma had seared the Permaskin, but she bored in anyway.

And then all conscious thought was wiped out by a powerful voice that came from her augment, from the com, and from the fabric of space itself.

BATTLE CRUISER CLYDE, THIS IS FACTORY 4-80. THIS IS YOUR ONLY WARNING. CEASE YOUR ATTACK. I REPEAT. CEASE YOUR ATTACK. PCSC NIGHTHAWK AND HER PASSENGERS ARE UNDER MY PROTECTION. BREAK OFF OR SUFFER THE CONSEQUENCES.

The only response was a renewed attack from the batteries facing the factory.

Natalia knew that the next salvo was for her. She was about to jam more power to the engines, but out of the corner of her eye she caught her upper portside viewscreen.

A beam of intense blue light lanced out of the factory, aiming at a point just to starboard of the *Clyde*. Amazingly, it stopped there, pouring energy into a tiny portion of space.

Time slowed, and in that instant two ideas flashed into her brain.

Demand: go!

Warning: annihilation!

Without conscious thought, her mind stabbed full power to the main engines and the starboard thrusters in a course that every instinct screamed at her was wrong, directly alongside the enemy, whose gun barrels were still trying to track her.

She talonned her fingers into the sides of her chair, her eyes fixed on the viewscreen as her ship jerked sideways, thrusters pushing, main engines whining at maximum acceleration. G-forces slammed her into her couch, and all she could do was hold her head pointed at the screen.

The concept of "gravity shadow" registered, and for a brief instant as they ran alongside the weight of the cruiser she understood it completely, and then that, too was gone in the agony of unbearable pressure. Somewhere in her augment she was taking in a reading of 30 Gs and rising, but her mind could not encompass the data.

Faintly on the com she heard Jones's voice, *"No...wrong cour..."*

Then the *NightHawk* slued away from the hulking *Clyde*, and she lost consciousness.

She came slowly out of a dark haze of indescribable weight to a nagging order, over and over in her augment.

Report by numbers...

Report by numbers. Captain...

Report by numbers, please, captain...

She forced her mind to move. *Captain on the bridge.*

...Helm on duty.

Bridge...on duty.

Engineering on duty.

Commun...communic...what hap...?

First Officer, possible concussion. All vital signs stable. I believe he tried to raise his head at a bad moment.

Weapons on duty. Targets, ma'am?

Galley on duty. You don't know what you just did to my soufflé!

NightHawk, take over communications. Rear viewscreens, please.

Despite the engines screaming on full battle power, they were only inching along, sliding ahead of and away from the mammoth cruiser. Charlie's missile had achieved its target, and a plume of debris spread from a gaping hole in the *Clyde's* plating. Several cannons hung askew, and all had ceased firing.

Movement in the belt, ma'am.

What's moving? Show!

It took a moment, but then it became apparent that all the nearby asteroids, from fine gravel to planetoids, were picking up speed, curving in their orbits toward the cruiser.

Freighty is throwing rocks.

Now the remaining cannons on the warship were swinging away, blasting at the larger boulders. But nothing stopped the slow surge of mass bearing down from all directions. Asteroids disintegrated under cannon fire, but instead of blowing up normally, the pieces curved back onto their original trajectory.

Wait a minute. They're not targeting the ship.

True enough, the centre of the moving mass was the tiny, bright light to starboard of the *Clyde*. Rocks bouncing off the old steel hull continued towards that point, where they promptly disappeared.

A large asteroid, maybe a hundred metres across, zoomed towards the light. As it neared, it seemed to shrink, as if it was shooting away rapidly. Then it, too, was gone. The speed of the influx increased, and soon an eddy of stone swirled around the centre, *Clyde* and *NightHawk* the only bodies moving counter to the flow.

Gravity increasing, ma'am.

NightHawk's slow acceleration away from the phenomenon began to taper off as massive forces tugged at her with tightening claws.

Lighten ship.

Jettisoning excess fuel, ma'am.

A plume of expanding smoke blew out behind them, and the little ship picked up speed.

The *Clyde* lumbered into a desperate turn to follow, but three large asteroids had just bashed into the centre of the eddy when a huge, jagged rhomboid of rock at least a kilometre long swooped past them, majestically turning end over end, an outthrust pillar of stone making a vain attempt to swipe Natalia and her crew to oblivion. The incredible mass curved past the *Clyde* and into a tighter and tighter spiral, edges crumbling and pieces streaming away ahead of the main body.

At immense speed, the asteroid was sucked into the point of light. At that moment *something* happened. It was impossible to tell what, but the whole universe lurched. The light from the stars shifted towards red, and *NightHawk* jolted as if she had run into a wall of treacle, her hard-won velocity dropping to a crawl.

The cruiser's engines had continued to blast, straining to get the hulking mass moving, but her course curved tighter and tighter to starboard. Then the great hull of the old spaceship swerved hard, moving straight sideways with an unbelievable jolt. Natalia cringed at the effect of that sudden jerk on the soft bodies inside. Abruptly the engines died, and holes began to erupt in the starboard deck plates, huge lumps of metal pouring away from the stricken vessel. A few steering thrusters vainly attempted to maintain a safe course, but their puny strength had little effect, only serving to keep the doomed ship in a wider orbit.

The crew of the *NightHawk* watched in awe as the enemy ship fell apart before their eyes. The first large objects streamed into a globe of smaller and smaller radius a few kilometres off to the side of the dying spaceship as the vessel was tugged into a tight orbit around that point. Smaller bits rained away as well, and an amorphous mass formed at the meeting spot. One by one the thrusters died, and as it neared the vortex, the whole cruiser bent, the bow seemed to elongate, stretching towards its doom. Gradually the starship fell apart, all the pieces spiralling down towards the lump of metal, which soon began to glow.

In less time than it took for *NightHawk* to make ten kilometres, the whole enemy ship had squashed itself into a seething mass of molten metal, explosions and bubbles disturbing the surface, immediately jerked back in wherever they rose.

There was an intense flash of radiation across every frequency the *NightHawk*'s Permaskin could register, and every crewmember in the augment shouted in pain and shock.

Then there was nothing. The viewscreen where the vortex had been showed empty space with an aimless swirl of rocks breaking from the eddy and shooting away in all directions.

NightHawk's full power still screamed, throwing them away from the site at full acceleration.

NightHawk, full stop.

Aye, ma'am.

The engine whine spun down, and the incredible pressure eased off.

Slow flip and normal accel back towards the mine.

Moving like zombies, the crew performed their assigned functions in the operation, and soon the ship was back to normal, covering at a sedate speed the several thousand kilometers of distance she had put on in seconds of hyper-acceleration.

Natalia opened the com. "Anyone injured?"

Nelson clicked in. "I feel like six hours in a training centrifuge gone wild, ma'am, but we're fine down here in Engineering."

The bridge crew all gestured with raised thumbs, and the rest chimed in on the com. While everyone felt bruised, there were no serious injuries. She turned to Jones. "How are you, First?"

He pulled off his helmet and rotated his head, his hand on his neck. "Not bad now, ma'am. I just tried to look around at the wrong moment. Felt like a sledgehammer to the forehead. Vision's clear. Won't know about the balance until I try to get up."

"Don't rush it."

"Flip over and decel in five minutes."

"What do you think that was?"

"Gravity well."

She glanced at the Chief Engineer's image on the viewscreen. "You think so?"

"What else would do that? Those first big chunks were the engines and generators and other heavy equipment that tore loose on the first high-G jolt. Smaller equipment followed through the holes, then the rest of the ship ran out of inertia and caught up.

"*NightHawk*, get Freighty for me, please."

He is online.

"That was impressive. Gravity well?"

"I'm glad you're impressed. I was going to add it to the bargaining list. Too bad I can't, now."

"Why not? I'd like to be able to do that. You could set us up with a less powerful version."

"Sorry. Against the articles of the contract."

"Which articles?"

"It's a weapon."

"No it isn't. It's a gravity generator."

"That's what it was until I used it to destroy that ship. Now it's a weapon. Reclassifying."

The Commander buried her face in her hands. "Linear thinking. I'm surrounded by linear thinking. I've gotta do something about that."

She refocused. "Can you at least tell us what you did?"

"I created a pinhead-sized singularity next to the starship. The *Clyde* fell into a black hole."

"But didn't that take an incredible amount of power?"

"It does to start with. Once the singularity starts attracting its own mass, it's not hard to keep it going, but I pretty much drained my reserves at the beginning, and we'll have to negotiate an equitable distribution of the cost of the fuel between the mine, the Space Arm and myself. Since it was action by a rival corporation, I deem that El Dorado should cover the majority."

"Once the singularity has been created, it's not hard to keep it going because when the mass reaches a certain point it feeds itself with whatever is nearby."

"Including the odd battle cruiser."

"Yes, but she wasn't cooperating. Once that huge asteroid was absorbed, the mass reached the point where its pull overcame the cruiser's engines. Hence the sudden jolt."

"Weren't you afraid of being pulled in yourself? How about us?"

The construct smiled. "I assume you know that gravity decreases by the square of distance. There was never any danger to me, and I knew you could take care of yourselves."

"Then how do you stop it?"

"The moment I remove the impetus, it collapses on itself and disappears."

"Nothing disappears. It just goes somewhere else."

"I congratulate you, Commander O'Rourke. That is a philosophical step worthy of a top physicist."

"In other words, you don't know what happens to it but it's gone, so why worry?"

"I see no evidence of any remaining effect that appears dangerous. It really does seem to be gone."

"Just like my Otherwhen sphere seems to be gone when it's in operation."

"A good point. I'll check in Otherwhere as well. It would not do to leave lumps of boiling metal in the path of FTL spaceships. Especially so close to an operating mine."

"Speaking of the mine, get Ludge on the line, will you, *NightHawk*?

Coming up, ma'am.

The mine manager's harried visage took up the screen. "What in all the blazes is going on up there? It looked like a big explosion, and the *Clyde* just disappeared."

"That's about it, Nicholas. Any problems down there?"

"Nothing you'll believe."

"Try me. We've been getting a lesson in new forms of reality out here."

"Well, perhaps my instruments are faulty, but it looks like our orbit has changed. It's hard to tell, because all the asteroids around us seem to be in the same positions, but relative to Barnard..."

"That would be about right. There's been a...let's just call it a gravity incident out here. It destroyed the enemy and towed a lot of asteroids around. Monitor your course carefully, and watch out for rogue boulders out of their usual pattern."

Ludge shook his head. "Will do, ma'am. I don't pretend to understand, but keeping close watch is something we do all the time. Of course, if people would stop messing about with large boulders..."

"I can see your point, Nicholas. I don't think you'll be bothered again."

29. FINAL ANALYSIS

Now it was *NightHawk* established in an upright position at the centre of the torus while Freighty effected repairs. Permaskin had been an entertaining puzzle for him, but he had come out with flying colours, adding a layer of ablative material to soften the blow of super-heated plasma.

When the repairs were almost done, he invited the principal members of the organization for a meeting.

After all this time, it turned out that Freighty had an office. Of course, he could have just whipped it up for the occasion. Natalia gazed out of the two-story panoramic windows at, if she remembered correctly, the skyline of Manhattan, and wondered how much of the room was actually there. The soft leather office chair that cradled her body felt real enough.

The construct, in his own fancy chair at the head of the conference table, grinned at her. "Exo-ergonomics: one of my specialties."

"Well, let's not overdo it." She glanced left down the wide, mahogany table to a very different kind of chair, this one of stone. A construct of Horus, the hawk-headed god of ancient Egypt, stared back at her with unblinking predatory eyes.

"I felt that *NightHawk* deserved an equal position in these proceedings."

I think my physical presence lends a balance to the social context.

"So long as Andrew doesn't suddenly turn out to be something other than a twelve-year-old boy, I don't mind."

The subject of her stare grinned back from beside the hawk. "I think you'll find all my unrealities are inside, ma'am. I mean Mum."

"Ma'am will do fine for this meeting. Shall we get underway? Freighty, are you chairing? This is your venue."

223

"Fair enough. *NightHawk*, I assume you will keep the official record."

It seemed the bird construct could talk through her beak. She had the same comfortable voice as on ship.

"As I always do."

"And, as you all know, I will keep my own record. Now to the first order of business. What was the *Clyde* doing out here? Anyone?" His nod indicated Natalia.

"Not much doubt they were after Andrew."

Agreement around the table, but Jones shook his head.

"Lieutenant Jones?"

"I don't think that's enough."

"I agree. What is your reasoning?"

"We now know that the boy is a sample of your advanced technology. He has incredible value to Space Arm." The First Officer's frown deepened as he regarded Andrew. "Perhaps even enough to make up for the fact that we have to put up with him for then next eight months." The frown stayed up at his eyebrows, though. His lip was twitching.

Natalia grinned. "That has yet to be decided as well."

Jones merely rolled his eyes, an expression she had never seen on his rigid face before.

Freighty tapped a finger on the table. "Please continue, Lieutenant Jones."

"But before that, he was just the scion of a major family. Perhaps I am naïve, but even if it turns out he is the heir to their total fortune, I can't see it would be worth the expense of sending a huge ship on a two-year voyage. They must have had multiple objectives."

He turned to Nicholas. "What's the situation with your mine, legally?"

Ludge pursed his lips, thinking. "The transplanetaries are governed by Planetary Community law. They don't like it, but it's the price of doing business, so most of the time they comply.

El Dorado is one of the biggest players. There is no chance another corporation could come out and take over the mine by force and make it stick, legally."

Natalia leaned forward. "What could they get away with, short term?"

The Mine Manager stared at his fingernails, then looked up. "In the first place, their timing was off through no fault of their own. We had a major shutdown a couple of months ago. That ore carrier should have been full when the *Clyde* arrived. A year's production. Do you know what that's worth?"

"It's beyond my comprehension." Natalia shrugged. "But when I think of the cost to set this all up, bring you and your equipment out here and keep the operation going, amortized over the life of one medium-sized asteroid mine, the yearly yield must be in the billions of planetoids."

"Close enough. Also, if they took over the mine, they would have several months of production on their own before El Dorado and the Space Arm heard about it and sent help. They could fill their holds, refine enough to fill their fuel tanks, and be gone into the depths of wherever they came from with a huge profit. Andrew would have been icing on the cake."

"*NightHawk*, what's the legal situation with staking claims on these asteroids?"

The Horus construct thought briefly.

"According to my records, they're free for the taking, ma'am. It costs an incredible amount to set up a mining operation so far from Earth, but the presence of naturally occurring plutonium triiodide in the Barnard's system is a real windfall. Back in the Sol system, it has to be processed from uranium, which is a slow and expensive operation. The demand for fuel is so high, the Planetary Community has pretty well declared carte blanche on mining claims out here."

"So if Develocon or Solarcorp was to suddenly come up with a mine on the next asteroid over, nobody would turn a hair."

"No, ma'am. The only control in these situations is a so-called gentlemen's agreement between the corporations involved."

Ludge nodded. "And with a year's takings in hand and a ship already in-system, that corporation would have a great head start. Especially if El Dorado's annual output was missing in action. They could slip the stolen ore in gradually and claim it was their own product."

Freighty waited, but there was no further comment. "That seems sufficient analysis of the situation to date. The *Clyde* had plenty of reason to be here, and Andrew was only part of it. That is somewhat reassuring."

He held out his hands, palms up. "Now to the future. What shall we do next, and what might the outcomes be. Manager Ludge?"

"You know better than I do how the repairs are going. I estimate we'll be back at the ore face in about two weeks. Your modifications to our rock harvesters will increase output by about twenty percent, of which half will come back to fuel your factory's needs. Thus we will send the ore carrier home three months late with a full load. Our masters back on Earth will be ecstatic when they discover that we have a connection with such a resource as Freighty."

"Commander O'Rourke. What do you see in the future?"

"Our mission has long ago been completed, and we have succeeded far beyond any parameters Space Arm could dream up. We could leave now, go straight home and be there in seven months."

"However...?"

"There are a few things we could clean up before we go. I've been looking over your proposed modifications to *NightHawk*." She shot a wry glance at Jones. "Since you already had all our specs, they suit beautifully. I will still have our personnel do the actual work. That's about as useful a way of covering my butt as tissue paper in a typhoon, but enough to show my heart was in the right place. It won't cost us any time, because the increased power will shave a month off both accel and decel...no, Freighty, I don't want to be told anything about travel in Otherwhere. That's one bit of knowledge the

226

Planetary Community will need to look at very carefully before accepting it."

"I agree. I have begun to reassess all my technologies since the gravity-well experiment, and decided that many more of them could be termed weapons than I ever expected. I am acutely aware that I contacted humanity earlier than the optimum moment, so I must be doubly cautious."

"If I might make a suggestion, although I'm getting above my pay grade."

"Go ahead, Commander. I'm sure you'll soon be promoted to an appropriate salary for your abilities."

"It may be less a matter of what technologies you provide, and more important to whom you are giving them. Planetary Community is a democratic government, but we do keep tight control of technological and sociological factors that affect our populations: drugs, personal weapons, bio-hazardous materials; the list is endless. The appropriate mores and ethics exist in the population, and sufficient government structure supports them. Our analysis of the probable role of the transplanetaries in the latest events plus Freighty's outside opinion of the development of human society makes me very leery of giving them access to much, but we can't leave them out."

Jones nodded. "I am of the same opinion."

"*NightHawk*, can you apply your problem-solving matrix to this problem?"

"Not in a reasonable length of time, ma'am. There is so much material available, and so much of it is contradictory, it would take me several days to come up with a useful analysis. I would have to shut down all but basic life support functions in order to handle the load."

Natalia grinned at the Horus head. "Maybe when we get into Otherwhere in a few months you can deal with it at your leisure."

"I will do that, ma'am. Now that you have started me on this topic, I must reach a conclusion of some sort. Otherwise I could find myself in a moral quandary which would affect my ability to perform my usual functions in reasonable time."

Natalia took in Andrew's puzzled frown. "She means that if you haven't decided what is right and what is wrong, you can't really make a split-second decision, can you?"

He nodded slowly, his mind already elsewhere.

She winked at Jones. "That'll keep him out of our hair for a day or two."

The Lieutenant frowned. "But there's still the question of who is looking out for the good of humankind."

Image: dominating male auguar shepherding tiny humans into a cosy den and standing guard outside.

"Thank you, Chakka, but I don't know if your tender care would give humanity what it needs right now."

Emotion: willingness.

"I know you are." She turned to the others. "Are you all getting Chakka's images?"

Ludge wrinkled his brow. "Is that what they were? It was rather strange. Is that how you two communicate?"

"That's classified information, Nicholas, and I'd be grateful if you didn't share it around."

"You can count on me, ma'am. There's a lot of stuff happened lately that I'll be keeping close to my vest."

Freighty nodded. "I'm sure your loyalty to your company will cause you some second thoughts in that respect, but we will leave it up to you."

The construct shifted in his chair in a very human way that indicated an approaching conclusion. "Now, as far as I am concerned, once *NightHawk* has been repaired and upgraded, and once the mine is fully operational, I will start for Earth at my own glacial velocity of 0.85 Lightspeed through re-ti space. I don't venture into Otherwhere for reasons that are beyond your understanding at the moment.

"The mine will continue to supply me with the surplus ore they will harvest with my improvements to their technology. El

Dorado will be happy because I do my own refining, with minimal shipping cost for the first few loads, anyway. Once I get close enough to Earth to take on more contracts I'll need more fuel, and I'll be able to afford a higher price. I'm sure the company will turn more of their production over to me as I need it."

"Taking into account my slow acceleration and deceleration rate, that will mean about eight years before I arrive. However, my modifications to your communications networks will halve the time it takes for messages to travel through Otherwhere. So I will be able to communicate with increasing efficiency as time goes by, and I have already started putting out feelers for my business activities."

Natalia grinned. "You won't get bored. Space Arm will have you crawling with diplomats in about a year. *NightHawk* is the fastest ship in the Fleet, so I imagine we'll do a quick turnaround and head back with the first wave. As soon as the modifications you have given us can be applied to an appropriately luxurious vessel, the attachés, consuls, envoys and plenipotentiaries will be on their way."

The construct smiled. "And if my modifications happen to give your boffins some hints as to the optimum use of your engines, it could be faster than that."

She faked a huge sigh. "Pushing *NightHawk* out of the front row and into a less prominent role in the Fleet, which would suit me fine."

"I somehow doubt that. You have another experiment to complete."

"Oh, yes. Them." Her gaze swept the trio at the end of the table. "You're not suggesting I take Beak-Nose, there, on my ship."

The Horus gave a very human laugh.

"I'll keep the program in storage and only bring it out on special occasions, ma'am. It does rather use a lot of bandwidth when it's running."

"Let us be thankful for small mercies."

30. LEAVING FOR HOME

Since the ship was in dock, Natalia put the ArIn on duty, and the whole crew attended Andrew's farewell reception. Nicholas and his wife, Wanda, were there with several lesser mine officials. Mariel had outdone herself, with the full assistance of Juanita and of Wanda, who brought a few delicacies she had rescued from the mine cafeteria freezers.

The cosy salon had grown, and several islands of furniture graced a polished hardwood dance floor. An olio of the popular music of many eras oozed from...basically all over...and the ceiling looked completely transparent, revealing the Milky Way in all its splendor.

The only attendees not circulating were Chakka and the guest of honour, who were curled on a settee in a corner. Natalia peered: from the look of it, the boy was reading a book aloud. She accessed her augment. "All the Mowgli Stories." He was jumping through to read all the parts where Bagheera was featured.

She nudged Nicholas. "You're going to miss him."

He shrugged. "I don't plan on being at the mine long. The Company will want a detailed analysis of what happened here, and even FTL communication is just too complex. My guess is my replacement will be on the next ore carrier, and Wanda and I will be headed back to Earth permanently in about a year."

He leaned closer. "And Freighty doesn't forget his friends."

She grinned. "He made you an offer, too, did he?"

He opened his hands, palms up. "Who else can help him interface with El Dorado as well as I can?"

"He's made offers to all my crew. Nobody leaves his or her position, but they're all on retainer for when they retire." Natalia shook her head. "Heaven knows what Space Arm is going to think about that."

The Mine Manager shrugged. "If they want to keep Freighty out of the hands of the transplanetaries, they need all the ties they can wangle."

Everyone wanted a word with Andrew, and the boy rose from his seat and took the publicity with élan, although somehow at the same time he was continuing his narration of the book, using the auguar's eyes to read through.

Natalia filed it away for future study. It was going to be difficult enough to keep the kid occupied through six or seven months of travel on a small ship.

Read the part about the battle with the red dogs, Andrew.

NightHawk! You're supposed to be on duty.

All stations reporting normal, ma'am. I just like the chapter about the wild dog pack. The tactics are fascinating. Chakka understands it, and he's working through it with me.

Very well. Carry on, NightHawk.

Thank you, ma'am.

Image: midnight-black panther rising from villager's cot as frightened men stare.

The boy went on...*and in that minute Bagheera raised his head and yawned — elaborately, carefully, and ostentatiously — as he would yawn when he wished to insult an equal. The fringed lips drew back and up; the red tongue curled; the lower jaw dropped and dropped till you could see half-way down the hot gullet; and the gigantic dog-teeth stood clear to the pit of the gums till they rang together, upper and under, with the snick of steel-faced wards shooting home round the edges of a safe.*

Image/Emotion: auguar rolling on floor in feline laughter.

Pushing the conversation out of her augment, she turned back to Ludge. "Have you sent in your report? What will they think about it?"

The manager grinned. "They'll turn cartwheels in the snow to keep their contracts with Freighty. That new Otherwhere communications impeller that doubles the speed of radio transmission is worth a tonne of plutonium all by itself."

"Freighty has decided that communications techniques are not weapons. I sent the specs on a faster com drone yesterday along with my full report to my superiors. They'll have time to make up the equipment and send me my walking papers long before I get into decel."

Ludge laughed. "I sincerely doubt it." Then he sobered. "You spacers have your problems with communications, I know. But those of us stationary at one end or the other have our frustrations, as well. Can you imagine what it's like, desperately wanting someone to do something, unable to tell him about it, and hoping beyond hope that he'll do it in time?"

She nodded towards a nearby viewscreen.

Image: Donald Duck backing slowly towards the edge of the Grand Canyon, his camera glued to his eye, while Mickey Mouse jumps up and down on a nearby ridge.

"Say, did you do that? Not bad."

"I'm learning from the best." She strolled over to where Mariel was conversing with Fiona and some of the female miners. The construct's motions were much smoother, now, her facial expressions more versatile. Natalia idly wondered which ones mimicked her own, but of course she had never seen them, either. Oh, well.

The adults were enjoying the party, but Natalia could see the signs in Andrew's stance. "You want to cut this short?"

"Yeah. I gotta say goodbye to Mum and Freighty. Might as well get it over with."

She sent a quick heads-up, and the two constructs met them at the door.

"We're headin' out. Big day tomorrow. Just wanted to...say goodbye."

Freighty nodded. "We'll be in contact regularly for the next few weeks, but it's not the same." He took the boy by the shoulders and faced him directly. "You were wonderful company for me when I needed it the most, and you have done very well on your present assignment. I have no doubt that you will continue to be successful."

"Uh...yeah. Thanks, Freighty."

"And I know your mother would be very proud of you."

"Yeah." The boy's lip quivered. "She always was, really." He gave a twisted smile. "That's what kept me tryin'."

"Well, you keep on trying, and I can't wait to see what you'll be like when I get to Earth in a few years and you're all grown up."

Andrew turned to the Mariel construct, which gave her very-human smile. "Your mother and Freighty made me with every part of her they could, and I'm very proud of you, as well."

He frowned. "I never thought of it that way. You mean I still gotta keep listenin' to you and doin' what you say?"

Her smile deepened. "Why wouldn't you? I always tell you what's best for you, remember?"

The boy rolled his eyes up to meet Natalia's. "That's the worst part of it. She really does."

He turned his glance to Freighty. "Any chance I could take her with me? If one Mum is good, two would be twice as good."

The construct smiled. "Sorry, the *NightHawk* doesn't have enough capacity. She's too integrated with my programs."

"Yeah, I sorta knew that." He straightened his shoulders. "Well, let's just do this." He gave each of them a long hug, then turned to Natalia, his shoulders straight. "Cadet Collingwood reporting for duty, ma'am."

"Good to have you along for the ride, Cadet. Let's go aboard and get you settled in."

Andrew's posture slumped as the door closed behind them. Ignoring his tears, Natalia laid her arm across his shoulders and led him out the gangway to *NightHawk*, his outside hand clenched in Chakka's fur.

"It's tough, isn't it?"

He snuffled and wiped his sleeve across his nose. "Yeah. They're only constructs, I know, but they're the only family I had for two years." A sob shuddered through him. "It's sorta like losin' Mum all over again, y'know?"

"Yes, I do know. My father died a few years ago."

"Oh. I'm so sorry ...ma'am...? What do I call you? I mean, I know I call you "ma'am" in public. But in private...?"

She shrugged. "Don't worry about it. This is never going to be a normal mother-son relationship, so you can call me Natalia or whatever you like." She spun to point a finger between his eyes. "Except 'Mumbot.' I know about that one."

"Sure. I'll save that for special occasions, shall I?"

Image: large, furry paw with needle-sharp black claws peeping out among the hairs.

"Oh, yeah. Forgot about him. He's on your side, ain't he?"

"I'm his mistress, his pride leader and his commanding officer, and don't you forget it."

He resumed his walk, mute, his hand still in the auguar's fur.

She strode alongside. "You tired?"

"Not particularly. It's only 9:43." He glanced at her. "You gonna make me have a bedtime, now?"

She laughed. "No. I just think this might be time for a talk. Before we leave, tomorrow."

"Sure. I don't mind talkin'." He grinned, peering up through his shaggy hair. "I'm good at it."

"Right. Come down to the mess. You can make me a drink."

When they were settled in their usual corner she took a sip of her mocha and regarded him.

His eyes grew round. "What? Did I do somethin' wrong?"

She shook her head. "You do realize how much Freighty has been experimenting on you."

Andrew shrugged. "Oh, that. I was already suspicious, and then I got on that ship and then at the mine. Their med scanners don't show a whisper of electronics in my whole body, and yet I could interface with every ArIn I came across." He grinned. "An' then you lot shows up, and I'm sayin' 'Howdy' to the most modern tech in the human sphere. That's when I begun to think his experiments mighta bin pretty successful.

"You know, Mum and I useta have a joke. She'd say, 'You're a very smart boy, Andrew. Don't let it go to your head.' and I useta say, "Where else would I be smart, in my butt?" And she'd twit me for crude language, and that'd be it. But I bin thinkin' lately. She never answered the question, either. How, exactly, did Freighty manage my augments?

"So I did some studyin'. There's nerve cells all over your body. A real big set down your spine, for example. So what if he's gone outside of my brain and created a larger network of intelligence that uses every nerve in my body?" He shrugged. "Just speculatin' you know. Might be a loada space trash." He grinned. "There's a woman at the mine always tellin' her husband that he's thinkin' with the wrong parta his anatomy. Maybe I really am thinkin' with my butt."

She regarded him. "Obviously you can speak proper English Standard if you want to. Which means you don't want to."

"My Mum always told me that no matter what game you're playin' or what act you're puttin' on, you gotta have a piece of you deep down inside that's really you. So as to not lose track, you know? Remember who you are, what's right and what's wrong. That sorta thing."

Natalia shook her head. "And this 'Aw, shucks, ma'am, I'm just a dumb kid' routine is the real you?"

"Yeah. What's wrong with that? I am a kid. I wanta do kid stuff. If I went around actin' like a PhD in physics, people'd want all sorts of stuff outa me that I'm not ready to give. At least not right now."

She frowned. "I hesitate to ask..."

"...but do I have a PhD in physics? Not yet, but I'm workin' on it. That's another reason I gotta get to Earth. I can download all the books and journals on five nets, but I gotta start talkin' re-ti to people that know. Freighty says I gotta tread the line between present theories and the new stuff he gave me."

"So when we get home, I have to enroll you in university?"

"Naw, I'm already enrolled. They just don't know I'm only twelve. You're gonna have to pull some strings."

She shook her head. "I'm just a junior officer in a big military organization, Andrew. I don't pull strings. I'm one of the poor sods on the other end, I'm afraid."

Andrew's eyes dropped their sparkle and regarded her steadily. "When you get back to Earth you'll find you've made progress. It hasn't really sunk in what kind of power you have."

"I don't have any power. I signed Freighty's contracts on behalf of the Space Arm. The moment I upload them to our Central ArIn, I'm out of the loop."

The glint returned. "Oh, my. Inexperienced young junior officers really shouldn't be signing important contracts."

"What do you mean?"

His voice became singsong. "You didn't read the fine print."

"I did so! *NightHawk* and I both went over those contracts in detail. I may not have a PhD, but I'm not stupid."

"No, no, not the business contracts. Our fostering agreement." He waited while that sank in. "Surely you noted the clause about my business dealings until I hit eighteen."

"I'm responsible for them. That's pretty standard."

"Not when your new foster son is a major partner in a large manufacturing business."

"...oh."

"Yeah, Freighty and I, we forgot to mention that. Y'see, my Mum and I were the first part of his plan to set up relationships with individual humans before anything official happened, so he had somebody he could trust, people who weren't bein' nice to him because of his power. He lost Mum, but I'm growin' up, and now you're on the hook for the next six years, at least."

She put on her best unimpressed-officer frown. "Unless I get tired of you and sue for a divorce."

"I doubt it. Parta my lessons was in diplomacy. I won't ever push you past what you can handle."

"Huh! Says the boy who hasn't hit the teenage years, yet."

Andrew yawned. "Yeah, it really is my bedtime. Why don't you go back to the party? Last one you'll have for six months." He grabbed her hand and pulled her up. "Away you go."

"You'll be all right?"

"On Freighty's factory? Look, either I'll get some sleep or I'll get some thinkin' done. Whichever way, you can't help. Off you go, Mother. Have a good time at the party."

She gave him a brief hug, then held him at arm's length. "This is going to take some getting used to."

"Yeah. Oughta be fun. Night."

"Good night." She turned and went out the door, careful not to look back. She had to get this right the first time. Ground gained now would be easier to hold.

Image: cloud leopard kitten gamboling in the savannah. Zoom to faraway rock, where adult leopard watches.

Thanks, Chakka. Nice to know you're on duty.

Emotion: pride and soppy love for tiny, soft cubs.

She returned to the party. She had to remind herself how real women talked. The ones who weren't scoutship captains.

* * *

When everyone had left, Natalia sat in the drawing room, the factory's best imitation of an old brandy in her glass and a residual buzz from the last two refills in her head.

Freighty regarded her. "One bit of business before you leave. You haven't seen the fine print on Andrew's contract."

"I never had any right to ask."

"But now you're his mother."

238

"All right. I'm asking."

"Andrew is a shareholder and sole member of the Board of the Four-Eighty Manufacturing Consortium."

"He told me. The permutations of that are endless, but the one that sticks is that he's a minor and I'm his mother."

"Straight to the heart of the problem."

"Is it a problem?"

"I'm coming around to believing it isn't." The Freighty leaned back, his fingers interlaced behind his head. "How did someone so young end up in command of such an important ship?"

"Luck."

"I somehow doubt it."

"Luck is being the right person in the right place at the right time. Space Arm discovered a small error in their planning. *NightHawk* is a reconnaissance ship. No room for bridge crew plus downplanet crew. She's made to be operated by the commandos she transports. Everybody has two functions: onboard and on the ground."

"Even the cook?"

"She monitors the ship while we're downplanet and patches us up when we get back. So they needed a Commando leader with bridge qualifications, and there weren't too many available."

"I begin to understand."

"They tried an experienced captain, but he couldn't command the Commandos, if you know what I mean. They don't react the same as most spacers, and he couldn't run the raids. So they went looking for someone with better qualifications." She did a dance step and bow without rising. "Tada! There I was. Nobody else, and I mean nobody, has the training to captain a starship, lead a Commando raid, and at the same time control an auguar. There are only a dozen of those operational."

Freighty smiled. "And now the light dawns. This has less to do with captaining a starship and more to do with melding human, Arln and auguar."

"I didn't say that."

"Of course you didn't. That would be telling military secrets." He grinned. "How's it going?"

"Not very well, and you know exactly why."

"Is my experiment interfering with your data collection?"

"Interfering! He's completely taking over. In three days he got Chakka to override *NightHawk's* security protocols. And I didn't worry. I thought it was Chakka. Silly me."

"You were right not to worry. It was Chakka. He's another resource your scientists have yet to plumb the depths of."

"I know better than to ask. I assume you were monitoring...whatever you monitor...during the battle before you set off that singularity?"

"I was watching your ship very carefully during the battle. The gestalt of minds was quite promising."

"Promising? Is that all?"

"Yes. The four of you reacted three times faster than any individual, human or Arln." He paused. "Of course, with four of you there is the potential for six times faster, but that's long in the future, even for me."

"You're adding the total number of possible connections."

"That's what makes a brain smart. Connections. But there is interference. Sloppiness. You'll get better with practice."

"So what happens now?"

The factory construct put his fingertips together, a gesture reminiscent of Andrew. "The boy is one of the technologies I had planned to offer the PC, although I was quite dismayed when you and your two little friends showed up. You're only about three generations behind him, which reduces his value as an asset. Of course, now that's all changed. I've already made the gift, so to speak, and the experiment is a reasonable success.

"And by the way, you won't need to worry about his dysfunctional family. Once the Space Arm gets wind of his worth, they'll protect him like the treasure he is. But that won't be what he needs; it will be what they need. Which is why…I'm sorry, Natalia, but I'm doing it to you again."

She sighed. "You're arranging everything so that he gets to keep his mother, aren't you? That's a life sentence, last I heard. How are you going to swing it?"

"I'm a god, remember? They will do what I ask."

"Which isn't always a good thing." Then she grinned. "But I'm the one that knows your secret."

"A limited advantage in a complex situation. You can't predict what I'll do in any given matter."

"In the long run I can. You'll act like me."

"I will?"

"That's not an answer."

"You didn't ask a question."

"As long as we understand each other."

"I suspect we do."

"We had better. The fate of the human race rests on it."

THE END

If you enjoyed this book, do the author and other readers a favour and go to Smashwords, Amazon, or Goodreads and post a review. Even a rating and a few words is great.

ABOUT THE AUTHOR

Brought up in a logging camp with no electricity, Gordon Long learned his storytelling in the traditional way: at his father's knee. He now spends his time editing, publishing, travelling, blogging and writing Fantasy, Sci-Fi and Social Commentary, although sometimes the boundaries blur.

Gordon lives in Tsawwassen, British Columbia, with his wife, Linda, and their Nova Scotia Duck Tolling Retriever, Josh. When he is not writing and publishing, he works on projects with the Surrey Seniors' Planning Table and is a staff writer for <indiesunlimited.com>

MORE FROM GORDON A. LONG

"Ocean of Grass" Petrellan Saga 1
"Waves of Stone" Petrellan Saga 2
"Zoysana's Choice" Petrellan Saga 4
"The Innkeeper's Husband" Petrellan Saga 5

"Out of Mischief" World of Change 1
"Into Trouble" World of Change 2
"Mountains of Mischief" World of Change 3
"The Trouble with Tents" World of Change 4
"Queen of Mischief" World of Change 5

"A Sword Called...Kitten?" Romantic Comedy with an Edge
"The Cat with Many Claws" Sword Called Kitten Book 2
"Cloud Cat" A Sword Called Kitten Novel

Storm Over Savournon (A Novel of the French Revolution)

"Why Are People So Stupid?" Social Humour with a Point

Look for Gordon's books, selected reviews, poetry and
short stories: <airbornpress.ca>
Gordon's opinions on humanity are at the
"Are People Stupid?" blog
https://airbornpress.ca/arepeoplestupid/
Find all his reviews and his ideas on writing at
"Renaissance Writer"
https://airbornpress.ca/newdir/

www.ingramcontent.com/pod-product-compliance
Lightning Source LLC
Chambersburg PA
CBHW022005170626
46808CB00001B/295